"You really think you___ ___ ___ ___ fences with me all day?" Ian asked.

Andrea nodded. "I want to try."

"Well, maybe I don't want to play nursemaid to some greenhorn." The moment the words were out of his mouth, he felt a stab of regret. He was being a jerk, he realized, punishing her for...

Had she broken up with him, or was he the one who'd left her? When he reached back for the memory, he found only a black fog of loss and pain—that, and the nameless anxiety that stalked him day and night.

There's something important you're forgetting. Something so big the weight of it will crush you flat when it finally comes.

"You don't know what you want, Ian. That's the problem. But I might be able to help you with that."

"I want to be left to my work, alone."

"I'm coming with you," she insisted. Emotion rippled through her words, real emotion as the mask of compassionate professionalism slipped a little. "I've really missed the man I knew."

"That man's gone forever."

Dear Reader,

I've always loved stories of second chances, of lovers or siblings or parents and lost children reunited long after hope was lost of a successful reunion. There is something about severed bonds that the mind keeps turning back to in quiet moments, probing the wound the way one might check an empty socket for a missing tooth.

Maybe because we've all pondered impossible reunions I was drawn to this story of a "lost soldier," Ian Rayford, who, long after having been presumed dead, miraculously finds his way home, his journey made possible by the memory of the woman he loves. But so many other memories are missing, from those of what really happened during a torturous period of confinement to an earlier breakup with his love and the estrangement with his proud but troubled ranching family.

Finding his way back home from hell required one miracle. But finding his way back to his grieving family and especially to Andrea, who believes she has moved on with her life since Ian's death was initially reported, may take the greatest miracle of all...especially when it's clear that someone— perhaps the government itself—is willing to go to almost any lengths to stop Ian from remembering the secrets still locked up inside him.

I hope you'll enjoy this story of a true Lone Star survivor and take a moment to appreciate the sacrifices of so many still struggling to find their own way home.

Colleen Thompson

LONE STAR SURVIVOR

Colleen Thompson

H HARLEQUIN®ROMANTIC SUSPENSE

Recycling programs
for this product may
not exist in your area.

ISBN-13: 978-0-373-27899-2

Lone Star Survivor

Copyright © 2014 by Colleen Thompson

Printed in U.S.A.

Colleen Thompson

After beginning her career writing historical romance novels, in 2004 Colleen turned to writing the contemporary romantic suspense she loves. Since then, her work has been honored with a Texas Gold Award, along with nominations for a RITA® Award, a Daphne du Maurier Award and multiple reviewers' choice honors. She has also received starred reviews from *RT Book Reviews* and *Publishers Weekly*. A former teacher living with her family in the Houston area, Colleen has a passion for reading, hiking and dog rescue. Visit her online at www.colleen-thompson.com.

Books by Colleen Thompson

HARLEQUIN ROMANTIC SUSPENSE

Passion to Protect
The Colton Heir
Lone Star Redemption
Lone Star Survivor

SILHOUETTE ROMANTIC SUSPENSE

Deadlier Than the Male
"Lethal Lessons"

HARLEQUIN INTRIGUE

Capturing the Commando
Phantom of the French Quarter
Relentless Protector

Visit the author profile page at Harlequin.com for more titles.

To the father who first taught me that
a true hero is not the man who talks about it
but the man who quietly, steadfastly loves
and supports throughout the years.

Chapter 1

Waves of searing heat shimmered above the empty road, the endless road he had been walking for hours or days or all his life. How long didn't matter, only that blurred spot in the distance, beyond the sea of dry, gold stalks, where the blazing sun reflected off what had to be a lake. The sight of it made his parched mouth ache with the memory of water, cool and fresh and unimaginably luxurious as his body slipped through it, graceful as a seal's.

While his blistered feet stumbled forward, the walker's mind returned to a jewel-bright pool of turquoise. As he sat along its edge, lush green fronds waved in the sultry breeze and giant coral blossoms spilled their honeyed fragrance. A woman in big sunglasses swayed toward him, a floral sarong molding to the sweet curve of her hips and a deep blue bikini top holding her firm, round breasts in place. But it was her smile that sent lust spearing straight to his groin, that dazzling smile so white against her summer tan.

"Ready for another?" she invited, offering him some creamy, icy beverage in a clear plastic cup. A chunk of juicy pineapple balanced on its rim, so vivid in his memory that he could almost taste it. He could almost taste *her* on his lips, too, just as he could feel the dark river of her long hair running through his fingers, gleaming strands of chocolate he'd watched her brush so many times.

He smiled, reaching for her. And felt the pain of his chapped lips splitting, tasted the thick, salt tang of blood instead of the hallucination's sweetness. The mirage teased in the distance, a lie woven from refracted heat waves. *You'll never make it back to her, not even if you walk to the earth's ends.*

But he didn't stop. He couldn't, not while every step carried him closer to the oasis he dreamed of. Toward it and toward a woman, her name as lost to him as his own.

He knew one thing, though. He'd loved her. Loved her even if… The rest shimmered in the heat and vanished, an absence permeated with the bitterness of loss. There was fear as well, the anxiety that he'd done something unspeakable to poison what they'd had. That he'd *been* someone who deserved the scorched red skin, the knotted beard and the half-healed scars he'd glimpsed in the window of the pickup that had pulled over to offer him a ride an hour earlier. Or maybe it had been yesterday. Impossible to know, since time had grown as slippery as a live fish squirming in his grasp.

A single, splintered second pierced through his confusion: the moment when he'd met the driver's eyes. Dark eyes, shaded by a broad-brimmed hat. A cowboy hat, like the ones they wore back in Texas. Like the ones he'd used to…

Before he'd been able to wrap his parched brain around the thought, those dark eyes had flared wide. The driver had hit the gas too hard, the back end of his pickup sliding around to spray the walker with pebbles.

An instant later, the truck sped away in a plume of dust that he could still see hovering above the oasis.

The walker stopped and rubbed his eyes in an attempt to clear them. Because that growing smudge on the horizon—that was from now, not before. For a moment, he wondered if it could be the same truck whose driver he'd frightened away before with his appearance. Some buried instinct warned him the man might be returning to mow him down or shoot him, leaving his body to the blistering sun and the scavengers that he'd sensed watching, following his movements with hopeful, hungry eyes.

At the thought of dying here, of finally stopping, he felt an odd blend of disappointment and relief. Resignation, too, since there wasn't a damned thing he could do about it, with nothing but flat, oddly familiar rangeland on either side and no strength left to flee. So instead, the walker kept putting one foot before the other, figuring that if he died, it might as well be one step closer to the mirage on the horizon…and his memory of the poolside beauty who'd meant everything to him before he'd somehow, he felt certain, driven her away.

It was a blue-eyed man who pulled up beside him minutes later in a newer-model truck, a dark-haired man who reminded him of someone. Maybe of himself, or at least the version of himself who'd swum through cool blue waters.

Taking off his straw cowboy hat, the driver jumped down from the cab. Tall and muscular, he wore a rolled-sleeved cotton shirt, worn jeans and a single bead of perspiration, running from his temple to his jawline. Color draining from his tan face, he stared directly at the walker, searched his eyes with an intensity that made his heart hammer.

The walker took a step backward, glancing over his shoulder, his muscles coiling as he looked for an escape route.

"I told that fool pup of a cowhand to quit talking crazy," said the driver, unblinking as he stared, "telling me he'd seen a man who looked like—looked like my dead brother out here on our land. Then I cursed him for leaving some poor, lost stranger way out here on his own in this heat, without even offering a drink of water."

"You—have w-water?" The idea of it, the possibility spun from his dreams, was so powerful that he stumbled closer, forgetting his fear as trembling overtook him.

"Yeah, sure. Here you go, man." The driver reached back inside the truck and pulled out a plastic bottle beaded with condensation. He cracked open the sealed lid and handed it over.

The walker was so overwhelmed by the cold moisture in his hand that he barely noticed the uncertainty darting through the other man's eyes or the moisture gleaming in them.

"Ian, is it really you?" he asked, letting the question hang as the walker chugged down half the bottle.

When he started choking, the driver warned him, "Slow down. Slow down and take it easy. There's plenty more where that came from. Food and clean clothes back at the house, too."

His coughing over, the walker glugged down the rest of the bottle. When he was finished, he peered suspiciously into the blue eyes. "Why?" he asked, searching the stranger for some agenda. "Why would you do all that for me?"

"Could be one of two good reasons. Either because I don't cotton to the idea of a stranger dying on my land.

Or because you're a walking, talking miracle—my only brother, Captain Ian Rayford, come back from the dead."

Andrea Warrington stared down at the file her boss, retired army colonel Julian Ross, had handed her, her throat tightening the moment she read the name *Captain Ian Rayford*.

What she had to tell the man sitting behind the battered desk, his shirtsleeves rolled up and his tie loosened against the late summer heat, would be awkward enough under any circumstances. But despite the fifteen-year difference in their ages, Andrea had recently accepted the handsome forty-six-year-old's proposal, so bat-sized butterflies attempted to flap their way free of her stomach.

Telling herself that putting it off was no longer an option, she drew a deep breath and squared her shoulders, just as she would have advised the wounded vets she counseled here at the Marston unit of the Warriors-4-Life Rehabilitation Center. "I—I'm afraid I can't take this assignment, Julian. There's something I've been meaning to tell you about myself and Captain Rayford."

"Sit down, Andrea, please." He gestured toward one of the mismatched folding chairs in front of his desk, the rich bass of his voice warmed by a gentlemanly Southern accent. Six months after the ribbon cutting that had opened this donation-supported unit, they were still getting by with whatever castoffs they could scrounge, mainly because Julian, who had been named director shortly before the center's opening, insisted on using every penny of the funds raised to provide services for their growing roster of military veterans. Though many bore physical reminders of the ordeals they had endured, the majority had come to Warriors-4-Life to deal with the fallout of combat-related brain injuries or post-traumatic stress disorder. The workload kept Andrea, the center's one practicing psychologist, along with two counselors and a psychiatric nurse-practitioner who worked under her direction, hopping, but she didn't mind her packed days—not when she knew for a certainty that she was saving lives.

Besides, the crazy hours and emotional challenges had drawn her closer to the handsome older man who had started out as her boss before evolving into much more. She admired him; she respected him, but it was love that was making the words knot in her throat.

She claimed a seat where a rattletrap oscillating fan on the desk could swivel back and forth between them. "I think I mentioned to you I was engaged before," she admitted, the breeze blowing a strand of long, dark brown hair—an escapee from her clip—into her face. "It was one of those whirlwind affairs, everything moving at light speed."

She flushed, remembering the heat of it, the passion, how exciting it had felt to be caught up in something so out of her control. But thrilling as they might seem, whirlwinds had the potential to cause a lot of damage. The kind of heartbreak she'd sworn she would never risk again.

"It didn't take long for me to realize he was lying about his deployments. There were other disappearances as well, with no warning and no explanation. I couldn't deal with the uncertainty, so I broke it off."

A smile touched Julian's brown eyes like a warm breeze from his Savannah boyhood. He'd promised he would take her one day, to see the historic Victorian home where he'd grown up before it had passed out of the family. "Everyone has a past, Andrea. I didn't imagine you'd lived underneath a bell jar for thirty-one years before you'd met me."

"Yes, but bizarre as it might seem, it was this man, Ian. Captain Rayford. He was still just a lieutenant then, and I was working on my doctorate. I—I should've told you, I know, after the news broke that he was found alive."

For weeks following his return, the "Texas miracle" was all anyone could talk about on the morning shows and social media. While Ian himself refused all interviews, the army had been left scrambling to explain how one set of charred remains could have been mistaken for another after some overworked soldier in the military's mortuary center had failed to follow proper DNA procedures to identify the body.

"So why didn't you say something?" he asked. "Surely, you can't imagine I'd hold you accountable for any of the suspicions brought up about his escape from the terrorists holding him?"

"No, of course not. It's just…" Though she couldn't put an answer into words, she felt it in the warm flush that rose to her face, the aching heaviness in her chest.

"You still have feelings for him," Julian suggested, though his sharp, brown gaze seemed more curious than judgmental. "Is that what you're saying?"

"No, it's not that." She raised her hands, not wanting to hurt this good man's feelings. "It's only—when he was reported killed in action, it brought back a lot of memories. The good, along with the bad."

Her gaze dropped, avoiding his, but because she'd learned the hard way that lies of omission could be the worst of all, she forced herself to look up. "I cried a lot at night. For months, I cried for him." Even after she'd met Julian, she'd come to work some mornings with her eyes red and swollen. His unfailing kindness, his steadiness had planted the first seeds of healing in her.

"I'm sorry for your grief," he told her. "But I assure you that I understand it. Possibly better than you can imagine. You see, the army personnel who debriefed the captain passed on his full dossier with the referral. I saw your name listed on his contact list, to be notified in case he was killed in action."

The burning in her face intensified. "He must have added me two years ago, when we were still together." She still remembered the horrendous shock that had followed the knock at the front door of her apartment back in San Diego.

"That's not my point, Andrea. My point is, I feel certain—and the army psychologist I consulted is in full agreement on this—that your past connection to Ian Rayford could be the key to recovering his missing memories."

She shook her head. "You mean he's still suffering amnesia? Was he found to have a brain injury?"

"If you'll take a look at the file—" the fan swung around to ruffle Julian's short, bronze-colored hair, a crop of silver threaded through it "—you'll see that's not the case, though he does have some residual scarring. From the torture, they believe, in attempts to extract intelligence on US targets."

"But he was cleared of those suspicions," she was quick to say. "And anyway, after a soldier's captured, codes are changed, right? Sensitive locations scrambled?" She was aware American civilians working in a war zone office had died or disappeared soon after Ian's capture, but few details had been reported, and surely, the bombing of their building could not be laid at the feet of a man who had suffered heaven only knew what torments.

Julian nodded, but his brown eyes looked troubled. "Officially, he was absolved of any responsibility in the bombing and given a medical discharge. Considering the hero's welcome drummed up by that Rayford woman's story—"

"Jessie Layton is his brother Zach's wife, isn't she? The journalist?" Andrea narrowed her eyes, trying to get it straight in her mind, since she'd never met Ian's family. They'd been estranged for years, he'd told her, though he'd avoided going into details—something that should have raised another red flag. But then, Andrea had her family secrets, too, issues so painful they'd sent her into counseling when she was in her teens. The relief she'd gotten, the insight into the dynamics that had destroyed her family, had led her to pursue the study of psychology.

Julian nodded in answer to her question. "Cutting Captain Rayford loose, giving him the benefit of the doubt, was the only thing the military could do, especially since he was diagnosed as having dissociative amnesia as a result of torture."

Andrea lifted a brow. "Not to mention all the suffering the screwup over the body caused both his family and the other soldier's. What a PR nightmare that boondoggle's been."

"So I'm told," said Julian, "which brings us back to you."

Apprehension crawled over her skin like live ants.

"Let Michael take him. Or Connor. He's a real pro, and the guys love that he's ex-military himself."

"Neither of the counselors will do, or Cassidy, either, for this case," Julian said, though as a psychiatric nurse-practitioner, Cassidy had both the experience and the ability to dispense any necessary medications. "You see, Captain Rayford has refused to come here. Refused to leave the family's ranch at all. Says he's had enough of shrinks poking through his head—"

"So you want to send me, a psychologist?"

"The man doesn't need or want a psychologist right now, but a friend, he might accept. And a trained friend, someone with your sensitivity, might find a way to break through. A way to help a man whose plight has drawn so much attention—and a way to help us, too, at Warriors-4-Life."

She folded her arms beneath her chest. "Really, Julian? That's what this is all about? The money?"

He sighed. "Come on, Andrea. You know I'm 100 percent focused on these soldiers. But as director, fundraising is a big part of my job description, and if we don't get donations up before next quarter, we're going to have way bigger problems than a broken AC system."

Worry fluttered in her stomach. "I know we're working on a shoestring out here, but what do you mean, way bigger problems? We're not—tell me we're not in danger of shutting down already. We've barely gotten up and running, and more and more returning soldiers are applying for our help every day. They need us, desperately. Where else can they go, if they don't have places like this when their lives come crashing down around them? Who else will prepare them to reintegrate into their families and meaningful employment?"

He held up a hand to stop her. "You're preaching to the choir. There's no need to sell me on what we do. I never would've come aboard if I weren't 100 percent behind it."

"I know that. I do." Like everyone else who worked at Warriors-4-Life, Julian had accepted little more than the use of one of the center's Spartan housing units and a nominal salary in exchange for his sixty- to eighty-hour workweeks. He even donated a portion of his military retirement pay to the cause, saying he couldn't encourage others to do something he wasn't doing on his own. Inspired by his generosity, Andrea gave whenever she could, as well, despite the mountain of student loans she would probably still be paying into her dotage.

"Then don't look so shocked that I'm thinking practically. I have to. Otherwise, we'll have no choice but to scale back the number of young men and women we can assist—and reduce our staff levels, as well."

She gritted her teeth, thinking of how overworked all of them were already, how many sacrifices they had made. And the look in his eyes told her that if the cutbacks didn't solve the issue, the doors they'd fought so hard to open might be forever shuttered. What would happen to their clients, then, people like twenty-year-old Ty Dawson, who'd gone missing for hours just yesterday after a lawn mower had kicked up a stone and cracked a window. He was found shaking and hiding in the darkened corner of a storage closet.

"All right," she said. "I'll rearrange tomorrow morning's schedule and try to get back by—"

"Your schedule's cleared, for the time being. Michael, Cassidy, Connor and I will all pitch in while you're away."

"Away? What do you mean? It's, what, an hour or so

from here to Rusted Spur? If I leave early, I'm sure I can be back by lunchtime to help cover the afternoon group sessions."

Julian shook his head. "For the next two weeks, you'll be staying at the ranch."

"Staying at the ranch? With my ex-fiancé? Are you serious? You won't— This won't worry you at all?"

She studied his face and caught the flicker of discomfort. But he quickly squared his shoulders and reclaimed his usual composure. The composure that had made her feel so safe.

"I'll admit I was hesitant at first. You know about my ex-wife, about what happened between us?"

Andrea nodded, remembering what he'd told her about a marriage in his twenties—and a wife who'd eased her loneliness with multiple affairs during his deployments. He'd spoken of it matter-of-factly, but she had seen the hurt, the vulnerability lurking behind his solemn brown eyes. And she'd sworn to herself she would be the wife that he deserved.

He reached across the desk and found her hand, then squeezed it. "I refuse to let it change me, let that pain turn me jealous and suspicious when you've done nothing to deserve it. When I could never imagine a consummate professional like yourself—a generous, decent woman—betraying what we have."

"Of course, I wouldn't." She'd learned her lessons young; she would never be her father. "Especially not for a man who broke my heart. But I will do my best to help him, just the way I'd help any other client who was hurting."

"Then it's settled," he answered with a nod. "I'll need

you to log in and update your contact records daily, but I'm told there's wireless available."

"When have I ever forgotten my logs?" It was a protocol she frequently reminded the counselors to follow, since the portion of their funding received from government grants depended on the number of recorded contact hours. The case notes themselves, however, remained password protected, covered by patient confidentiality.

"Also," Julian said, "I thought you'd like to know that when Captain Rayford's family extended the invitation for you to come, they mentioned they'd set up a suite of rooms for your use."

"A *suite* of rooms, just for me?" It sounded like paradise, since her own quarters consisted of a single bedroom in the women's dormitory, where female staff and clients alike shared a communal bath and kitchen.

"Play your cards right, and I'll throw in some bubble bath." From across the desk, he winked at her, a gesture so at odds with his usual demeanor that it made her laugh with delight.

"Ooh la la." She waggled her brows at the man who'd asked her to keep their engagement under wraps for the time being, to avoid causing any suspicions of favoritism among the staff. And given that there was no way either of them could visit the other's room without drawing speculation, the physical side of their relationship had been largely confined to their imaginations—a situation that was growing more frustrating by the day. "But it'd be ever better if you could join me in that bathtub."

He smiled. "With or without strategically placed bubbles?"

"Up to you, Colonel," she teased, standing when he left his chair and came around the desk.

He pulled her into a warm embrace. "I promise you, my darling, by the time you come back to me, I'll have figured out a way to break the news to the others. And after that, no more sneaking around like a couple of teenagers."

"In that case—" she smiled up into his brown eyes "—I promise you, I'll do everything I can think of to get Captain Rayford's memory back in record time."

Chapter 2

Funny what it was his mind chose to remember, Ian thought as he curried the palomino, a sturdy gelding known as Sundance. Though Ian had been told that he hadn't set foot on the ranch since the day of his high school graduation, he remembered the order of operations he'd been taught to the last detail: currycomb, then dandy brush, followed by the mane and tail brush and the hoof pick. He remembered to lay the saddle pad over the withers and slide it back so the golden hair would lie comfortably and to walk the horse a few steps before cinching up the saddle so it would be tight enough. He knew to mount from the left side, too, just as he could still not only ride but rope a calf or cut a heifer from the herd with ease.

Procedural, semantic and short-term memory intact, one of the army shrinks had written on his report, which meant that Ian also remembered the meaning of words and could acquire new information. But it had been the next part that disturbed him, the notation: *Retrograde biographical memory continues impaired—psychogenic origin likely due to emotional trauma.*

In other damned words, they figured him for some kind of nut job. Not a veteran who'd lost his memory due to the injuries he'd clearly suffered, judging from the scarring on his back, his arms and legs, but a head case too soft to handle the stress of the ambush that he'd been told had killed a fellow soldier, along with the captivity that followed. Insulted by their insinuations and sick of being poked and prodded, he had gone back to the ranch and vowed to stay there, with the people he was learning to accept as his family…slowly.

He led the horse out of the barn and into the bright September morning, happy that last night's shower had knocked down the dust and cooled the temperature. Zach kept telling Ian he didn't have to work like a hired hand to tackle any of the never-ending chores that kept the cattle ranch's wheels turning, but he found it far easier than staying in the house to be watched, fussed over and treated like a ticking time bomb by his mother or stuffed full of pastries by their cook, Althea, who apparently took it as her God-given duty to help him put back on the forty pounds his ordeal had cost him.

His older brother was easier to deal with, maybe because he'd served as a marine corps fighter pilot before his return to run the ranch following the false reports of Ian's death. Ian had found Zach steady, supportive and respectful of his privacy, but always there if he wanted to talk or ask questions. Along with Zach's journalist wife, Jessie, he did his best to keep their little girl, Eden, out of Ian's hair, though the rambunctious five-year-old was forever finding ways to corner him and wear him out with innocently awkward questions. Questions that he couldn't answer, for the most part, no matter how damned cute she and the pair of young Australian shepherds who followed her everywhere were about their interrogation.

Mounting up, he looked beyond the ranch's outbuildings and toward the open rangeland, where a herd of red-and-white cattle grazed off in the distance. Farther afield, he'd been told one could find the fresh drilling that marked the promising new natural gas find that had recently sent the family's fortunes soaring. But Ian left the worries about the operation and the money to Zach while he focused on the hard manual labor that was not only helping him recover his physical strength but would leave him exhausted by the day's end. Too exhausted, he hoped, for the disjointed nightmares that had been waking him several times a night. Like his past, their content was largely forgotten the moment he returned to himself. But that didn't keep him from racking his brain for hours, no matter how frustrating the attempts.

He nudged the palomino into an easy lope, eager for the freedom, the peace that he found only with the prospect of a day alone in the saddle. But it had barely lasted for an hour before he spotted a lone rider making his way toward him: Zach, aboard his big bay, Ace, irritation casting more shade on his expression than the wide brim of his hat.

As his brother's mount clattered to a stop, Ian sucked a breath through his clenched teeth and raised a palm to hold off the complaint he knew was coming. "Sorry, man. I'm sorry. I did it again, didn't I?"

"Apologize to Mama, not me," Zach told him. "Do you have any idea how panicky she gets when you take off without a word to anybody? Jessie thought she was going to have a stroke when she found your bed empty after you didn't show for breakfast. Mama broke down, asking if you were really still dead, if she'd dreamed all that part about how you'd come back home."

Ian screwed shut his eyes and blew out a long breath, hating himself for causing her more suffering. "But you knew where I was, right? You told her, didn't you?"

"I told her you were sure to be around, yeah. But the fact is, Ian, I got lucky figuring out where you were because you didn't tell me, either."

"You could've called instead of riding all the way out…" But as he felt his pocket for the fancy new smartphone his brother had bought him, Ian's mouth went dust dry. "Oh, shoot. The damned cell—"

"Works a lot better when you remember to take it with you, bonehead."

Ian opened his eyes and faced his older brother's disappointment. "I know I screwed up. But I swear, I'll do better."

"Yeah, you damned well will." Zach's glare faded, his blue eyes softening. "Listen, man. I know what it's like, going from a place where you have only yourself to think of, yourself and your mission. But things are different now. You're part of a family again, with people who care, who worry about you, who want to help you finally come home."

"I *am* home," Ian insisted, the edge in his voice making his mount shuffle and toss his mane. Clutching the reins tightly to keep Sundance in hand, he added, "Against all odds, I made it."

The government's investigators had tracked his northbound progress through Mexico and into Texas, where he'd hitchhiked, walked and at one point trailed "coyotes" smuggling their human cargo across the border during his months-long odyssey. There had been some speculation about how Ian might have gotten out of the Middle East and into Mexico, but he'd been unable to contribute anything beyond a fragmented memory of himself clinging to a coarse scrap of threadbare blanket in the dark hold of a cargo ship.

"You think you've made it, brother," Zach said, "but I'm telling you, you've still got a ways to go. Which is why you're coming back with me right now, to meet our visitor."

Ian's gut clenched. "I told you, no more shrinks. No counselors. None of Mama's preachers, either, here to save my lost soul. This range, this work, is the only salvation I need."

Zach gazed out over the undulating golden waves, over a land that looked flat to those who didn't know the deep furrows that could lead a man to its hidden places. "I remember a time when you couldn't wait to get the hell off this land."

Old resentment squeezed in Ian's chest. Because since returning, he had remembered enough fragments from their upbringing to resurrect some old grievances. "You should talk. You took off before I did. Left me here, with *him*."

At the mention of their father, Zach's shoulders fell and his gaze drifted. It served as a reminder that some of the memories Ian had recovered would be better off forgotten.

"I know, and I'm sorry, bro," Zach said. "Sorry for leaving you and Mama both behind. I was just trying to survive those years without ending up in prison. Because I would've damned well killed the son of a bitch if I'd stayed one more day."

Ian nodded, understanding the same desperation that had driven him away from their father's brand of torture as soon as he'd been able. Like Zach, he'd left their mother here to face it, since she'd refused to admit to what her husband was, much less abandon the material comforts and social status she'd enjoyed as a Rayford. As sorry as he felt for the suffering she'd endured when he'd been believed dead, Ian still hadn't entirely forgiven her for refusing to protect him and his brother back when it might have mattered.

But there was nothing to be gained by treading that old minefield, and he quickly changed the subject. "I'll apologize for scaring Mama. I'll remember my phone next time. But I won't be coming back with you now, not unless you tell me who's there waiting."

"I'll tell you this much. It's a woman. A woman from your past."

Ian frowned, wondering which past his brother meant: the one he couldn't bear to think of, or the dark, erotic glimmers that invaded his dreams every night.

Andrea had known Ian grew up on a working cattle ranch in North Texas, but she'd had no idea that he'd come from money. Maybe she'd been projecting the hand-me-downs and frequent moves that had defined her own hardscrabble upbringing or maybe she'd judged Ian by his rare comments about living hand to mouth after going out on his own right out of high school, but the ranch itself, especially the opulent white mansion at its center, convinced her she'd had it wrong. As did the fact that a heavyset woman with her pinned-back gray hair and a starched uniform wheeled out a real, honest-to-goodness tea cart with a silver pot and baskets of delicate confections to the fussy formal living room where she waited while Ian's mother, Nancy Rayford, did her best to pick Andrea's brain.

"So, dear," said the neatly dressed, silver-haired woman over the gold rim of her teacup, "you were saying, you met my son in California?"

Andrea didn't answer, too distracted by the heat rising to her face as the maid offered her some cookies. "Th-thank you very much. These are lovely." Andrea chose a chocolate-centered square to be polite, nearly choking on the thought of how her mother, who had waited on more than a few pampered rich ladies in her day, might have looked a lot like "Miss Althea" had she lived.

The maid nodded and excused herself, leaving Mrs. Rayford to repeat her question.

Andrea nodded. "Sorry. Yes, we met on a country road not far outside of San Diego. I was out riding when the chain came off my bike and sent me flying." She shivered in the air-conditioning, remembering the moment she'd gone over the handlebars. "Fast as I was moving, it's a wonder I didn't split my skull along with my helmet." As it was, she'd been a bloody mess, with the frame of a bike she'd scrimped and saved for for two years bent so badly it was never again race-worthy.

Mrs. Rayford frowned. "You don't mean to tell me you were riding one of those noisy *motorcycles*, do you?"

Andrea nearly laughed aloud at the horror souring the woman's prim face, as if a female on a motorcycle would have been the scandal of the century. "Not a motorcycle, no. A racing bike, for the triathlons I used to compete in before that crash. I tore up my knee pretty badly in the fall. If it hadn't been for Ian pulling off the road to help me, I could've lain there for a long time before anyone else came along."

She remembered the moment she'd first seen the tall,

dark-haired man jumping out of his SUV and racing toward her, gorgeous as any guy she'd ever met in real life, but in a masculine, clean-cut way that left actors and male models in the dust. Hurting as she'd been, she'd still felt sucker punched by his blue eyes, the intensity and concern in them as real as anything she'd ever seen.

"He was always a bighearted boy," his mother reminisced. "Always dragging home strays."

Jolted by her words, Andrea wondered if she'd just joined their ranks in his mother's eyes, if the woman somehow saw through the tan slacks and coral shell she wore with a light jacket, through the fake gold earrings and the thrift-store beige pumps and all the way back to the scabby-kneed, motherless girl she had once been. Telling herself that couldn't be, that Nancy Rayford only knew her as Zach's former fiancée, a psychologist who happened to work an hour away in Marston, Andrea said, "He didn't exactly drag me home, but he did drive me to the ER."

Behind her, the floor creaked, and she turned to face the man she'd met that long-ago day. Though his face was leaner and his tan deeper, she recognized those deep blue eyes and came to her feet at once. But his eyes were different, too, she realized, haunted by events he could not consciously remember.

"Ian," she managed, pulse revving as she fought an instinct to run to the man she'd once loved and throw her arms around him. "I'm so glad to see you, so relieved that you're..."

He stared into her face, his gaze as unreadable as it was disconcerting. Her stomach fluttered in response, and she felt an outbreak of tiny beads of perspiration.

"He won't remember you, of course," his mother announced. "He didn't know any of us here at all, not for days and days—"

"Andrea?" he asked, taking two steps closer. Close enough that she saw his color deepen and recognized what looked like pure relief wash over him. "Andie, is it really you?"

Andie, he had called her, using the nickname no one else did…

Before she could react, his mother scolded, "You'll need a shower before you come in on the good furniture. I can smell the horse on you from here."

Paying her no mind, Ian took two more steps and claimed Andrea, pulling her into his arms and kissing her for all he was worth.

The connection arced through every nerve ending, raising each fine hair and jolting her with memories of how incredibly well their bodies worked together. The searing contact made her ache for more, forgetting all the ways they'd wounded one another.

Forgetting, at least for a few moments, the other woman who stood gaping at them and the man Andrea herself had so recently promised to marry, a man whose face she struggled to recall.

Finally, she pulled away, a red-hot tide of embarrassment scorching her face. Shaking her head, she stammered, "I—I'm sorry. S-sorry, Ian, but what you're remembering—that was two years ago. It's been a long time since we—"

"I remember the trip we took together to Key West in Florida," he said, the words coming in a rush as she took two steps back. "There was a little bed-and-breakfast, and you wore—there was this blue bikini. I've been dreaming of that trip, of all that color, of you for so long now."

The professional in her noticed the way his eyes had dilated and the light that had come into them, extinguishing the pain she'd first glimpsed. As much as she hated dimming that excitement, she told herself that letting him go on believing would be crueler.

"You're right," she said. "What you remember really happened. But afterward, so did a lot of other things. We're not—we're not together anymore, not in that way. But that doesn't mean I don't care about what's happened to you. It doesn't mean that I can't be your friend."

"We're not…we're not together anymore?"

Confusion shifted through his handsome features, followed by a sorrow so profound it reminded her of the day she'd told him they were finished. *Of course*, she realized, because for him, it was happening again right now, the boom lowered only seconds after he'd consciously accessed the memory of one of the happiest times of their eight-month relationship, a time before she'd grown aware that it was all built on a raft of lies.

"I'm sorry," she said, meaning it—and acutely aware of the disapproval emanating from his mother. She couldn't say whether it was because he'd made the sexual side of their relationship so obvious or because Andrea had so clearly broken her son's heart, but she knew one thing for certain: the woman didn't like her.

Andrea shook it off, reminding herself her visit was about Ian's well-being, his healing, not her comfort level. "We've been apart for two years," she said. "I have a new fiancé."

"So we're engaged—or we were?" He shook his head, offering the wry smile she'd always found so irresistibly disarming. "I must've been an idiot, letting a woman like you go."

She smiled back at him, pretending not to hear the fresh grief behind his words. "Your brother thought that we might visit for a while and talk. He thought that seeing me might help you remember."

Ian snorted. "Well, at least you're a damn sight better looking than any of those shrinks they keep pushing at me."

She sighed but realized there was no way around what was sure to be another troubling disclosure. "Do you remember why we went to Key West? What we were celebrating?"

He shook his head.

"You surprised me with the trip after I completed my doctorate."

"So you're a doctor? Like an MD?" He winked at his mother. "I always did go for the smart girls, at least, the pretty ones."

"I'm a psychologist," Andrea admitted.

He laughed, his smile turning bitter. "So that explains why you're here. One more shrink to poke around my skull. Tell me, are you working for the army these days, or the Department of Defense?"

"Neither, Ian. I'm here because I care about you. And your brother, Zach, really did speak to my boss at the center for—"

He waved it off. "I don't give a damn who sent you."

His mother looked up sharply over the gilded rim of her teacup. "Language, young man."

"I just want you out of here, right now," he finished, anger and betrayal competing in his voice.

"Please, Ian," Andrea said. "I've come a long way to see you."

"Not half as far as I've come to be left the hell alone."

With that, he showed her his back as he stalked toward the stairway. A few steps up, he paused and turned to look down at his mother, his voice gentling. "Sorry for the language, and I'm sorry I upset you earlier. I'll remember next time to let you know when I have plans."

"It's all right, Ian. It's just—" she answered nervously "—I do worry so about you, with everything that's happened."

"I'm headed upstairs for that shower now. But while I'm gone, would you please show *Dr.* Warrington the door."

On his way upstairs, he nearly ran into a strawberry-blonde woman close to Andrea's and Ian's own age as she was heading down, a purse over her shoulder and a set of keys in hand.

"Excuse me, Jessie," he said, his voice tight with impatience as he angled his way past her and the muscular black-and-tan Rottweiler at her side.

"Sure thing, Ian." Jessie raised a speculative brow as he charged upstairs. At the bottom of the steps, she paused, glancing back up toward the landing at the sound of a door slamming. "Is he mad that I sent Zach to find him?"

"I'm afraid he's upset with me," Andrea admitted as she walked up to the woman and offered her hand. "Andrea Warrington."

"The psychologist, right, and ex—the old friend." Jessie shook her hand in greeting, looking up to meet Andrea's gaze. "Hi. I'm Jessie Layton."

"Jessie *Rayford* now," her mother-in-law corrected, that same disapproval in her tone.

"I thought we'd had this discussion. Several times, as I remember." An undercurrent of annoyance rippled beneath an attempt at pleasantry. "Since I write under my maiden name—"

"But you're not writing now, Jessie. This is a social situation, and as Zach's wife and Eden's mother, I'd expect you'd want to—" Nancy Rayford cut herself off as the Rottweiler interposed herself between the women, as if to ward off her harsh words. Scowling, she added, "Really. That animal."

"Gretel, *platz*," Jessie said, and at the command—which Andrea thought might be in German—the dog dropped into the down position. "Sorry, but whenever she perceives a threat—"

"So what happens if you have an argument with my son?"

Jessie smiled at the Rottweiler. "Big traitor usually takes his side."

Eager to defuse the tension, Andrea cleared her throat. "I read the article you wrote on Ian's return. It was incredibly well done, very moving."

Jessie ducked a nod, the relief in her green eyes making it clear she appreciated the diversion. "Thanks, Andrea. It was important. To get the word out quickly, I mean. Ian might not remember why, but he's pretty paranoid these days. When he first came, he worried that someone might come take him away in the dark of night if the public didn't hear he'd come back. He's pretty short-tempered these days, too. But I guess you've already found that out for yourself."

"Please, Jessie," Nancy Rayford said. "He's been

through so much. And you're making him sound like some sort of madman."

"I promise you, I'll never think of him that way," Andrea assured her. "I work with returning vets. A lot of them have anger issues, and it must be even more confusing when he doesn't consciously recall the reason why."

"It was those horrible terrorists," Mrs. Rayford whispered, tears shining in her eyes. "Heaven only knows what they did to my poor boy for almost a year. When I think of how he's suffered…"

"It must be hard for you, too." Andrea looked from one woman to the other in an effort to remind them of their common ground. "Not knowing what might set him off, not knowing what will help him."

Jessie gave her a look that seemed to weigh and judge her. "*You'll* help him. I see that."

"It's a shame that Ian won't allow it," her mother-in-law said, talking right over her. "But you heard him a moment ago. You'll have to leave, Miss Warrington."

"But I just—" Andrea started, more concerned about the swift dismissal than she was the omission of the "Dr." before her name.

"He's been through enough. We mustn't upset him."

Jessie looked down at the small, frail woman, the impatience in her expression melting into compassion. "You want him to get better, don't you?"

"I do, more than anything."

"Then can't you stick with the plan we made, you and Zach and me?"

The older woman hesitated. "I only want to be a better mother. I swear I do, but…she *confuses* him." With this pronouncement, she pinned Andrea with an accusatory gaze. "He thinks she's still his fiancée."

This time, however, Andrea heard the fear behind the woman's words, the terror of losing her son all over again. "He knows the truth now, and if he forgets it, I'll remind him…gently, carefully. I promise you that. Believe me, I don't want to hurt him any more than you do. But I also don't want to leave him in pain the way he is."

She knew the grim statistics too well, had seen up close in her work how many returning soldiers suffering untreated PTSD chose to end their lives. Or to obliterate their pain with drugs and alcohol, which often amounted to a slower form of suicide.

Ian's mother hesitated, but for Jessie, this was apparently good enough.

"Let me show you to your room," she said. "Then, if you want, you can ride along with me to pick up Eden from her playdate, and I'll fill you in on everything you'll need to know about this family."

Andrea didn't miss the panic that flashed through Nancy Rayford's blue eyes. But for the moment, Andrea pretended not to see it as she took up Jessie on her offer and followed her to the wing that housed the mansion's guest quarters.

Still, she couldn't help but wonder, *What is it Ian's mother is so afraid I'll find out about the Rayfords? And how can I enlist this frightened woman's help to save her son?*

When he couldn't convince his brother, Jessie or even his pushover of a mother to send the shrink packing, Ian decided instead to ignore Andrea's presence. It was a hell of a lot easier said than done, though, since his mind kept replaying the warmth of her curves when he had pulled her into his arms and the strength of the connection he'd felt coursing through him that moment their lips met. The only way he could manage, could keep his eyes from locking on to every move she made, was by avoiding her as much as possible.

Over the past two days she hadn't made it any easier, "happening" upon him whenever he came inside and pretending to be no more than a *concerned friend*. But he'd brushed her off in a hurry and retreated to his room each time, not giving a damn about the look of disappointment on her gorgeous face.

What difference did it make anyway? Whether or not he ever spoke to her, she was sure to get paid for her efforts. He was a job to her, or at best some pet project, a screwed-up loser she'd dumped so she could ride off into the sunset with a guy whose brains weren't scrambled eggs.

This morning, it was the sunrise that he planned to ride off into after leaving a note in the ranch office, a space more like a studio apartment, with its own seating area, kitchenette and a small bath where Zach could wash up after getting dirty with the livestock. His brother had taken the opportunity to expand the office, which had been built into a corner of the barn after an arsonist had burned down the entire structure last year. Ian knew his family had gone through a rough stretch, a time of grief compounded by intense fear and worry, but at least some good had come of it, if his brother's relationship with Jessie was anywhere near as solid as it looked to Ian. Though yesterday he'd overheard them squabbling over Jessie's "scaring the liver out of him," as Zach had put it, with her refusal to share details of the new exposé she was working on, it was clear they loved each other deeply, and they had fun together, too.

Seeing how they worked as a team with Eden and how much joy the little girl, who'd started school just last week, brought them struck Ian with a sense of loss—and anger, sometimes, creeping up on him when he didn't expect it—for the life he'd been missing out on, a life centered on a family he'd never even known he wanted. Or maybe that wasn't true. He couldn't say for certain these days. Along with his memory, he'd lost so much more, including a true sense of who he was.

He left a brief note on his brother's desk, grateful that Zach would be running later than usual this morning since it was his turn to drive Eden into town for school. If he were here, Ian knew, there'd be another lecture and maybe an argument like yesterday's, when Ian had told his brother what he could do with his advice to quit acting like a stubborn jerk and give Andrea a chance.

He did miss his brother's coffee though, he thought as he eyed the fancy espresso machine longingly. But no way was he taking a chance on messing with Zach's prize possession, which had enough buttons and levers to rival the fighter jets he'd once piloted.

Ian thought of heading back inside to cadge a quick mug of Althea's simpler brew—and maybe a couple of his favorite raspberry thumbprint cookies—before he rode out, but that would bring the risk of running into Andrea since she'd been getting up earlier each day in an attempt to catch him alone. He felt idiotic sneaking around his own home—and more aggravated than ever with her for forcing him into it.

Which is why he swore under his breath when he saw her standing by the hitching post, next to his saddled palomino. She held two insulated travel mugs, one of which she offered with that gorgeous smile of hers, so white it competed with the glorious September dawn. Sleek and straight, her dark brown hair had been brushed back, with a clip keeping the front sections out of those long-lashed hazel eyes he'd always loved.

"Peace offering," she said, looking more casual today in a pair of jeans that drew his eye to other favorite parts of her anatomy. Places he'd awakened hot and hard from dreams of touching, tasting and claiming as his own again.

When he reached for the mug, she didn't let go, locking in on him with a take-no-prisoners gaze instead.

"Didn't realize there'd be strings attached," he said, looking at her almost straight on, since she wore a pair of riding boots that brought her to within a couple of inches of his own six-four.

"Life is a series of negotiations, Ian. The question is, what will you bring to the table?"

He lowered his hand and shook his head. "Thanks for bringing out the coffee, but I prefer mine black, not tarted up with a bunch of shrink talk. Or any talk at all, as far as that goes."

"Then how 'bout if we ride instead? Just ride and see how that goes?"

He chuckled to himself, getting the point now of the boots and jeans. "You really think you're up to riding fences with me all day?"

"I want to try."

"Well, maybe I don't want to play nursemaid to some greenhorn. Or ride back for a ladies' room when we're a couple hours out." The moment the words were out of his mouth, he felt a stab of regret. He *was* being a jerk, he realized, punishing her for… Had she broken up with him, or was he the one who'd left her? When he reached back for the memory, he found only a black fog of loss and pain—that, and the nameless anxiety that stalked him day and night.

There's something important you're forgetting. Something so big, the weight of it will crush you flat when it finally comes.

"You don't know what you want, Ian. That's the problem. But I might be able to help you with that."

"I want to be left to my work, alone. And that's not gonna change, not even if you start staying up all night to try to catch me before I ride out."

"I'm coming with you," she insisted.

"Do you even know how to saddle a horse? Or where we keep the tack?"

She shifted uncomfortably. "Well, no. I was hoping you could help with that part."

"But you've ridden before? I see you've got the boots for it."

Her cheeks reddened. "Well, actually, Jessie was nice enough to lend me these. Turns out we wear the same shoe size. And she's tied up doing some research for a story she's been working on, so she told me I could take her horse, too. Um, Princess, I think her name is?"

He felt a tug at the corner of his mouth. "My five-year-old niece named her, which means she could've done a lot worse, considering that Eden calls the barn cat Fizzy Fuzzbutt."

"So you *do* still smile," Andrea said. "In a nice way, I mean. Haven't seen that for a long while." Emotion rippled through her words, *real* emotion as the mask of compassionate professionalism slipped a little. "I've really missed that, Ian. Missed the man I knew."

"That man's gone forever."

She nodded, her eyes somber. "You're right, I'm afraid. Experience changes people. Even experiences you're not ready to remember."

"I'm ready. More than ready. I just— It's gone, no matter what I do. No matter how hard I try." He shook his head, his sore fist curling—the same fist that had punched through the wall of his bedroom in frustration. "What the hell is wrong with me?"

"I don't think anyone has all the answers. In a lot of ways the mind's still the same uncharted wilderness it was in Freud's day. But I may have a few insights for you...if you'd like to hear them."

His knee-jerk reaction was to shut her down, to say *hell, no.* But something in the way she'd looked at him in that single, honest moment had touched off a yearning to see more of the real Andrea, the same woman who still lived in his dreams.

Besides that, he was getting sick of himself, of the way he had been acting. And if she knew something that might change that...would it really hurt so much to try?

He reached out for the coffee, their fingers brushing as he took it. Her skin felt so soft and tender beneath his calluses. So warm.

Taking a sip of the dark brew, he was relieved to find it black and bitter.

When he murmured his thanks, she shrugged. "I remembered how you took it."

"As opposed to yours...right?" he asked, as an image of her pouring cream into a porcelain mug came out of nowhere. She'd been wearing a loose white robe, her hair a jumble around her shoulders. Her lips were puffy and her smile warm, her eyes misted with a contentment that told him they'd just made love that morning.

A sense of loss sent a pang through the hollow of his chest. Of all the people the government could have sent to see him—and he felt sure they were behind this, somehow—why did they have to torture him with her?

"You're right," she confirmed, smiling sheepishly. "Two sugars and real cream whenever I can get it. I still eat pretty healthy, but I'm hopeless on that front."

"I'll saddle your horse, Andie—"

"Please, call me Andrea. All right?"

Ignoring her, he finished. "If you'll agree to wear a riding helmet. Horses can be dangerous enough when a person knows her way around 'em."

"So if I agree, you'll take me?"

"Only because I want to get my brother off my back about it. Well, that and to see how you walk tomorrow morning." Ian smiled, figuring it would be no hardship to watch the sway of her hips under any circumstances.

She winced and said, "Oh, boy. I haven't ridden very much, but I do remember that part."

"It only lasts a few days. Then you'll get used to it. Or die."

"You are teasing about that last part. Aren't you?"

He snorted. "Right. You'll only feel like dying."

He left her with a smile and went to retrieve Jessie's mare.

Chapter 3

The pinto was pretty enough to lead a parade, with bold black patches over brilliant white and a full and flowing mane and tail. But she seemed to have a mind of her own, a quality she demonstrated when Andrea tried to hold her back after she had mounted.

"You don't need to haul on the reins like that," Ian told Andrea, amusement written on his face. His own mount's golden hide gleamed in the early-morning sunlight, the well-muscled animal as handsome as his rider. "Her mouth is sensitive."

"Oh, am I hurting her? Should I— What do I do to keep her from running off with me?"

"Loosen your fingers, for starters, and grip her body with your knees, not your hands."

Embarrassed to be caught holding on to the saddle horn, she gave the reins a few inches of slack. But inside, her muscles quivered, ready to bail if Princess took a notion to gallop away.

Instead, the pinto exhaled, sounding more relieved than about to race away, and Andrea found the courage to tuck an irksome stray lock back up beneath the riding helmet and out of her eyes.

"That's a little better," said Ian. "Now breathe deeply,

from way down in the bottom of your belly. And ease up on the reins a little more. Like that, yes. Now move them both to one hand. All you'll need to do is lay the reins on her neck, to the right to turn right, to the left for left, just like I'm doing here. See?"

She was grateful when he demonstrated, his amusement giving way to patience as he took her through the nudges, clicks and reining that he claimed would be enough to get her started.

As he expertly guided his mount and closed the paddock gate behind them, he eyed her critically. "We'll still have to work on your seat."

"I'll bet you say that to all the girls." Her breath caught as she reminded herself that the light teasing, the innuendo, was no longer appropriate between them.

When he laughed, though, she decided it was worth it. Worth easing her professional demeanor to help him relax around her.

"Hardly," he answered as they headed for the range, riding side by side, "but mostly because the only girls I see around here are married, five years old or my mother."

"What about Miss Althea? And there must be maids, I'm guessing?" Judging from the size of the house, it would take a team to clean it.

"Miss Althea'd crack me upside the head with a wooden spoon if she ever caught wind I was thinking about her or the maids' seats. And you're the first visitor we've had staying here since…" The spark in his blue eyes dimmed. "Since I…"

"Since you've been back?" she prompted.

She saw his throat work as he swallowed, caught his haunted look as he nodded in answer.

They rode in silence for a while, the creaking of the saddles and the clopping of the horses' hooves the only conversation. She fought back her impatience to get started with her counseling, to finish this job and head back to Warriors-4-Life, where the lines between the past and present didn't blur like hoofprints in the wind. But she reminded herself that Ian's healing was what mattered and that pushing him too quickly would only shut him down again. So instead, she took a deep breath, forcing herself to enjoy the mildness of the morning sunshine and reminding herself that the ability to wait and to listen was worth twice as much as anything a mental health professional could ever say.

She was lost in thought when Ian told her, "We'll pick up and catch the fence line I've been checking about a half mile up ahead."

"How can you know where anything is? It's like the surface of an ocean. I don't see anything but grass."

"That's because you haven't learned to really look yet, to see it like the horses or the deer or the coyotes. A lot of what's out here lies beneath the surface. There are gullies and old streambeds, hidden groves of trees and cow paths."

She looked around, still seeing nothing, then turned in the saddle and realized with a start that she'd lost track of the mansion and the ranch outbuildings, too. How was that even possible, if the land was as flat and featureless as her senses tried to tell her? "Guess you have to be born to this land. I'm so turned around, I have no idea of the way back."

"I can teach you," he assured her. "Show you, so you can always find your way back home again."

"Like you did…" she said quietly, so quietly that she

wasn't certain he had heard her until she marked the way his shoulders stiffened.

"There," he said, pointing to two tufts that were a brighter green than the mostly golden grasses. "Those are the upper limbs of cottonwoods we're heading toward. They're actually good-size trees—and you see the notch between them where the creek's eroded a ravine?"

"So you go by the color of the treetops?"

He nodded. "And the time of year. Whenever you see that shade this late in the season, you know you're close to flowing water—cottonwoods usually crowd the creek beds, and the cattle like to lie in the shade beneath them."

"Sounds like an oasis."

"Oasis…" he echoed, frowning over the word as if it had stirred some dark association. Before she could decide whether to follow up with a question, he added, "It can be until a storm rips through and sends a flash flood roaring though that ravine. Then it's a damned death trap, those high walls hemming you in, heaven only knows who looking down on your location."

Andrea's stomach tensed as instinct warned her he was referring to a harsher territory. Did he himself even know what he was doing, or was she hearing from that part of him still wandering through foreign lands among those who meant to kill him, a part of him still desperate to get home?

"Thank goodness it doesn't look like rain, then." She gestured toward the thin silvery wisps painted over the blue sky, her need to reassure him stronger than her desire to draw him out. "And no one for miles around."

"No one," he repeated, his blue eyes unfocused until he shook off whatever reverie had gripped him. "Right. Of course, you're right. Our nearest neighbor's a half-day's ride, and I always check the forecast. Every single day before I ride out."

"You used to like surprises," she said, remembering how she'd always been the one who'd wanted things locked down and certain. Remembering how she hadn't been able to deal with it when he couldn't give the security she craved.

"Not anymore, I don't."

Something in his tone had her feeling a little skittish as they rode single file down into the ravine. The narrow, crumbling walls seemed to close in on her, even after Ian stopped and pointed out a low rock outcrop behind them that marked the way back to the mansion.

Soon, however, Ian eased her worry, straightening in his saddle and leading the way with the natural air of confidence she had been drawn to from the first time she'd met him. Her faith in his leadership was soon rewarded when the ravine opened to a green and grassy hollow bisected by a swift but shallow creek splashing over rocks. The air cooled as they continued downhill, riding beneath the spreading arms of the cottonwoods and provoking a symphony of morning birdsong.

Mooing to protest the invasion, cattle rose from the hollow they'd claimed as a resting place and trotted along the barbed-wire fence line on the other side of the creek.

"It's beautiful," she said, marveling at the hidden world he'd shown her.

"Beautiful and a pain, too, sometimes. Cows are always using those fence posts to scratch whatever itches—if they're not pushing 'em over, it's some thunderstorm that's washed them out. Look, there's one now that needs attention." Dismounting in one smooth motion, he used rock from the creek bottom to brace a tilted post.

"Want some help there?" she asked, though she wasn't entirely sure she could get back on her horse without a mounting block.

"I've got it covered. Just relax and enjoy the view."

She didn't have to be told twice, her gaze seeking out one singer and then following the progress of a pair of bright red wings flitting among branches. She tracked the movement until she was distracted by what looked like the metallic glint of something moving above them on the hillside. Something that didn't belong.

She stood in the stirrups and leaned to the right, trying to see it through the branches. "What's that? I saw something move. There." Though she'd lost sight of the movement, she pointed in the direction she'd last seen it.

He looked up from the strand of barbed wire he'd been tightening, a pair of pliers in hand. "What? You mean a bird?" he asked. "Or maybe a—"

She shook her head. "Something man-made, I think. A windshield, maybe, or something metal. Could someone be—"

He swore and rushed at her, his movement so abrupt the pinto shied away from his reach.

"Get down!" He closed in, grabbing at her leg. "Off the horse now. Gun!"

"No, Ian," she said, recognizing the panic ripping through his voice, the glazed eyes seeing a time and place she knew was as real to him as this one. Clearly, he had tipped into a flashback, something she had witnessed so many times in clients. "It was only a reflection, I'll bet, maybe some piece of trash blowing in the—"

"Gun, damn it!" This time when he lunged, he caught

her belt from behind, and she screamed as he pulled her down. Her terror echoed with the horses' whinnies as they bolted for the ravine's entrance, the clatter of their hoofbeats followed by a shattering boom.

Lightning strike, she thought as Ian caught her in his strong arms and started dragging her toward the shaded hollow where the cattle had lain. She'd heard of bolts from the blue, even on the clearest days.

The second blast convinced her she was wrong, the loud *plunk* as the post Ian had been working on exploded. Someone was really shooting, firing on them here and now and not in Ian's imagination. Had some out-of-season hunter mistaken them for game?

"No!" she shouted. "Don't shoot at us! We're down here!"

Ian clapped a hand over her mouth and ordered, *"Quiet. Now,"* through clenched teeth. One arm around her waist, he hauled her forward. Already knocked askew, her riding helmet fell as another shot echoed through the creek bottom. Grit spattered the back of her leg from where another bullet drilled the ground behind them, right where she'd been standing a half second earlier.

As her survival instincts kicked in, Andrea quit fighting Ian. Because whether or not this nightmare was rooted in his missing year inside the war zone, there was no denying it could kill them in the here and now.

His heart thundered in his chest, but Ian's mind dropped into mission mode as he guided the civilian with him under branches and around rocks. Because the civilian *was* the mission, her safety paramount in his mind, no matter how confused he was to have Andrea here with him.

Hadn't he left her behind in the peace and safety of Southern California? And hadn't she left him, too, a memory slicing through the darkness like a shard of broken glass, saying that she wanted another kind of life, a life without his secrets? So it made no sense that he was half leading and half dragging her here across this shallow creek, in a place where he used to hide out when his old man got that dangerous look in his eyes. But with no time to stop and think it through, Ian accepted this bizarre tangle of the half-remembered like another of his convoluted nightmares.

He searched the deepest shadows, focused on finding the one spot where he knew Andrea would be safe. A few steps beyond the water, he pointed out a horizontal shelf of weathered rock that had been undercut by past flooding. Partly filled in by damp pebbles, it would be a tight squeeze on her hands and knees, but if she could wedge herself in that space, she would be well hidden from the person up top with what sounded like a rifle.

"Crawl under there, where he won't see you."

"Down there? In that hole, you mean?" Her eyes were huge with disbelief.

He nodded. "Back yourself in, and don't come out, no matter what you hear or see."

"What about you? There's no room for both of—"

"Just do it, Andrea, and I'll come back for you. I swear to you, I will."

Their gazes locked, his blue with her hazel. And in that fraction of a second, some understanding passed between them. Face pale with terror, she blew out a shaky breath.

"You'd better," she whispered, grabbing handfuls of his shirt, "because if you leave me out here all alone, I swear to you, Ian, I will… Hunt. You. Down."

Dire as their situation was, he grinned at her bravado, then ducked his head to briefly touch his lips to hers.

Shock mingling with confusion on her beautiful face, she took two steps back and then crouched to do as he'd asked, crinkling her nose as she backed into the dank space. "There'd better not be spiders in here, especially those ones with the nasty, hairy legs."

"You'll be just fine," he assured her, not wanting to mention that a scorpion encounter was a lot more likely.

Still able to see her eyes, he dragged a tree branch to disguise the opening and moved off without another word. Stooping to palm some stones, he hurled them farther downstream, setting off a clatter.

The sniper didn't take the bait, probably wanting to get a visual before wasting another bullet. Or maybe he'd decided to cut his losses and get out, now that he had lost the element of surprise.

Whichever was the case, Ian zigzagged up the steep hillside, his progress as silent as the animals so often drawn here by the water. When he heard the deep thrum of an engine, he picked up his pace, not wanting to miss a glimpse at the SOB who'd tried to shoot them here, on his family's spread.

Remembering his brother, Ian paused and pulled the phone out of his pocket—the phone that he had, thank God, at last remembered to both charge and bring along. But down in this damned ravine, it was showing zero bars—no service. He tried sending a quick text, but it just sat in the outbox.

Jamming the cell back in his pocket, he continued his

climb. With every stop, he fought to hold on to his focus, but his mind kept slipping backward, toward a past that had the blue sky above him and the brush before him fading to the ink-stained silhouettes of buildings along a blackout-dark street, where he craned his neck to see a minaret against a star-strewn sky. The crescent-moon shape at its top marked it as a mosque. He breathed in the dense smells of a city, the cooking smoke tinged with exotic spices, the animal dung mixed with burning sandalwood. A reminder that life mingled with death here, death that waited to jump out of the shadows...

As the thrumming sound receded, he wondered, by returning here to Texas, had he brought death back with him? Were the gunmen who'd abducted him heading to the house to storm its walls?

He staggered to a stop, the realization ripping through him that he hadn't lost his freedom in a remote desert ambush as he'd been told. Hadn't been knocked unconscious and captured when an explosive device overturned his Hummer and killed one of his comrades. Hadn't been in Iraq with his unit...because he hadn't been a member of an army unit at all.

The knowledge doused him like ice water, the certainty that he'd never been what he'd told his family, friends and Andrea. *So what the hell were you, if you weren't really army? And how'd you get so screwed up you'd swallow your own cover story?*

Not only that, but the army itself had backed the whole sham, sending officers to debrief him, military shrinks and doctors to poke around his head. Which had to mean they were operating under someone's orders. Or more likely, some of them had really been CIA agents, trying to determine what he knew. And whether he was capable of accidentally spilling truths they preferred to remain hidden.

Was it possible they'd sent a team to guarantee his silence? Could one or more gunmen be waiting on the prairie above, knowing he must eventually emerge from cover?

Frozen to the marrow, he was blindsided by more fragments of the past, each more horrifying than the rest. A dark cell so cramped he couldn't stand up, so rank that he could scarcely breathe. A pang of horror as the door clanked open and two pairs of rough hands dragged him out for yet another beating. A coil of loose chain in the filthy straw, dripping with his blood and buzzing with flies.

As he crouched among the bushes growing along the side of the ravine, he slowly became aware of the shifting of rock and the crunching of leaf litter, the thud of fast-approaching footsteps.

Footsteps of a new threat coming up behind him, the fate he'd let himself imagine he'd escaped.

Between Andrea's cramped, uncomfortable position and the fear that at any moment, a killer would appear and shove a gun in her face, she was miserable enough without the ants that had found their way into her boots, crawling up her pant legs and stinging her for all they were worth. She shifted her position, trying to escape them, but pinch after pinch assured her that now that they had gotten past the protection of her boots and clothing, they meant to defend their home from her invasion—to the death, if necessary.

With no other choice, she crawled out of her hiding place and brushed at, swatted and stamped out every fire ant she could get to before she was hit with more venom. Shuddering with revulsion, she took a deep breath and assured herself that the stinging devils were gone and she would be fine, save for the itchy welts that would erupt.

As she pulled her boots back on, she nervously looked around, her stomach spasming with the fear that someone might have seen her wild "ant dance" or heard her muffled yips. But she spotted no one and heard nothing, no sign of the person who'd fired on them or Ian, either.

She tried to remember how long she'd waited, still and hidden, before the stings had become too much for her to bear. Five minutes? Ten? She couldn't be certain, especially not with her heart thumping so wildly she wanted to crawl out of her skin.

She relocated to another patch of shade, where she crouched and fought to calm herself for the next few minutes. But no matter how many times she assured herself that an experienced soldier like Ian, who had survived so much, knew what he was doing, phantom worries stung every exposed inch of her heart.

Before he'd left, he'd seemed so sure of himself, so tough and so cocky, the way he'd smiled and ducked his head to surprise her with a stolen kiss. Her stomach fluttered with the memory, with the knowledge that she'd have to talk to him about it later. But other thoughts troubled her more as she recalled those moments when his blue eyes had drifted, his expression troubled as something she'd said left him grappling with memories. Memories his conscious mind remained too shell-shocked to face.

She'd seen flashbacks before, had read case reports of terrible things happening—accidents, assaults and even murders—in the wake of something as innocuous as a backfiring car, a slamming door or a loud scene during a movie. In a situation as reminiscent of wartime as this one, would Ian's struggle with the buried ghosts of his past endanger him in the present?

As more time passed, she fought to hold back the rising tide of panic, telling herself it was a good sign that she'd heard no more shots. Reminding herself of how present and centered Ian had been when he had promised to return.

But eventually, her worry overwhelmed her, and there was nothing to be done except follow in the direction he had taken. As she walked, she prayed she would encounter Ian rather than the shooter.

She prayed even harder that when she did, he would still be the man she knew.

Chapter 4

Like horses, cattle were first and foremost prey animals, ruled by their adrenaline when anything strange spooked them. A half-dozen head charged toward Ian, their eyes rolling in their broad heads as they sought a path out of the ravine, back up to a place where they wouldn't feel trapped.

"Yah, yah!" Ian shouted, waving his arms at the dumb beasts so they would veer around him instead of crushing him to the ground. Startled by his movement, they broke and headed downhill, their oversize calves bawling in protest, their hooves clattering noisily over the loose rock.

"Nearest exit's *that* way, beef-for-brains," he said, jerking his chin in the opposite direction the frightened animals had taken. But at least their presence had served to yank his mind back to the here and now and the threat that might even now be drawing a bead on him, thanks to all the racket he had just made.

No shot rang out, but as he climbed higher, he heard Andrea calling his name, her voice strained and her breathing heavy. Scanning the rocky incline below, he spotted her, except she wasn't moving his way. Instead, she was following the cattle, her attention clearly drawn by their noise.

Had nerves driven her from her hiding place? Or had something down there frightened her into leaving safety?

Strength thrumming through his limbs, he moved downhill to intercept her. Before he could reach her, though, she slipped as a patch of loose earth shifted under her feet. Sitting hard, she slid with a miniature landslide of stones, her shriek echoing as she picked up speed, hurtling toward a pile of jagged rock some thirty feet below.

Though Ian was surer on his feet, he had trouble, too, as he broke into a shuffling run. His progress sent more scree rattling downhill and bouncing toward her. Arms flailing, she managed to grab on to a jutting tree root and break her fall, only to cry out as a fist-sized stone struck her above the left eye.

"Andrea, hold on!" he called, more worried about her passing out and falling than the chance that the shooter remained nearby.

She jerked her gaze in his direction, fresh blood streaming down her pale face from a small cut above her brow. "Ian? Ian, are you all right?"

She squinted and blinked at him as he picked his way toward her, as if she couldn't focus. Concussion, maybe, he thought, cursing himself for sending the rocks raining down on her.

At last, he reached her and took her free hand. "Don't worry about me. Let's just get you someplace more stable. I know it's pretty steep here, but I'm going to help you move to safety." He pointed out a spot about twenty feet to the left. "The trick is to go slowly and slide your feet. You ready?"

She shook her head, her eyes rounding. "I'll fall again."

"Take some deep breaths though your nose if you can. That's it. In and out."

He betrayed no hint of the urgency he was feeling as he waited, though he desperately wanted to get them away from this spot where they'd made so much noise.

She darted a glance up the hillside, her nails digging hard into his palm. "Is whoever—whoever shot at us still up there? Did you see him?"

"I heard a vehicle drive away a while back," Ian told her, not mentioning his worry that someone might still be waiting above, staking out the trail they'd taken to descend into the ravine. "Would've had to be a truck or Jeep—something with four-wheel-drive—to be out here."

"So he's gone, then," she said, her grip on his hand easing.

"That's right, darlin'. Now you need to let go of that root you're holding on to, and we'll get you up on your feet, slowly."

"I—I'm too dizzy. And my head hurts."

"I know, and I'm really sorry. I think I might've accidentally knocked down—"

"Don't be sorry. Just get me back home."

He wondered whether she was referring to the place she worked in Marston, some kind of rehab center for former military, he understood from what he'd read online. Or did she mean all the way back to where she'd grown up in Southern California?

"We're going to get you out," he said, "get you help as soon as we can. All you have to do is trust me. All right?"

"Okay. I can do this." She pressed her lips together, pushing aside the fear and pain with a look of intense determination.

The expression sparked another memory of the afternoon he'd met her. Ian recalled how impressed he'd been by her courage, despite her cuts and one very torn-up knee. Rather than giving way to hysteria, she'd focused on what had needed to be done.

Now she reclaimed that survivor's strength, standing with him on her own power and carefully choosing her footing as he steadied her with an arm around her waist. Together, the two of them made their way to stable ground before heading back down to a shaded spot beside the creek.

"How 'bout you sit right there, on that boulder?" he suggested. "I'd like to wash your face if you don't mind, check out that bump on your forehead."

"This time, I'm going to check for fire ants first." She eyed the ground suspiciously, kicking at the coarse gravel around the rocks.

"Ants?" He winced at the thought of the aggressive little hellions. "Is that what happened with the place I left you?"

Sighing with relief when nothing stirred at her feet, she sat down and nodded. "You really know how to show a girl a good time, don't you? Flying bullets and stinging ants, followed by a hard crack to the noggin."

"It's a gift, my way with women. But at least I held off on the tarantulas." He smiled down at her, his hand digging in a back pocket for the clean bandanna he'd tucked inside that morning. Taking it to the creek, he stooped to dunk it in the cool, fresh water. "But then, it's always good to hold back something for the second date."

She managed a smile, but what came out was more groan than chuckle.

He squeezed water from the cloth and returned to the spot where she was sitting. "This could sting a little."

She nodded and closed her eyes, her body tensing while he washed the red streamers coating the left side of her face. He dabbed gently at the wound itself, not wanting make the bleeding any worse.

"Do you think I'll need stitches?" she asked.

"Maybe a couple," he said, blotting the wound again. "You have a pretty good goose egg coming up, too, but that's all superficial. I'm more worried about a possible concussion. Can you tell me what day it is?"

"I'm fine."

"The date, Andie," he pressed.

She grimaced. "Everybody calls me Andrea. And it's Monday, September...the thirteenth, right?"

"The fifteenth, but we'll call that close enough, at least we will if you can tell me where we are."

She rolled her eyes. "A heck of a long walk from the mansion, since both the horses took off."

"It's not a mansion."

"Not in *your* world, maybe. But you haven't spent the past six months living in a dormitory."

"And you haven't spent the past year living in a cell." Quick and vicious as a slashing switchblade, an image of the dark and filthy hole where he'd been kept made him swallow hard.

"I'm so sorry," she said, sincerity shining in her eyes. "I wasn't thinking."

He wanted to tell her it was all right, but it was easier to change the subject. "Your idea about walking back home in the open might be a bad move. Down here, at least, there's cover."

Her gaze locked in on his. "I thought you said the shooter left."

"I *think* he did, but I'm not willing to gamble our lives on the theory." If Ian were here alone, he'd take the chance, but he couldn't bring himself to risk Andrea's safety.

He still had feelings for her, he admitted, feelings that refused to stay buried. She might have left him long ago, might be promised to another man now, but his heart and Swiss cheese memory had conspired to make all of that irrelevant. He'd tried, these past few days, to fight it, had fought to keep her at arm's length. But seeing her bruised and smeared with dirt and blood, her hair as tangled as a little girl's, ignited a fierce instinct to keep her safe.

"It makes sense that he'd leave, doesn't it?" she argued. "He probably panicked after realizing he was shooting at human beings, not a deer or something."

"It would make sense if I believed for one minute it was just some poacher hunting out of season. Or even some dumb teenager out with daddy's rifle playing Let's Shoot Anything That Moves."

"But you don't think that."

He shook his head. "I don't. Which means it's possible someone's still up there, waiting for us to make a move so he can take me out."

He went back to the creek to rinse out the bandanna, creating eddies of pink water that quickly dissipated. Wringing out the thin cloth again, he took it back and gave it to her. "You'd better hold on to this, keep it pressed to your head until the bleeding stops. Since my phone won't work down here, we could be in for a long wait before someone from the ranch comes looking."

She dabbed at the wound and frowned at him. "This theory of yours, about someone waiting for us... Is there some reason you suspect someone might be after you?"

"Other than the bullets, you mean?"

"Just now, you said *for us.* But a moment ago you used the word *me.* You said, *waiting for us to make a move so he can take me out.*"

"If it makes you feel any better, he'd probably shoot you, too, to eliminate the witness."

She snorted in response, intelligence glittering in her narrowed eyes. "Witness to what, Ian? Are you suggesting some kind of a—of an *assassination*? Your sister-in-law mentioned something earlier, some worries you had when you first came back that someone might try to take you away if the public didn't know you were here."

Anger flared, like a match struck in a dark cell. "So you've been talking about me, have you? Asking family members just how crazy this situation's made me? Did they tell you it all started years ago, that Zach's and my old man beat us so often we couldn't get away from this ranch fast enough? That our mother turned a blind eye and explained away our bruises, since she didn't have any of her own to worry over."

"Oh, Ian. I'm so sorry," she said, her beautiful eyes glittering with compassion. "I had no idea."

"Maybe I am insane, to want to come back to a place with such bad memories—"

"There must be other memories, too, good memories that helped draw you back here. Or maybe you unconsciously sensed that you needed to forgive to heal. I would never call you insane for returning to your family or for worrying about how your more recent past might come back to haunt you, either."

"No, I guess you shrinks have fancier words for it. You'd call it paranoid, right? Or delusional or some other psychobabble. But I didn't make up those gunshots, did I? You heard them, too. You saw the reflection from the gun above us."

She hesitated, and his heart stumbled. He wasn't *really* crazy, was he?

She nodded, and he breathed again. "I heard the shots, Ian, and I saw something. Which means it's possible the reason for your fear might be real, too. So let's explore that for a moment—"

"I don't want to *explore* it. I don't want to *dialogue* about it, or *own my feelings*, or any of that BS you picked up in shrink school. Can't we just talk, Andrea? Talk the way we used to, back before you kicked me to the curb?"

Her cool look lasered through him. "I'm going to blame that on your memory, but the fact is, I didn't *kick* you out of my life. You made that choice, refusing to tell me where you'd been when you disappeared without a word two days before our engagement party. Refusing to tell me why, when I was worried enough to call the army post where you'd told me you were stationed, the MPs I spoke of had no record of you."

"And I said I couldn't tell you," he said, more pieces of the puzzle spinning together in his brain.

"Couldn't. Or *wouldn't*." She looked away, but not before he saw pure anguish shifting through her expression. "And all I could think of was that, for all the counseling I'd gone through, everything I'd done to start a healthy new life, I was repeating my mother's mistakes after all…"

"Your mother's?"

She nodded. "Yes, my mother's. You don't remember, do you?"

He grimaced, his mind snatching at memories that darted from his grasp like minnows. Unexpectedly, he caught one. "Your mom's dead. You found her, after. After she'd taken a whole bottle full of—"

Seeing the pain flash over Andrea's expression, he cut himself off. "Sorry. Didn't mean to blurt it out like that. It's just—when something comes back—"

"No, it's good. It's true, that's what happened," she allowed. "And I'm glad your memory's returning. That's a good sign."

He opened his mouth to ask her what their breakup had had to do with her mother's "mistake," as she'd put it. But something else occurred to him first, something he couldn't wait another minute to get off his chest. "I've remembered other things today, too, when I was climbing up to try to see the shooter."

"Flashbacks?" she asked. "I was worried the gunfire might've triggered—"

"I know the reason I lied to you in California. Why I felt I had to."

She dabbed at her dripping forehead. "I thought you might be married, but I didn't see a word about a wife or ex-wife in your file."

"You thought I might be—? Hell, no. I'd never do that. Lie to you like that, I mean. There was no other woman."

"But you *did* lie to me, about your military post, at least."

He sighed. "Believe me, it wasn't by choice. But when you're involved with clandestine services, it's easier to use a cover story than—"

"Clandestine services?" She blinked at him. "Do you mean—you were some sort of *spy* or something? Is that what you're telling me?"

"Not a spy, exactly," he said. "My work with the CIA involved cultivating relationships with foreign resources."

"So you were a spy*master*, then. Really?"

"Something like that," he admitted, though even now, with his once all-consuming career in tatters, it went against the grain to talk about his work.

"Then what were you doing in California?" she asked. "I thought people like that were all overseas or in D.C."

"Not all of us, not all the time. But as I'm sure you guessed, I was called on to travel quite a lot—especially when there was a lot of chatter about planned terrorist activities targeting our country's citizens."

"So you were overseas, then, when something went wrong?"

The dark city street came back to mind, followed by a blinding flash, a deafening boom and crumbling masonry—then nothing. "It sure as hell wasn't like the army claimed, but there was an attack when I was on my way to meet a potential asset who'd promised to turn over sensitive information. An explosion, and then…"

Overcome by a dizzying sensation, he sank down to sit beside her on the boulder. He couldn't think, couldn't speak, panic racing with his pulse as the ravine whirled around him. Panic that pushed back the onslaught of memory that threatened, the tidal wave of shame that left him shaking. If he'd only seen it coming, recognized the subtle clues that he was being set up for an ambush, he could have avoided capture and the torture that had made him—

"No wonder they want me to die," he murmured, rising to stagger away where he could retch again and again, bringing up nothing but his own icy terror. *What the hell did I do? How many deaths did I cause?*

Rising from the boulder where she had been sitting, Andrea fought to hold herself back, to give Ian the space to pull himself together. Not so much for his benefit, she realized, but because she felt so vulnerable herself. So at risk of forgetting who she was and what she'd come to do.

I'm here as a psychologist, she reminded herself, *drawing on my professional experience with PTSD survivors.* Not so much as a friend, no matter what had been said, and definitely not as Ian's lover. So why was it she ached to touch him, to comfort him not with words, but...?

No. She wasn't going to chance it. To risk confusing Ian, risk disgracing herself. She pressed the damp bandanna to the wound on her head harder than she meant to, the resulting stab of pain a penance for what she had been thinking.

No, not thinking, she realized. *Feeling.* Succumbing to memories of falling headlong into a love affair that had proved such a bad idea on the first occasion.

She walked away, holding her hands over her stomach, knowing that, in returning to him his past, she risked losing sight of her own present, not to mention the future she had planned with Julian. She fought to focus on the man she'd fallen for, the man whose vision for the center had captured her imagination. She remembered how he'd invited her to lunch at a seminar on post-traumatic stress disorder, how his passion in describing Warriors-4-Life had lured her from a better-paying job in a place that wasn't located in the dead center of nowhere.

He'd explained to her how costs were so much lower here in Texas. It was only by sheer chance that the vacant nursing facility the organization had restored had ended up being so close to the Rayford family's spread. Chance, not fate, had brought her here.

But the harder she struggled to picture Julian's face, to enumerate his noble and inspiring qualities, the more she kept glancing back at Ian, who was now crouching by the water, jeans straining against his strong thighs, his lean, muscular arms scooping handfuls to his mouth to drink. When he turned to glance back at her, the sight of him nearly took her breath away, the high cheekbones and deep tan that spoke of native blood in his lineage, the contrast of his deep blue eyes—eyes that glittered with unspeakable pain. With the need for reassurance that only she could provide.

Seeing him like that, her brain shut down completely and muscle memory took over. Her mouth drying in an instant, she started toward him. At the same moment, he moved toward her, his steps longer, swifter, unstoppable.

Helpless to resist, she hurried, too, her every cell crying out for the necessity of contact. When he took her into his arms, she felt the rush, heard the *whoosh* as her willpower caught flame, all her resolve burned to ashes the moment their mouths came together.

She tumbled to temptation, to the desperate press of lips and tangle of tongues, the hunger to taste what she'd never guessed she had been starved for. Pleasure arced through her entire body, a buzzing need that made her breasts ache for the sensation of his hands, his mouth on them. Between her legs, an even deeper yearning set in, an ache that left her wondering how she could have lived so long without his touch.

His lips slid to her neck, the hot moisture of his mouth moving over sensitive skin beneath her ear. She moaned aloud, felt herself grow hot and wet as sensation spiraled though her. Her hands rubbed at his back, pulling him even closer.

He yanked her shirttail from her jeans, then reached up beneath her top, finding and tweaking a hard nipple. She remembered how it felt—the moist heat of his mouth suckling—and the memory was so strong, her desire so sharp, that she nearly came right then. Her knees buckled from beneath her so suddenly that Ian had to make a grab for her to keep her from collapsing.

His eyes found hers, their electric blue intensity cutting through the past two years, cutting through her willpower. "I know the timing's bad—worse than bad—stuck out here with heaven knows who waiting to take another shot at us the second we leave cover. But I'm putting you on notice that I want you. I need you. And the first chance I get, the first damn moment we can find a private, safe spot, I mean to make you forget there's ever been anyone besides me. Because there damned well never should've been. It was all one big mistake."

It would've been so easy to nod her head. To forget the danger, forget herself, and give in to the chatter of the little creek, the sunshine slanting through the green leaves, the unbearable hunger building in her body and provoke him to make love to her here and now. But in the depths of his gaze, she read the terror of the unknown, his desperation to latch on to those few things that seemed familiar.

That was all she was to him, a solid rock to cling to at the center of a rushing torrent. A torrent that seemed to echo his words: *All one big mistake...*

She pulled free of his embrace, blinking and shaking her head as she struggled to clear the flood of hormones. The physical attraction she'd already allowed to carry her far past her normal boundaries.

"No, Ian. This is crazy. I don't know what's got into me to—" Seeing the hurt wash over him, she ached to return to him, but she couldn't risk the contact. "I was in the wrong here, clearly. This is totally unethical."

"Don't do this to me, Andrea," he said, his gaze a raw wound that made the cut still oozing on her forehead fade into insignificance. "Don't treat me like I'm nothing but your patient."

"But you *are* my patient, in a sense, and I was wrong to forget that for a single second." The trembling that racked her found its way into her voice. "Wrong to come here, clearly, to imagine I could put the past aside."

"You can't put it aside—can't put *me* aside—because you still love me," he insisted, "just the way I love you. Those old feelings, they're all still there. I dreamed of your face, your body for so long. I followed the memory of you home."

She closed her eyes. "Please don't, Ian. Don't put that on me. I do care for you, really. I think I always will. But I love another man now, a man I owe my loyalty—" She put a hand over her mouth in an attempt to stifle the sob that she felt coming. Because she hadn't proved worthy of the trust Julian had offered. She'd been every bit the faithless cheater his ex-wife had been. Worse yet, she'd lived up to her father's legacy—a father whose broken faith had cost her family everything.

"If you love this man so much, what are you doing kissing me?" Ian asked.

She opened her eyes, blinking away their dampness. "Getting tangled in old emotions, echoes from the past. In my own grief after learning—did you know the army sent a chaplain and an officer to notify me you were dead?"

"Oh, Andrea. I'm sorry. I meant to change that after we—"

"It doesn't matter now, and I don't blame you. But it did tear open old wounds and make me think what might have been. If it—if it hadn't been for meeting Julian, I don't know how I would have—"

"Julian. So that's his name. The man I'm going to make you forget."

"I'm sorry, Ian, but Julian's the man I'm going to marry." A lump swelled in her throat, so painful it made her eyes brim over. "At least if he'll forgive me, after this."

"You'll tell him?"

She nodded, a yawning chasm opening in the hollow of her stomach. "Of course, I will. I won't start a life with him with secrets between us."

"Then I hope he's a jealous ass. I hope he—"

"Don't talk about him. Please don't. I feel horrible enough already. And he's a great man, really. You'd like him if you ever met him, if you heard him talk about the center, about the need to help the soldiers coming back from war with so many terrible…" She realized she'd said the wrong thing as color suffused Ian's face.

"You mean poor broken wrecks like me. Pathetic losers you would never dream of—"

"Stop it, Ian. Please, stop. Let's not make this any worse."

"I'm not sure how it could get worse," he said, "unless the sniper—"

As if conjured by his words, the rumble of an engine silenced the singing of the birds. An arrival that drove home the realization of just how vulnerable they were.

"Ian, are you down there? Dr. Warrington?"

Ian's tension dissipated when he recognized his brother's deep voice, calling him from the mouth of the ravine.

"We're down by the creek!" Ian called, watching from the corner of his eye as Andrea hurriedly tucked her shirt back into her jeans. "We're coming up now."

She looked up, catching his eye, and he noticed the flush of redness beneath her collar.

"Don't worry," he assured her. "I'm not the type to kiss and tell—even if you're still planning on it."

Avoiding his gaze, she went to rinse out the bandanna in the creek one last time. Once she was done, she followed as he retraced the uphill path they'd originally traveled, where both Zach and Virgil Straughn, the long-time ranch manager, stood outside of Zach's four-door pickup, their faces drawn with worry.

"Thought you must've run into some trouble when the horses showed up at the barn," Zach said. "I tried calling your phone—could've wrung your damned neck when I couldn't get through."

In spite of the harshness of his words, Ian saw Zach's tension in the stiffness of his shoulders, saw how badly he had scared his older brother. "I had the phone with me this time, and I swear I tried to call you. But there's no signal down there. Couldn't even get a text out."

Zach thumped him on the back a lot harder than was strictly necessary. "Thank God, you're still in one piece, man. My life flashed before my eyes at the thought of having to tell Mama you'd been..."

"That makes two of us," Virgil put in as he pulled off his sweat-stained hat and raked his fingers through his thinning gray hair. "Poor woman would've had another breakdown for sure."

Zach caught sight of Andrea pressing the cloth to her forehead. "Are you all right? What happened?"

"Just a little bump," she said, sounding surprisingly subdued. "I'll be fine, I'm sure."

"Here, miss." Virgil hurried to the truck with surprising speed, considering his slight paunch and the hitch in his gait. He opened the passenger-side front door and waved her over. "You should sit down here in the cab, and I'll get you some water and—how about some Tylenol? I think we've got some in the first-aid kit."

"That'd be fantastic," she said, heading for the pickup.

Hearing the exhaustion in her voice, Ian realized how rough the ordeal had been on her, both physically and emotionally. He'd been wrong to take advantage, to come on with all the finesse of a charging bull while she was so vulnerable.

But that didn't mean he hadn't meant every word he'd said. He wasn't sorry he had kissed her, either—a kiss that had cut through all the fog of his confusion like a beam of pure white light. Complicated as their situation was, his feelings for her were the only thing he trusted, the one thing he could see that was still worth fighting for.

While Virgil fussed over Andrea, Zach gave Ian the

full big-brother stare. "So what the hell went on here? How'd you let her get hurt?"

Ian scowled at him. "I'm glad to see you, too, bro. Especially glad it *was* you and not the son of a bitch who decided to use the two of us for target practice."

"Target practice?" Zach's gaze narrowed, sweeping the prairie in all directions. "You're telling me someone *shot* at you two?"

"I am. And as you can probably imagine, our horses took exception."

"I figured something was up when I spotted 'em making for the barn like their tails were on fire. So who was shooting? Did you see 'em? And are you sure they meant to shoot at you?"

"Damned sure, considering how close those bullets came—and how the shooter fired again after Andrea called out that we were down there." Ian's throat tightened as it hit him how close they'd both come to being killed out here. "And no, I never saw him or heard anything except an engine when he took off. Thought we'd be better off, though, waiting for help down where there's good cover."

"Smart move," Zach allowed, "and I was damned glad to find that note you left saying where you and the doc were going." He glanced back toward the truck, where Virgil was rattling around in the backseat cooler to get Andrea some ice. "That bump on her head—"

"It was a falling rock that did it, one that I'd kicked loose. We'd better take her into Marston to get checked out. I think she might need a couple stitches."

"All right, but before we go, have you come up with any idea, any theories at all, why somebody would be out to kill you?"

Ian thought of telling his brother what he'd remembered about the true nature of his work for the government, but this wasn't the time or place. "Same as I've said before," he answered. "I have this feeling not everybody's happy to have me back from the dead."

Zach's gaze zeroed in on him. "You know, when you first came back and started talking about somebody wanting to make you disappear, I chalked it up to dehydration mostly, or the hell that you'd just been through making you a little…you know."

"In light of the fact that you invited a shrink to stay with us, I guess I do."

Zach grimaced. "Now, though, I'm beginning to see your point, especially considering how long the odds are of some random nut job coming on you out here accidentally." His gesture took in the broad sweep of a land that went on unbroken as far as the eye could see. "But why now? And why not wait to catch you alone instead of when you had a witness with you?"

"Could be that just maybe, Andrea's what set this all off," Ian said in a low voice, his gaze swinging toward Zach's truck. "Maybe whoever shot at us is worried she'll unlock something they'd just as soon stay secret. A secret—"

Zach interrupted, his face hardened as he finished his brother's sentence. "A secret so big and so ugly, someone's willing to shoot down both of you to keep it."

Chapter 5

While Zach drove them back to the house, Andrea sat in the front-passenger seat holding the ice pack Virgil had improvised for her. The cool pressure felt soothing, and it offered her a chance to hide her face—and her silent struggle to regain her composure.

It was ludicrous, she told herself, that she was far more upset about kissing Ian, now seated behind her, than she was about the fact that someone had tried to kill them. Still, she would rather dodge more bullets than try to explain her behavior to Julian.

Oh, he would be stoic about it, if she knew him, understanding even. With his own training in psychology—though he had always worked on the administrative side—he might even offer her excuses, citing her emotional trauma and her head wound, both of which had left her vulnerable to a retreat to the past. But inside, he would be devastated, left to wonder what it was that drew him to unfaithful women. Or what it was that he was lacking, when the flaw was hers alone.

As they rode, Ian and Zach discussed calling local law enforcement to report the incident.

"Not that I imagine Canter'll do much in the way of an investigation," Zach said morosely. "He's mad as hell

I put a stop to him coming to Mama with his hand out every time the department needed something."

"So you have something against spreading around a little Rayford money in the public interest?"

"It's the sheriff's *self*-interest I'm worried about," Zach said. "I don't trust the SOB as far as I can throw him."

"You aren't the only one," Virgil said. "I tried to tell her it wasn't right, him coming by so often…"

Zach glanced over his shoulder, looking at his brother. "You remember Canter at all from back before we left home?"

Ian went quiet for some time before saying, "I remember a stiff-necked deputy with a hatful of attitude threatening to haul our gold-plated Rayford butts to jail when we raised hell around town. Tell me you don't mean that jackass."

"The very one. He's sheriff now, and I can tell you, he was all about kissin' up to Rayfords back when Mama was alone and half-looped most of the time with all those damned pills she was popping."

Miserable as she was, Andrea perked up a little to hear that the primly proper Nancy Rayford had had a substance abuse issue. So that was what was behind her brittle and tiresome behavior, especially toward her daughter-in-law. Andrea felt certain that the family matriarch's snootiness was nothing but a facade, hiding the flaws she feared would be exposed.

"Maybe we should just look into this ourselves," Ian suggested. "Keep him out of it entirely—and away from Mother."

"Much as I'd like to, I think we at least need to report what happened. After he blows us off, we can try digging into it on our own—"

"Or maybe Andrea can help me figure out what this is really all about…" Ian reached forward from the backseat and laid his big hand on her shoulder. She felt the warmth of him radiating through the fabric of her shirt, heard the concern in his voice as he gave her a gentle squeeze. "Almost home. You hanging in there?"

"Just trying to let everything sink in," she said. "And trying not to scratch those stupid ant bites." The itching had begun already, though she was doing her best to ignore it.

"We'll have ointment for that at the house," Ian assured her. "But we'll want to get you checked out at the nearest ER anyway."

"That's not necessary. The ice is helping, and the bleeding's almost stopped."

"Don't try to minimize it," Ian said, giving her shoulder a firmer squeeze. "I saw the way your head snapped back when that rock smacked into you. And you looked dazed or worse when I—"

She jerked away her shoulder and angrily demanded, "When you *what*?" When he had kissed her until she'd forgotten the danger they were in? Until she'd lost all sense of who she was, much less the professional and personal obligations she was honor-bound to live by?

"When I *reached* you, that's all," he said shortly. "No need to jump down my throat about it. And no damned chance of getting out of an emergency room visit, so quit arguing about it."

Zach sent a measuring look their way, his expression telling her he'd figured out there was something more than met the surface going on between them. After letting them settle for a few moments, he said, "I understand your not wanting to make a fuss, Doctor—"

"Please, it's Andrea." She'd asked the family several times to call her by her first name, just as she did with those clients she saw at the center.

"Okay. Andrea, then. But I'm going to have to side with Ian on this. There's no sense taking chances, not with a possible concussion. And since it happened on ranch property, I insist we cover the cost."

She opened her mouth to argue that wasn't the point but then realized it was useless. "I see that I'm outnumbered. But if I have to go all the way to Marston for the ER, I might as well pack my things. I'll send one of our other counselors, but I won't be coming back."

"What do you mean, you won't be coming back?" Ian demanded. "We were just beginning to make real headway. This morning, I remembered—" He cut himself off, leaving Andrea to guess he didn't want to go into his work with the CIA in front of Virgil and his brother. "I remembered so much more."

"Connor will be perfect for you," she said, pretending she hadn't heard the note of desperation in his voice. "He served in Operation Enduring Freedom, so he has a lot of personal knowledge of the effects of the war on—"

"He doesn't have personal knowledge of *me*, damn it. Not like you do, Andie."

She gritted her teeth to get past her knee-jerk desire to correct him—or tell him that his use of his old nickname for her only underscored the fact that he would never see her as anything but the woman he'd once loved…

The woman he *still* loved, she reminded herself, since he'd made it clear that in his mind, their relationship had never ended. And that he meant to do everything in his power to make her forget it had...

Even if doing so would destroy her completely. Which was why she had to get away from him the moment that she could.

Once they were back home, Jessie emerged from The Deadline Cave, as she called her book-and-paper-strewn study, and insisted on going upstairs to help Andrea clean up and gather her things. Ian had seen Zach whisper something to his wife—probably a directive to find out the real reason that Andrea was in such as hurry to leave. Seeing the fear in Andrea's eyes, Ian had already sworn that, despite what had happened, they could keep her safe here. She'd only shaken her head, her stubbornly clamped jaw telling him that she wasn't about to change her mind.

As soon as the two women disappeared into Andrea's suite, his brother turned on him and cuffed his arm. "So what the hell did you do to her, bonehead?"

Ian shoved him back, reminding the dumb lug that he might be skinnier than usual, but he was nobody's punching bag. "What makes you think I did a damned thing? Maybe she just doesn't like being used as target practice. Probably not what she signed up for after spending all those years in shrink school."

Zach mimicked an air-raid siren, a sound so annoying, Ian wanted to deck him. "You hear that?" Zach asked him. "That's my bullshit detector hittin' the red zone. Because it's obvious as the nose on your ugly face—"

"I don't care what anybody says. I don't look *that* much like you."

"—the reason she's bailing has nothing to do with

bullets and everything to do with you. Or something between the two of you, more specifically. Which brings me back to my question. What the hell did you do?"

Ian grimaced and paced past the bottom of the staircase as he attempted to cool down. Much as it griped him to admit it, his brother was absolutely right about why Andrea was leaving.

"If you're going to tell me, hurry up about it," Zach urged, "before Virgil finishes calling Canter or Mama gets back from her hair appointment."

Ian blew out a long breath. "Could be I was a little too direct in announcing my intentions to make her forget this other guy."

"The one she's engaged to marry? While she's trying to help you to get back your memory? Smooth move, brother."

"I can't help it when I'm with her. Can't help the way it all comes rushing back to me—how smart and brave and sexy she is, how meeting her again brought me alive." As true as everything he'd said was, the real reason remained unspoken: how the memory of her had sustained him, keeping him safe throughout a journey that had spanned continents and oceans, how he would walk forever to get back to where they had been…even if it was a place that no longer existed.

"So that's the trouble." Zach shook his head, something between a grimace and a wry smile pulling at one side of his mouth. "You remember the rush but not the rest. Thing is, though, Ian, there's gotta be a downside. Otherwise, you wouldn't have broken up two years ago."

Ian thought of telling him why it had happened, telling him about the clandestine services career he'd kept hidden for so many years. But before he told anyone else about his CIA past, he needed time to consider whether sharing the information might prove a legal problem or, worse yet, a danger to the people he loved.

It was just as possible, though, that getting it all out in the open might prove his best defense. But at the thought of allowing the viral sensation that would follow any report of how the government had spun up the feel-good story about a "soldier's" miraculous return, his throat clenched and icy chills crawled up the column of his spine. The white marble and carved mahogany stairway fell away, dropping him back to a time and place where...

Hunger and thirst, suffocating heat and numbing cold, and the cruel positioning of his arms as they bore his weight were bad enough. But the worst part was the hood that blinded him so that he couldn't see pain coming, couldn't see the chain begin its downward arc.

He soon learned to listen for the dark chuckle or the clink of metal, to scent the sour sweat of his captors as they approached, to brace himself for the beating that would follow. But his senses failed him sometimes, leaving him in the constant torment of anticipation, holding his breath and clenching his muscles, his pulse jumping at every scrape of distant footsteps or a whisper of rats' feet in the straw.

It was the anticipation, along with the memory of pain, more than the torture itself that broke down his mind, his body, his will to resist the questions that kept coming, each one hard and unyielding as another blood-caked metal link.

"Ian? Ian, you still with me, man?" Zach's voice was a mere echo, an imaginary strand of English woven through the rough fabric of the Pashto demands that he tell them where the listening post was.

But Ian knew it was illusion, another trick to break him, just like the hallucinations that tortured him each time he'd blacked out, impossible dreams where he'd managed to escape his bindings and strangle his guard with that damned chain. Dreams where he had somehow talked a sympathizer into helping smuggle him out of the mountains, out of the country. Where he had made his way back home...

Not to a place, so much as to a woman. A dark-haired beauty in a blue bikini, a woman who regarded him with green-gold eyes beneath the long fringe of her lashes...

"Ian!" He heard the semblance of his brother's voice again, this time coming with a hard grip that shook his shoulders.

Ian flailed to break free, his unbound arms swinging strong. His fist crashed into something solid, some*one* who shouted in surprise as he crashed backward into the banister before sitting hard on the pristine marble floor.

"What's going on, you two?" A red-faced older version of the Virgil Ian remembered stepped between the brothers, a phone forgotten in his hand. "What the hell's all this about? Show some respect in this house. Your mama could be back any minute."

Ian gasped for breath, his heart jackhammering its way through his sternum. His skin beaded with hot sweat as he looked around wildly, seeking somewhere to run before the other guards showed up to beat him, to kill him this time for daring to strike one of their own.

Before he could decide which way to run, the fog lifted, leaving him blinking down at his own brother.

At Zach, who was sitting on the landing floor and rubbing his jaw.

"It's okay, Virg," Zach said, his voice surprisingly calm for a guy who'd just gotten decked. "I've got this. You back here with us, Ian? You're safe. You're home now, and I swear to you, you're never going back."

Ian took a shaky step and bent, offering his older brother a hand up. "I'm sorry, man. I'm sorry."

"I know you are. I get it." Zach accepted his help, his steady gaze indicating that he did so more out of a desire to offer reassurance than out of any real need for assistance. Once he was on his feet, he tightened his grip. "Just let's not make a habit of it, all right? Because I can get past a sore jaw and some bumps and bruises, but what if it had been Mama? Or Jessie or even Eden?"

"I wouldn't have hit one of them."

"But you weren't swinging at *me* either, were you? Not that I don't probably have it comin' every now and then, but it was pretty clear that you were after somebody else. For one thing, you were yelling in some foreign language. Arabic, maybe? I don't know. I never had the gift for—"

"Pashto. It was Pashto," Ian told him, naming the language of his captors.

"So they were Taliban?" Zach asked him. "The ones holding you over there in—"

"I don't remember the details. And I sure as hell don't want to talk about it." It was bad enough knowing that his brother had seen the ropy, red scars across his back and shoulders. Bad enough that anyone knew that he'd been beaten.

Virgil shifted and cleared his throat, then let them know the sheriff had insisted on coming personally to take their report rather than sending a deputy to do it. "He wanted you both still here when he arrives. I told him Dr. Warrington needs a trip to the ER before she's questioned, said I'll take her there myself."

Zach scowled, looking as if he'd rather take another shot to the jaw than deal with Canter. "What about her car, though?" he asked, referring to the old blue Honda she'd arrived in.

"I'll drive her in it and one of the hands can pick me up there later. They're always itching for an excuse to head to town anyway."

"To head to the bars there, you mean. Try and keep 'em out of trouble, will you? Or at least don't let 'em drive after they've had a few."

"As long as I don't need to stick around to keep you two out of trouble." Virgil glanced from Zach to Ian, who was still grappling with the realization that the ranch in Rusted Spur, not the torture chamber, was his reality.

"We're just fine, aren't we, Ian?" Zach said.

"Yeah." Ian blinked, then rubbed at his knuckles, noticing that one was split and bleeding. "Leastwise, I've busted up my hand enough for one day on your big mouth."

Frowning at the uneasy look that passed between the brothers, Virgil said, "I'll—ah—I'll be out in the kitchen, then. Making up a couple of more ice packs."

"Don't worry on my account," said Ian.

"Mine, either," Zach tossed in. "We're done now. Aren't we, Ian?"

"You have my word," Ian told them both.

"Then I'll be out there pinching a couple of those molasses-spice cookies I smell baking." Virgil shared a warm smile that had served as a counterbalance for their father's scowls and curses for so many years.

Seeing it calmed Ian, a reassurance that kindness sometimes outlived cruelty.

Once he'd left the room, Zach asked Ian, "You ready to talk about it now, see if the two of us can figure how your past could be connected to what went down this morning?"

"I—I don't—" Ian felt the vault of words slam shut, the lock inside him turning. He tried to struggle past it, reminding himself that his brother was on his side, but his face grew so hot he imagined he must be glowing like an ember.

"Guess not." Zach rubbed his jaw again, but not before Ian saw it was already bruising. "But if you can't talk to me, you'll better damned well talk with someone. Before whatever's bottled up inside you finds a way out we'll both regret."

"B-but Andrea's leaving," Ian choked out, "heading off to Marston and never coming back."

"Then try that other guy she mentioned. Or anybody, Ian."

"I'm not spilling my guts to some damned stranger."

"In that case, you'd better do a little quick thinking about how to change her mind."

From the guest wing, they heard a door close, but to Ian's disappointment, it was not Andrea but Jessie who came downstairs, the loose waves of strawberry-blond brushed back over her shoulders.

"How's Andrea?" Ian blurted. "Is she all right?"

Jessie shrugged. "It's hard to tell. She's being awfully quiet, especially when I mention your name. You two have a fight or something?"

Zach snorted and looked at Ian. "Didn't I tell you it was obvious?"

Ian grimaced but was saved from responding when Jessie went to her husband and reached up to touch his jaw.

"What the heck happened to you? I could swear you were in one piece when I left you."

"Just a little bump, that's all. No need to start fussing."

Jessie swung a narrow-eyed gaze from one brother to another. "Don't tell me you two got into it. *Really?* I'd think you guys would want to circle the wagons right now, with somebody taking shots at Ian."

Zach stared at her for several moments before he asked, "So what if this person *wasn't* after Ian?"

Jessie shook her head. "In what universe does that make sense, Zach? Maybe I should be loading *you* into the car to get your head scanned, too."

"Just hear me out. It could be possible that—"

"Andrea Warrington's way too nice to have made enemies, especially the kind that would come gunning for her here."

Undeterred, Zach asked, "But what if the shooter meant to kill *you*, Jessie? After all, Andrea was riding your horse."

Jessie made a scoffing noise. "Seriously, are you really back on that again? I've already told you, I'm not giving up my work. It's too important."

"It's important to me that you stay in one piece, and these people you're investigating—"

"Are going to be totally blindsided when this story hits the news. Besides, even if it did somehow get out, these guys may be slimy and corrupt, but that doesn't make them killers."

"If you're not worried about these crooks, then why keep me in the dark about what you're really up to?"

She sighed. "Because I love you, of course, and would never want to see you accused of trying to influence—I'm sorry, but I can't discuss this. It's all irrelevant anyway. This shooting has nothing to do with me."

"What about those white supremacists you hacked off with your book last year. Who's to say those guys don't have long memories—and a longer reach? If anything were to happen to you—"

"I know you worry about me." Jessie's green eyes locked with her husband's. "But do you hear yourself, Zach? Think about it. Andrea looks nothing like me, with that long dark hair of hers."

Though Ian thought Zach's theory was a long shot, he felt bad enough about the lump rising on his brother's jaw to offer, "She did have on a riding helmet when we left. And besides, that flashy pinto of yours is recognizable from a long way off."

Jessie swung an annoyed look his way. "You might mean well, but stay out of this, or your brother won't be satisfied until he's locked me in a cage." Making a sweeping gesture that took in the entry and the living room, she added, "Sure, it's a *nice* cage, a first-class accommodation. But anyplace can be a prison, if you make the bars too tight."

"There's a big difference between being a damned prisoner," Zach told her, "and a treasure to be protected."

"Well, this *treasure's* taking Andrea to the ER in Marston. And I might even talk her into a little lunch at that cute little tea room if she's feeling up to it afterward."

"But Virgil's planning—"

"I'm sure he has better things to do," said Jessie, waving off the protest. "But the real question is, are you willing to cut me enough slack to do it?"

For several moments, the pair stared each other down, a clash of wills that made Ian want to excuse himself before any more was said.

Zach raked his fingers through his black hair, looking as if he were considering tearing it out instead. "Yeah, Jessie. I can do that. But you'll text me, won't you? Let me know you've made it over there all right?"

Jessie raised herself on her toes to kiss his cheek, then smiled at him. "I can do that, sweetheart. And did I ever tell you how handsome you are when you're being reasonable?"

"Don't push your luck," Zach warned, swatting her on the rump as she scooted back toward the guest suites.

Once she had gone, he sighed and turned to Ian. "You ever love a woman so much you can scarcely breathe for fear you'll lose her?"

Ian answered with a slow nod, a dark void opening beneath his heart. "The thing is, there're so many ways to screw it up yourself. And if you do, you'll end up like your little brother, full of nothing but regrets."

Andrea felt vindicated when the ER doctor ran her through a few perfunctory tests, used a special skin-bonding adhesive to close the cut on her head, and pronounced her good to go. Sure, she'd been warned to return if she experienced further head pain and nausea, but the instructions sounded purely precautionary to her trained ear.

"See?" she couldn't resist asking, as they climbed into the passenger seat of Jessie's blue Prius. "It's not that I don't appreciate the concern, but I told you, Ian and Zach were overreacting. It was nothing."

Jessie shrugged as they both clicked their seat belts. "It's the way those Rayford men are made. I swear they're like my dog, Gretel, on testosterone and steroids. I'll be the first to admit it can be aggravating as all get-out sometimes. But it means they care about you, that they want to take care of you."

Alarm zinged through Andrea's system, along with worry that she hadn't done enough to make her position clear to Ian's family. "Yes, but I'm not Ian's to take care of. I'm just his psychologist—and an engaged woman to boot."

"I know you are," said Jessie as she started the engine. "But does Ian really get that? Can he, even, with his memory like it is?"

Andrea sighed. "I thought I could get through to him, but what happened this morning made it obvious he's not capable of putting our past relationship behind him."

"You mean...somewhere between the flying bullets, you two managed to—" Jessie's sharp eyes asked a question that brought swift heat to Andrea's face.

"He kissed me," she admitted in a small voice. "And heaven help me if I didn't kiss him back. I—I got caught up in the moment, the adrenaline. It's disgraceful. I'm not like this. I lo— I've made a serious commitment to my—to Julian, and I do have ethics."

Jessie was quiet for a long while before saying, "You

also have a history with Ian. A history that apparently includes a good dollop of unfinished business."

"Maybe in his mind, but not in mine."

Jessie looked over at her, her green eyes sympathetic. "The words are loud and clear, Doc, but if you want anyone to hear them, you're going to have to figure out a way to keep your voice from shaking and your face from blazing red."

"I'm just— I'm tired, that's all. And maybe a little hungry."

Jessie smiled knowingly but allowed the change of subject. "All right, then. How 'bout that tearoom I mentioned earlier? We can have a nice lunch before I take you—"

"I just want to go back to the center, all right? I need to talk to my—"

"Come on, Andrea. I scarcely ever get a chance for grown-up girl talk anymore, and I swear I won't bring up Ian again or the shooting, either."

Andrea held out for a few moments before asking, "What do you mean, you don't get a chance for girl talk? I mean, with your mother-in-law right there in the house, how could it possibly get much better?"

Deadpan as Andrea's delivery was, Jessie tried to control herself, her mouth twitching before a distinctly unladylike snort broke free. Then both women erupted into laughter, assuring Andrea that no matter how disastrous her trip to Rusted Spur might have proved, at least she'd made a new friend.

It was midafternoon by the time she finally returned to the Warriors-4-Life Center on a grassy country road outside of town. As she pulled her suitcase from the back of the Prius, Jessie promised to have one of the hands deliver her car later that afternoon.

"That is, if I can't talk you into coming back with me to give working with Ian one more chance," Jessie added, putting a hand on the hatch to close it.

Shaking her head, Andrea glanced toward the entrance of the Warriors-4-Life center, a long, low tan brick structure. In front of the building, a wheelchair-accessible walkway looped around a small pond partly hidden by a grove of trees. Park benches had been donated, creating a peaceful respite from the building's more institutional interior. But it was the people inside that Andrea both looked forward to and dreaded getting back to. Or one of them, at any rate.

"I have to go," she said, foreboding rippling through her at the thought of the confession to come. "Thanks for treating me to lunch. That was really sweet of you."

"Least I could do after bending your ear about my—my little issue."

"I'm not sure there's anything *little* about it, Jessie," Andrea said, recalling the dilemma Jessie had talked to her about as they'd lingered at the table once the meal was over. Though Jessie had declined to give her the specifics, she'd made it very clear that her story would open a Pandora's box that could end up hurting loved ones. But with her professional integrity, her very identity, at stake, too, there was nothing clear-cut when it came to her decision. "You clearly have some soul-searching to do before you decide whether to go forward with what you've found."

"Just tell me, tell me, please, as a psychologist and as a woman. What would you do?" Jessie pleaded.

"First of all," Andrea told her, "I don't have nearly

enough information to say. Besides, I'm not you—and I'm definitely not in the business of making anyone's decisions for them. But I have faith you'll carefully think it through and figure out what's right for you."

Jessie snorted. "Spoken like a true headshrinker."

"Now you sound like Ian." Andrea's smile quickly faded. "And speaking of Ian, I'll have Julian contact your husband about the counselor I recommended."

"If this shooting business hasn't gotten him too paranoid to allow it." Frowning at the thought, Jessie added, "Though I guess it's not technically paranoia if someone's really out to get you."

Andrea felt the needle-sharp bite of fear because, no matter how enjoyable it had been to pretend that the two of them were a couple of old friends enjoying a lunch getaway, Jessie's words drove home the fact that only hours before, someone had peered down the barrel of a weapon, aimed at her and Ian, and then squeezed the trigger...

Someone who might very well do it again after discovering Ian had escaped unharmed. "No one *will* get to him, will they?"

"Zach'll see to it they don't, I promise. Ian won't be riding out alone again until we know what happened. If my husband had it his way he'd put me on lockdown, too, for the duration."

She looked so troubled that Andrea might have tried to talk more with her about it had Julian not chosen that moment to come through the front door, looking surprised to see her here, especially without her car. As he often did on days he wasn't meeting with potential donors, he wore a dark green polo shirt, the Warriors-4-Life logo embroidered over the left chest, neatly tucked into a pair of crisp chino slacks. Though he was several inches shy of Ian's six-four and fifteen years older, his warm, golden-brown eyes, his strong jaw and the dusting of gray at his temples lent him an air of authority. Fit and distinguished-looking, he strode toward her, the precision of his movements reminding her—strongly and for the first time—of the father she hadn't seen in nearly twenty years. The father she'd worshipped with a child's fervor, before she'd learned he had another family…and had left behind a third back in his hometown without troubling himself to divorce any of the women he had married.

She blinked and squinted at Julian, telling herself her suspicion wasn't true. Surely, she'd been attracted to his unwavering devotion to a greater purpose, to his leadership and kindness rather than some subconscious trigger buried in her past. She was especially sure she hadn't fallen for him because she was still pining for the father whose betrayal had shattered her family into a million pieces.

Still, nausea roiled in her stomach, her eyes stinging with suspicion.

"So that's him, is it? Ian's competition," Jessie asked her in a low voice. When Andrea couldn't find her voice to answer, her new friend added, "Guess I'll leave you to it, then."

As she pulled back out onto the road, Andrea waved goodbye before turning to Julian, dread pooling in her stomach.

"What are you doing back alrea—" The question died on his lips as his gaze latched on to the small white rectangle taped above her left eye. "What happened? Are you all right?"

She raised a hand. "Before I tell you, you need to know that everybody's okay. Doctor says I'm fine. I didn't even end up needing stitches."

He studied her for a moment before reaching to pull her to him, clearly forgetting that they might be seen by anyone. When Andrea stiffened in his arms, he broke off the embrace. "What is it?"

"Let's walk down by the pond," she said, leaving both her purse and suitcase on the first of the park benches that lined the pathway.

Though he walked beside her, he didn't try to touch her again as they descended the gradual incline leading to the pond's green-brown waters. A light breeze whispered through the tall grasses growing on the far end, and a few water lilies skimmed the surface, along with a trio of fat white ducks.

She recounted how she'd convinced Ian to take her with him out on the range that morning, saying, "It was the only way I could think of to get him to stop avoiding me and maybe open up a little."

"I had no idea you rode," said Julian, his gaze straying to the bandage once more. "Or do you?"

"Not very well, that's for certain, but I managed to stay in the saddle. Or at least I did until Ian dragged me down."

Julian stopped walking to stare at her, his face contorting. "He *attacked* you? What the devil happened?" Edged with anger, his accented words sliced like a saber.

"It wasn't like that, I swear," she rushed to explain. "It's more like Ian *saved* me. Otherwise, I might have been shot or thrown on my head when my horse spooked."

She told him what had happened, downplaying her

own terror and emphasizing Ian's efforts to keep her safe and then tend to her after she was accidentally injured.

"Even after he thought he'd heard the shooter drive off, Ian insisted we stay where there was cover and we'd be safe," she said. "We waited there and talked. It was an excellent discussion, leading him to remember more than ever."

"Remember what?" Julian asked, an unaccustomed urgency in his voice. "What did he say, Andrea?"

She stopped walking to stare at him. "More about his life prior to his capture, but I can't share any details. You know that."

His face reddening, Julian grimaced. "Of course, I know you can't break confidentiality. I only— Seeing you injured like this made me worry that these recovered memories came out of flashbacks. That you might have…*exaggerated* Captain Rayford's heroism in an attempt to downplay an unfortunate—"

"He didn't hit me. I swear it." But Andrea felt her own face heat with the knowledge that, in kissing her, the handsome agent-turned-cowboy had done something far more dangerous. "We were just talking, that's all, and then his brother and the ranch manager showed up looking for us."

Her heart stumbled and she felt the prickle of perspiration beneath her top. Because in her eagerness to reassure Julian, she'd left out the fact that she and Ian had done more than talk.

Guilt pressed down on her, along with a memory of Ian leaning forward to claim her mouth. And she'd kissed him just as fervently, the memories of their original attraction igniting like dry tinder. Because when it came to the gorgeous, maddening and persistent Ian Rayford, one intimacy would always lead to another.

"All I can think of is that you might have been shot down," Julian said, wrapping her in his arms again, now that they were hidden from view by the trees. "I might have lost you forever, in a single moment."

She pulled away and resumed walking, too nervous to keep still and too disgusted with herself for words. But somehow, she must find them.

Stalling for time, she instead answered Julian's questions about what had happened with the shooter and whether Ian had any idea of who or why the attack may have happened. "I understand the sheriff will be looking into it. But unless the gunman left behind some clue, I suspect he'll get away with it."

The injustice of the thought brought with it a rush of red-hot rage, the desire to see the guilty party punished. "It makes me absolutely furious to think that after everything Ian's been through, he'd have someone shooting at him in his own country, on his own property. How much does he have to sacrifice to finally come home?"

Julian did a double take. "You're upset. Not on your own account, but his."

"Of course, I'm upset. I care about—about my patients." She swallowed hard, a painful lump threatening to choke her. "And I can't help caring especially about Ian."

Julian stopped walking and studied her before nodding. "It's only natural, since the two of you were close once. A past personal relationship will always color—"

"The trouble is," she said, the thrumming of the blood in her veins a rushing noise in her ears, "Ian doesn't—he can't or he won't—remember that we ever broke up. It's been hard for me, too, Julian. Difficult to keep from… from being swept up in the past as I try to draw him to the present."

"What are—what are you trying to say, Andrea?" he asked, looking more concerned than ever. Or was it fear that she was seeing, a panicked pulse of déjà vu? As much as she wanted to spare him doubt or pain, she forced herself to remember how her father had once given that excuse when his acts had finally, horrifyingly come to light—and how that decision had left her mother shattered.

She shook her head. "I'm sorry, but I can't go back there. Not without risking—this morning, after we were shot at, emotions were running high. I was bleeding. He was helping me. And then—there was a kiss."

"He kissed you." Julian's voice went cool and smooth as plate glass. But there was a spark of heat in his eyes, the telltale twitch of a muscle in his clenched jaw.

She nodded, her face blazing. "I'm so sorry. I never meant to… I thought I'd made it clear to him that I was… But clearly, it didn't sink in, and in the heat of the moment, I'm afraid—afraid I forgot myself, forgot what I was there for. And I kissed him back."

"Andrea…" Julian groaned, his eyes closing as he raised a hand to pinch the bridge of his nose.

"It's not— I love *you*, Julian. I want to be with *you*, not him or anyone else."

He blew a breath through his nose before looking at her as if she were a stranger.

Shame took root in the pit of her stomach, spreading icy tendrils. "Can you— Do you think you can forgive me?"

His lips thinned and paled as he pressed them together. But he soon regained control of himself, looking far more like the man she'd come to know, the man whose squared shoulders and quiet dignity were so much like her father's. "As you said, emotions must have been—"

"That's true, but I have to tell you, it wasn't just the moment," she said. "It was… I'd grieved this man, thought he was dead. So to expect me to be able to wall myself off from all those feelings, to forget we'd ever been a couple… It's too much, Julian. Too much to expect from me and especially from him."

"I see," he managed, looking as if the two words left a bitter taste in his mouth. "Well, I suppose I should credit you for being honest. You tried to warn me from the start, I know. But this—"

"Please don't ask me to go back. I don't want to— I can't. Send Connor, please. I'll consult with him on the case from here."

Julian remained silent long enough for her to wonder whether he was considering or brooding. "As much as I'd prefer that solution," he finally said, "I'm afraid there are…there are other factors in play."

She stared at him, hot moisture welling in her eyes. "What other factors? You can't possibly be thinking about the money. This is—this is our future I'm talking about, Julian. And my mental health because I can't be the kind of woman who would—"

"I understand you're upset. You've been through a terrible ordeal and aren't ready to rationally talk this through, not yet."

"Talk what through? If you'd only tell me the real reason…"

"Come inside, Andrea. It's clear you need to rest now. Sleep, and then we'll talk again."

A spike of heat was her temper's only warning. "So you're putting me to bed now, like a misbehaving child?"

"I'm sending you to rest now," he said, a warning in his gaze, "because I truly do care about you. And because I need you out of my sight right now, before I end up saying something we'll both very much regret."

Chapter 6

Ian decided his brother had been right. Sheriff George Canter remained nothing but big hat and attitude, especially when it came anything to do with his two least favorite reformed hell-raisers. Tall and rugged-looking, with dark eyes and a perpetual sneer, he seemed more interested in finishing their meeting in the barn office so he could run to the house to *console* Zach and Ian's mother.

With every passing reference to their mama, the pulse point at Zach's temple beat a little harder until finally he erupted. "First of all, you've missed her. With my wife out for the afternoon, my mother was kind enough to volunteer to pick up Eden from school."

In their stalls, the nearest horses stamped and shuffled, as if they scented the tension in the air.

Canter glanced at his watch. "So what time is it that kindergarten gets out? 'Cause if she'll be back soon, it's only right that I should wait and pay my respects."

"Never you mind about that," Zach said. "You'll be out investigating the scene of the shooting by the time they're home. Before it gets dark."

Eyes narrowing, Canter pulled off his hat, revealing a full head of dark hair, highlighted by lighter patches at the temples. "Those cowhands of yours might jump to your orders, but last I checked, I work for the people of this county."

"Especially the people inclined to write checks for your next campaign."

Anger twisting in his rugged face, Canter opened his mouth to speak, but Ian broke in first.

"Let's head out now, together, and I'll help you look for shell casings. I have a pretty good idea where you might find them, after all."

The sheriff looked at him as if he were still the same dumbass tenth-grader he'd caught cutting class and drinking behind the Wheeler barn, though now he had to look up to meet Ian's eyes. Shaking his head, Canter said, "Can't have the victim along collecting evidence. Wouldn't some damned lawyer have a field day with that? No, sirree, soldier boy."

Ian's entire body clenched. "I'm not your *soldier boy*."

Canter looked him up and down. "You better damn well uncurl those fists, or maybe you'll get to be my *prisoner*. Again."

A buzzing built in Ian's head, the angry sound of a wasp's nest, as his mind whirled through several methods of overcoming and incapacitating an armed man. Methods he remembered being trained in. Methods he'd had occasion to use, even if they hadn't worked that night in Pakistan, where he'd been ambushed with another…

"Ian." Zach's voice filtered through the buzzing, and Ian recognized the warning in it. "Don't rise to the bait, man."

Zach stared at the sheriff, his voice going hard as steel. "He's a former POW, Canter. A national hero— didn't you hear it on the news? Be a damned shame not to give him the respect that he's got comin', the kind of disgrace that wouldn't look good on a campaign poster if it happened to get out."

Hero. The word lodged like a thorn in Ian's throat, as one of his captor's demands floated up from the black depths. An English-speaking captor brought in especially for this interrogation. *The listening post—you will tell us where it is. You will tell us today, or by all that is holy, you will not live to see tomorrow.*

Beyond that, he remembered nothing but a bolt of blinding pain.

Shaking if off, he grew aware of Canter, who was clearly weighing the chance of settling whatever grudge he held against the Rayford brothers and Zach's unspoken reminder that his wife was more than capable of influencing media coverage. After a bit of boot-scuffing, the sheriff said, "Don't you boys worry. I've got this covered. I should be able to find the place just fine, with those GPS coordinates you gave me. I'll head out now and collect any evidence around the rim where you said, then photograph any tire tracks, all that sort of thing."

Judging from the curdled-milk look on his face, he was none too happy about it, but at least he was willing to go through the motions.

"Track's pretty rough," Zach warned him.

"Shouldn't be an issue, with the new department SUV."

"Well, call us if you get stuck or run into any trouble. I can send Virgil or a couple of the hands out, no problem."

Canter nodded and donned his hat before leaving the barn but not before giving the brothers a look that said he wouldn't forget this indignity. The two Australian shepherds, who tagged along with Zach when Eden wasn't around, wagged their fringed tails after him, leaving Zach to shake his head.

"There's proof positive those goofball pups are no damned judge of character."

Ian laughed. "Where's Gretel when you need her? And what's the German command for 'Rip that ugly sneer off his face'?"

Zach shot him a wry grin. "She'd probably catch rabies."

"I wouldn't be surprised, but seriously, man. You need to watch your back around him. Because whatever your beef is with him, it's clear he'd love a chance to lay you low."

Zach's smile turned to a grimace. "Come here. I want to show you something. Something that might explain a whole lot."

He led Ian to the barn office and gestured toward the window. "You see that brand-new Tahoe he's heading out in? The one with every freaking option you can put on one? That was donated to the department by our mama this past November, when Jessie and I were off on our honeymoon."

"So Mama did it while you were out of sight, then," Ian said, understanding that in accordance with the terms of his father's will, he and his brother were each meant to have a vote on all large expenditures, as the three of them were equal heirs. Once Ian was reported killed in action, their mother—who despised dealing with the everyday decisions and recognized that her prescription-pill problem had caused her to make a mess of things in the past—had insisted on signing over her proxy to Zach.

Zach nodded. "While I wasn't around to guard the henhouse from one determined fox. She went all teary when I confronted her about it later, said she'd only wanted to 'give back to the community,' since we've been doing so well thanks to that natural gas find. I told her I'd be behind that idea 100 percent. I'd be glad to pitch in for a new truck for the fire department or a playground over at the school if she asked me, but no more to the sheriff. Not another dime."

"So what's his hold on her? Is it just he pays her attention, or does he have something on her?"

"He may've at one time, but that's all in the open now, and we have Eden," Zach said, referring to the dark time in his and Jessie's past that had ended up bringing them together as a family. "So I don't know what it could be. I only know it's been tough keeping them apart."

"You'd almost think he might suck up to us, too."

"Maybe he's too disgusted, remembering how he used to drag us back to the old man when we got rowdy, or he's just too eaten up with jealousy over the new money from the gas find."

Ian winced. "He wouldn't be so jealous if he knew how the old man lit into us whenever he brought us home."

"So you remember?"

"Not all of it, just bits and pieces I'd as soon've left forgotten." Only six months prior to Ian's disappearance, the old SOB had keeled over of a heart attack. Neither Ian nor his brother had attended the services that followed; nor had either one reached out to the mother who'd implored them to keep up appearances at all costs, never lifting a finger to protect them from his rages, not even when blackened eyes and broken bones were involved.

Still, for some reason Ian might never understand, this land had called him back to it, this once-shattered family drawing him the way a magnet pulled a compass needle.

When Zach said he had a call to make, Ian headed back to the house in hopes of scaring up an extra sandwich. When he'd first returned, weak and dehydrated, he'd had almost no appetite, but these days, whenever he wasn't working, he was hitting the kitchen between meals.

He forgot his hunger when he passed the little nook outside the kitchen, where he spotted Jessie at the built-in desk, completely engrossed in something she was reading. "What's wrong?"

As she turned to hide the folder behind her, he caught a glimpse of what looked like handwritten script. "Oh, nothing. Just going through today's mail, that's all. Nothing but the usual junk."

"You sure? You look a little— Is everything all right with Andrea? What did the doctors say about her head?"

"She's fine." The hand that had held the note came up empty as Jessie brushed aside his concern. "They used this glue stuff to close the cut and told her to take it easy for a few days, but she was feeling well enough to go to lunch—and I only had to twist her arm a little."

"Do you think there's any chance she'll come back? Any chance I haven't scared her off for good?"

When Jessie hesitated, he added, "I know you talked about me. I can see it in your face."

"I'm sorry, Ian." Compassion gleamed in her eyes. "I understand how confusing it must be for you, and I think it is for her, too. But it was probably a bad idea to invite her in the first place."

"I'm glad you and Zach did."

"I'm not, because it's obvious that both of you are hurting." She shook her head. "You have to understand, Ian, the way you feel about her has put her in an impossible situation. She could lose her license and hurt a man she seems to care very much about."

"I don't give a damn about him, only her. And if she can't come back to work as my psychologist, couldn't she at least come as a friend?"

"You need to understand. She's not coming back."

The pitying look Jessie gave him set his teeth on edge. He was more than just a victim—and he'd be damned if he'd be victimized by this. "What's that old saying about Mohammed coming to the mountain? Because if she won't come here, I'm heading into Marston to see her."

"I don't think that's a good idea."

"She's helping me remember. And besides, I—I still…" He couldn't get the rest out, couldn't stand to sound pathetic.

But Jessie seemed to understand him anyway. "I know you do. But you don't have a vehicle or a valid driver's license. Not to mention—"

"Yeah. Being declared dead is inconvenient that way." Ian had barely begun to tackle the reams of paperwork it was going to take to get everything sorted. "But if I didn't let those terrorists stop me, I'm damned sure not about to let a couple of small details like that get in my way."

"I was about to say, not to mention the little detail that someone's tried to blow your head off."

"I won't be caught off guard again."

Jessie frowned. "Just promise me you'll give her a little time, at least. Okay?"

"Time enough for you to talk my brother into putting me on lockdown?"

She crossed her arms in front of her chest. "We aren't your captors, Ian. But we do care about you. All of us. You're our miracle."

When he said nothing, she asked, "So are you and I good?"

He swallowed hard, then let out the breath he had been holding. "Of course, we are. And thanks, by the way, for taking care of Andrea."

"No problem. I really like her. She's smart, has a great head for people and has the driest sense of humor ever. But I'd better get up to our suite. I'm sure Gretel's more than ready for a romp outside by now. I can hear her whimpering from here."

"See you later, then."

Instead of heading to the kitchen, he grabbed this month's issue of *Working Ranch* and feigned fascination with a truck ad until he heard her footsteps heading upstairs. With Jessie safely out of sight, he went through the mail to find the note she'd hidden, but it was nowhere in the stack.

Had she slipped it under her shirt or tucked it into the waistband of her jeans? Possible, he thought, but tough to do one-handed. He took another look at the desk before trying the top drawer, though he dimly recalled that one had never slid smoothly, opening—when it did open—with a squawk of protest.

Apparently, someone had fixed it in the many years since he'd lived at home. The drawer moved freely, and sure enough, he found in it a folded piece of unlined paper.

"Gotcha," he said, but as he picked it up, a spasm of conscience tightened his gut. Did he really want to do this? Spy on his brother's wife? What if he discovered something terrible? An affair or—

No way would she do something like that, he decided, not when she was so clearly devoted to his brother and Eden. Besides, from what he'd seen of Jessie, she had way too much integrity to sneak around behind Zach's back. But he could easily imagine her trying to protect him by hiding something she thought might set back his progress, so he tamped down his reservations and unfolded the paper, then quickly read the five words someone had handwritten in block letters. Five angry words that had been clearly meant for him.

Humiliated at being sent to her room, Andrea found herself pacing its cell-like confines as the room's one window grew dark. As hard as it had been hearing the controlled anger in Julian's voice as he'd demanded she leave his sight, she'd expected—and deserved—no less. What had blindsided her, though, was his reaction to her plea to send someone else to work with Ian.

"I'm afraid there are...there are other factors in play," he'd said, but what on earth could he be talking about? Was someone pressuring him about it? Someone he knew from his former military career? Or what if he was still secretly working for the government?

She thought of how passionate, how persuasive he'd always been about the center and what he called the worthiest mission of his life. For more than six months, he'd poured every ounce of energy into Warriors-4-Life.

Difficult to believe he had room for another agenda, impossible to think his Southern honor would allow it.

But as she remembered how he'd pushed her to share confidential information, another possibility slipped like a shadow into her mind. What if Julian was one of the victims in this, a victim of blackmail? Someone might have something on him, some secret so devastating they could use it to bend him to his or her will.

So devastating he didn't care if it cost him the woman he had sworn to love for as long as he lived, the woman he wanted by his side as a life partner.

What if he'd been pressured into more than she guessed, if their relationship itself had been part of the sham? *He hasn't even taken the time from his work to pick out a ring,* some small, suspicious part of her whispered, though when he'd blushed, admitting he had found it so hard to believe a "beautiful, intelligent young woman" would accept his proposal that he'd been afraid to buy "the hardware" first, she'd blurted that she cared nothing for diamonds, only for him.

Her stomach flipped, and she told herself she was wrong, that Julian genuinely loved her. His coercion had to be more recent, for him to turn so suddenly.

When someone knocked at her door, she took a quick glance at the mirror and arranged her face into what she hoped would come off as a bland expression.

Their psychiatric nurse, Cassidy, stood there, grinning from ear to ear as she handed Andrea a key ring. "The cutest guy just dropped these off for you a while back, but I was on my way to do meds. But anyway, this cowboy? He had the whole hat, boots and license-plate-sized belt buckle going for him. Scrumptious!" A tiny redhead with a million freckles, she sighed happily and twirled one of the bright red corkscrew ringlets that fell over her shoulders.

Though she was only a couple of years older than Cassidy's twenty-nine, Andrea couldn't help but smile. Had she ever been so young or lust so uncomplicated? "Oh, yes. I remember," she said as she pocketed the keys. "They told me a couple of the hands would bring back my car." If Cassidy had gotten a gander at either of the Rayford brothers, she would have probably choked on her own drool.

"A couple? Darn it all, I only saw the one." Cassidy snapped her fingers before her smile abruptly faded. "Icy, what's that on your forehead? And what're you doing back so early anyway?"

"The short version is I bumped my head."

"I want the whole story. Come on. Dish it, sister."

Andrea looked down at the center's live wire before shaking her head. "You'd be bored to tears, and anyway, I'm exhausted."

Cassidy studied her, her eyes narrowing. "Something's bothering you. Tell me."

Though she hated to lie, Andrea pointed toward her forehead. "Kind of a bad headache. So let me rest now, and I'll tell you about the cowboys I saw on the ranch later."

Cassidy brightened instantly. "In *excruciating* detail?"

"So excruciating, you'll be begging for mercy."

"I'll hold you to that, then. Feel better."

Andrea was still smiling and shaking her head at her departure when she heard the harsh grinding of an ignition in the staff parking lot outside of her one small window. Frowning at the unpleasant sound, she peeked out from behind her curtain, curious about which staff member was murdering his or her ride.

But the SUV she saw whipping out onto the state highway was Julian's Ford Explorer. Though she couldn't see him through the tinted windows, he must be beyond upset to speed off like that. She'd never known him to be anything but a safe and cautious driver.

Could Julian be so furious thinking of Ian kissing her that he'd decided to go and confront him on the ranch? Almost instantly, she dismissed the thought. Julian wasn't the type to fly off in a jealous rage. Besides, if he had blamed Ian, he surely wouldn't have pressured her to go back into the proverbial lion's den.

Nor did she believe that Julian was so upset about her confession that he'd roar off to the nearest bar to drown his disappointment. He might have a stiff glass of bourbon in the privacy of his own room, but he was far too disciplined—and too proud—to risk making a public spectacle of himself or damaging the center's reputation.

More likely, she thought, he was desperate to speak to the person pressuring him to get inside information on Ian Rayford's progress. Though why he couldn't do it in his office, she had no idea—

His office.

She caught her lip between her teeth, thinking of how much time he spent there working on fund-raising campaigns, weighing the needs of the center's many applicants and conducting a host of other administrative tasks. Which meant, she decided, that if someone were putting pressure on him, it was the most likely place to look for evidence of whatever secret he was keeping...

Evidence she could use to save him from his blackmailer—and maybe their relationship, as well. *But is there really something left to save if you're willing to spy on him? And do you really want a man you can't be certain you can trust?*

A part of her cringed, knowing those were the questions she would ask any client she was counseling. But it didn't matter, not when the idea of getting answers had taken root so stubbornly and especially not when whatever Julian was keeping from her could be dangerous to Ian.

She slipped out of her room, avoiding her coworkers and the clients, who were sharing their evening meal in the dining room. Instead, she walked down to the building's front corridor and knocked at the door to Julian's office, as if she believed for half a second that he might be inside.

When there was no answer, as expected, she let herself in, grateful that he'd been too upset or distracted to lock the door. The office itself was moderately but comfortably decorated. Though Julian had chafed at the suggestion of putting up what he called "an ego wall," she'd talked him into hanging his framed degrees and photos of him smiling with illustrious donors, supportive politicians and several of the center's first residents to foster confidence from both the families of clients and potential contributors.

Now, though, those photographs came back to haunt her, staring down with seeming disapproval as she commandeered his leather chair and nudged the mouse of his desktop computer to wake it out of sleep mode. What came up, however, was a dialogue box asking for the administrator's password. She cursed under her breath; she had her own log-in to the network, but it was both easily traceable and useless in gaining access to his private messages.

Forgetting the idea, she started digging through drawers as she recalled the many times she'd seen him scribbling notes while he was on the phone. Surely, he must have saved some. In the top drawer, sure enough, she found a stack, each message so innocuous that she burned with fresh guilt and thought of giving up.

"In for a penny, in for a pound," she said. But it was Ian's lean and handsome face that moved her to flip through pages of Julian's calendar and then lift his desk blotter, where she plucked out a slip of paper.

Opening the folded square, she blinked and then gasped as she recognized her own passwords.

Her blood ran cold, chill bumps erupting as she realized he had not only her network and email log-in information, but passwords for the social network pages she used to keep up with old friends. He even had access to her online banking, a discovery that raised every fine hair behind her neck. She'd heard of keystroke-tracking software that could be secretly installed on a computer, but how on earth could he have gotten to her laptop? *Somehow, through the network. He must have—*

"What the devil do you think you're doing?"

She nearly jumped out of her skin at the sound of Julian's voice behind her. Hands curling into fists, she leaped to her feet, heart slamming wildly and body shaking so hard that her teeth were chattering.

"Never mind that," he said, eyeing the open drawers at the side of the desk. "The answer's quite apparent. What I want to know is *why* you're going through my things?"

Startled as she was, she could only say, "B-but I saw you race off."

"I loaned my truck to Michael. His engine wouldn't start, and he was late for what I take was a hot date with some local woman. So I ask you again, why are you spying on me?"

Swallowing back her panic, she mustered all her indignation and rattled the paper in her hand. "How *dare* you ask me that when it's even more obvious you've been spying on me for far longer than I've ever— I can't believe you. You're a total stranger. A fraud." Just the way her father had been.

At the sight of the paper, the color drained from Julian's face, his accent intensifying as he said, "No, Andrea. I'm still the same—"

"Liar," she said, flashing back to the terrible moment when she'd first accepted what her father was. Because this man, she understood now, had never been more to her than some sort of replacement for the love she'd lost as a child, though she would have sworn the wound had long since healed. "I can't believe I was so stupid to fall for your line. To imagine that I loved you."

"I still love you, Andrea. I do now and always will. But you have to understand…Marilyn destroyed me, so much that I swore I'd never again marry. So I had to be sure, dead sure, before I could possibly commit myself to—"

"Get some therapy, then. But don't count on me standing by your side while you pull yourself together. I'm finished."

"What do you mean, you're finished? Please, Andrea—"

"I can't be with you, not in a relationship. And not

professionally, either. When I resigned from the youth center in San Diego, my supervisor left me an open invitation to come back if I ever—"

"You can't leave. You can't leave Warriors-4-Life. We need you. Your clients need you. There's no one else your equal when it comes to—"

"Don't throw them up in my face," she said, yet her heart was breaking at the thought of all the vulnerable ex-soldiers she worked with, so many of them already rejected by family and friends, and the society who judged them "crazy" and turned their backs on them. And then there was Ian, caught up in a tortured no-man's-land between pain and memory.

"What about your lover?" Julian asked bitterly. "Will you really abandon him, too?"

"First of all, Ian's not my lover." Glaring, she held up the paper with her passwords as a horrifying new thought occurred. "And secondly, tell me this wasn't about him. All of it, from the start. That the rest isn't some cover story you've come up with to get to my personal case notes on him and turn them over to who knows who?"

She frowned, realizing, unlike the other passwords, her case-note log-in was outdated, since she was in the habit of changing it every week or two. "Wait— You didn't get it, did you? Not my notes." A measure of relief washed over her, a warm wave beneath a shell of ice.

"I didn't. But I'll need that password, Andrea. The latest one, right now. You can write it on the—"

"Have you lost your mind? I could lose my license, for one thing, to say nothing of betraying the confidence of all my—"

"Not all of them. Just one. The password, Andrea, before you leave this office."

She stared into his face, willing this to be a nightmare. What on earth would ever convince him to behave this way? "Just tell me, Julian, are you being coerced in some way? Blackmailed or threatened? Because if you are, I can help you. We'll call the authorities together to report it."

Standing as tall as he at six feet, she stared straight into his eyes. And saw the instant a wall slid down, cutting himself off from the possibility of redemption, of salvaging their relationship. She knew she'd never again fully trust him—or herself, around another older man. But Julian had the chance, at least, to save himself, the man whose passion and charisma had drawn her to this place...

A town only an hour's distance from the ranch where Ian grew up.

She couldn't let her mind travel down that path yet, couldn't pause to wonder if her recruitment, maybe even the establishment of the center itself, could be part of some grand conspiracy.

"You have to explain," she said. "Tell me why you'd be willing to forget every professional ethic you've ever stood for to look into a patient's confidential records."

"You talk to me about *professional ethics*—" a cold-steel hardness hammered through his words like nails driven through half-rotted wood "—when you were out there on that ranch swapping DNA with your own client—an admission that would cause you a world of trouble if I happened to report it to the state board."

"That's it. I'm out of here." She tried to step around him, but he moved to block her way.

"The newest password, Andrea. If you care about your country in the least, you have to do this for me."

"My country?" she echoed, a cold chill raising goose bumps. "Explain yourself right now."

"You'll have to trust me on this," Julian told her. "And trust me when I tell you this is a dangerous game you're playing."

"Trust *you*, a man who's lied to me and invaded my privacy on so many levels, over someone who's sacrificed so much for his country? I saw those photos in his file, Julian. I saw what Ian's captors did to him." Tears sparkled along the lower rims of her eyes at the memory of angry, raised scars that crisscrossed his back and shoulders. Maybe they would fade with time or a plastic surgeon could diminish their appearance, but underneath, they reached to his soul, wounds to the psyche that would never go away.

"You know, Julian," she went on, "I've wondered why you've held back all this time, why you've deliberately avoided getting physical."

"I've told you why. The other employees here, the possibility of—"

"I thought maybe you were just an old-fashioned Savannah gentleman, a little out of step with the times. But now, I have to wonder, was there another reason you were afraid to get too close?"

She waited for him to argue with what she'd said, or at least to elaborate a little more. Except he couldn't. Or wouldn't, preferring instead to fall back on his most authoritative stare.

Well, she had never been one of the soldiers he commanded, so if he thought she'd accept patriotic duty as a reason without the slightest shred of proof, he'd better think again. Only inches from his face, she leveled her coldest gaze on him—partly to disguise the way her pulse was pounding. "Step out of the way, Julian, unless you want law enforcement tangled up in this, too."

"In addition to refusing your duty to your country, you'd shut the center down? Stop all the good we're doing?"

"I'll do what I have to to get back to California—after I've warned Ian." She owed him that much, at least, even if she feared it might inflame his paranoia. Except that Jessie's words whispered in her memory: *I guess it's not technically paranoia if someone's really out to get you.* "I'm packing up my things and leaving, and if I lose my license to practice in Texas over this, so be it."

She tried again to pass him, and Julian's hand shot out to grip her forearm, hard enough that her attempts to jerk it back were useless.

Before she recovered from the shock, he spoke, his quiet words laden with an eerie menace. "If you cross me on this, I swear to you, you'll never practice again anywhere. I have connections, you see. Connections that will make certain that wherever you tried to set up shop, the charges against you will—"

"The *charges*?" She struggled again to free her arm, but his grip only tightened. "For a single kiss, shared with a confused man I was once engaged to? A man that you pressured me into seeing in the first place despite my strong reservations?"

"That's all *your* story." His gaze was as cold and level as the surface of a frozen lake. "But it won't necessarily be mine. It's counted as a sexual assault, you know, when a mental health professional has relations with a client. Especially one whose memory gaps would make him extremely vulnerable to—"

She shuddered, her skin crawling. She couldn't imagine how such a charge, without physical evidence or a client's testimony, would ever stick. But crazy as it was, even an accusation of sexual impropriety from someone as respected as Julian Ross would send her life spinning out of control. Using all her passwords, he could easily create incriminating emails, maybe even texts, too—at least enough to get an investigation started. If the media got wind of it, a female psychologist "raping" a nationally known male patient, she'd be the subject of a torrent of media and online commentary. And people would happily speculate that Ian, with his well-known memory issues, had simply forgotten what had really happened. Or enjoyed her attentions too much to complain.

"You're insane," she whispered, her tears leaking out the only warmth left in her.

"Insane?" His smile, too, was icy. "And here I thought you psychologists never used that word."

You psychologists, he'd said, as if the science were completely alien to him and not a world he'd supposedly worked with on the military side for decades. Shaking her head, she asked, "Who *are* you? Because you're certainly not my Julian."

His lips thinned and his mouth tightened, as if the question pained him. "No, I'm not. That version's gone now. Which means, my darling Andrea, that you're going to have to find a way to survive this one—you and Captain Rayford both."

Chapter 7

Ian went out to the barn office, a lump in his throat and the five words on the note echoing through his brain. He'd wanted to take it, get his brother's opinion on the handwriting, but when he'd heard quiet footsteps moving down the staircase, he'd replaced it in the same drawer where Jessie had left it hidden.

He'd retreated to the kitchen, where Althea, true to form, asked him to "taste test" the mouthwatering lemon squares she'd made a thousand times before. Unable to escape her well-meaning chatter, he smiled and made nice, praising her delicacies and gently teasing until he had the broad-hipped older woman blushing like a schoolgirl.

Then his mother came in with Eden, looking sleepy and bedraggled as a five-year-old can after a rough day in the kindergarten trenches. He'd cheered her up by sneaking her a lemon square against his mother's exhortations that she "save her appetite for supper" and telling her some silly riddles dredged up from the recesses of his memory.

Only after Eden had run off giggling to play with her dogs had he found a private moment to return to the little alcove, where he'd pulled out the drawer and found the note gone. Figuring Jessie meant only to protect him, he knocked at his brother's office door now, but there was no response. Instead, Ian found his older brother working with a coal-black filly in a nearby corral, soothing the tall three-year-old with big hands and soft words until she quit her fidgeting and trotted smoothly around the enclosure.

Not wanting to startle anyone and possibly get his brother thrown, Ian stood on the rails watching until Zach dismounted and patted the animal's sweat-soaked neck. "That's a good girl. You're going to be a real champ, aren't you?"

Ian smiled to see his brother's gentler side. "That's not the way our old man broke in young horses."

"Or sons, either," Zach said as he led the filly closer, "which is just one reason I'm going for exactly the opposite approach."

"Marriage has been good for you, ironed out some of the rough edges. Or maybe it's fatherhood that's doing it."

"Maybe it's both," Zach said, "because I'll tell you what. I had some issues of my own to work through when I came home, not the least of which was the news of my little brother's death."

He peeled off a leather glove and slapped Ian's arm with it. But Ian felt the affection in his gesture, just as he saw it in the look Zach gave him.

"So what's on your mind?" Zach gestured toward Ian's chest. "And why didn't you bring me one of those lemon squares that you've obviously been scrounging?"

Ian looked down, then brushed a few telltale yellow crumbs from the front of his shirt. "Too bad for you that Althea loves me more." The truth was, the old cook had always been more generous with her affections than their mother.

"She just feels sorry for your scrawny ass on account of you being so pitiful." Zach grinned as Ian leaned between the rails to punch his arm, a movement that had the filly tossing back her head and straining against the reins. "Come on, man, knock it off now. You're upsetting my girl here. If you want to talk, come walk with us."

Ian got serious and stepped into the corral to do as he'd been asked. Drawing a deep breath, he said, "I've gotta tell you something. Something about Jessie."

Zach stopped walking the horse to stare at him. "Just remember, that's my wife, before you start."

Ian threw his hands up. "Jessie's great, man. Really, she is. Whip-smart and beautiful and, for some damned reason nobody can figure, in love with your dumb ass."

Zach shrugged and said, "Some guys have just got it, man. I don't know what to tell you."

Ian made a scoffing sound before getting to the point. "Thing is, I saw her hiding something a little bit ago. Something I'm convinced was meant for me. She was trying not to worry me, I imagine, but after I read the thing—"

"What're you talking about?"

"It was a note, Zach, anonymous and to the point. Only thing it said was 'Your hiding days are over.'"

Zach's body tensed, a dangerous look hardening his features. Ian recognized the expression and braced himself for an explosion, but his brother's anger wasn't directed at him.

"Hold on a minute," Zach said, then raised his voice to call out, "Rusty?"

One of the younger hands looked up from whatever

he'd been doing beneath the hood of an old pickup in the lee of the barn, wiped the grease from his hands and came trotting over.

"Mind interrupting what you're doing and cooling down Onyx here before you put her up?"

"Sure thing, Mr. Rayford, sir," the kid said, for Ian realized that, despite his ox-like build, the round-faced cowboy with the ridiculously tall hat still hadn't lost all his baby fat. Not that there was much chance that ranch work wouldn't melt it off him in a few months.

"You don't have to *sir* me, cowboy. This isn't the marines," Zach said. "Be gentle with this filly, though, and give her a good rubdown, too. She's just getting started, and I don't want her scared or hurt, or to have any negative associations with the barn or human handling."

The kid snatched off the ten-gallon hat, revealed an unruly shock of red-brown hair. "Yes, sir—I mean Mr. Rayford, sir." Blushing, he added helplessly, "I'm sorry. But I won't disappoint you. I promise that I won't."

Zach nodded and looked after them as the hand led off the filly.

"That horse is special to you, isn't she?" Ian asked him, taking note of the animal's gleaming jet coat and rock-solid quarter horse build.

"Not half as special as that stubborn woman of mine."

Ian nodded, his throat tightening. "I get that, Zach. I do. First the shooting, now the note. I'm a danger to your family, aren't I, to Jessie and Eden? A danger to all of us, as long as there's a sniper gunning for me. Which means, it's time to move on. I've still got my savings." Though it had been part of his own so-called estate, Zach had restored the money, along with funds from the sale of his vehicle and the furnishings from his old apartment.

There would be government back pay as well, from the months he'd spent as a prisoner, and Zach was working with the family's lawyers on seeing that Ian would receive a healthy portion of the ranch's profits, too—a portion easily worth millions.

But his brother was scowling at him now, shaking his head and demanding, "Quit talking nonsense. You're not going anywhere. Mama would have a heart attack."

"You think she'll like it any better when a bullet comes flying through the window? And what if she ended up hurt, her or Jessie or Eden, or Miss Althea or Virgil or—hell, *you?*"

Zach managed a wry smile. "Glad you thought to add me in there, somewhere, bonehead. But we'll definitely be stepping up ranch security. And the thing is, Ian, we don't have any way to know if this note's got anything to do with you, not without a name or an envelope to go by."

"You've got to be kidding. Do I really need to remind you that someone's out to get me? And this time, I've got a witness to prove it's more than just my imagination."

"I realize you were shot at. But it could turn out that was some jackass kid out drinking with his buddies, thinking it'd be funny to see you and Andrea duck and cover. Or it could've been someone with an ax to grind against the family as a whole—a disgruntled former employee or somebody who's feeling resentful that the Rayfords keep getting richer while they're still flat broke."

"You could be right, I guess, but I'm right when I tell you that not everybody's happy I made it back home. I can't tell you exactly how I know it, can't remember why I'm so damned sure that whoever's responsible for that ambush is even unhappier about the fact that I'm starting to remember pieces of my time—" Ian's vision wavered like a mirage, his brother shifting, shrinking, his blue eyes going dark and hard as stone while the reins he was holding morphed into a blood-caked chain. But this time, Ian gritted his teeth and shook off the hallucination. "Of my time away. And I'm sure that this person won't care who he has to hurt to stop me from remembering the rest."

"If someone really wants you dead, why send a warning? Why not just take you out when you're least expecting it?"

Ian thought about it for a moment. "Maybe the sender changed his mind about what it was going to take to run me off. We ought to ask Jessie how and when it was delivered, take a look at any envelope, as well, to see if there's a postmark or any other clue to where it came from."

"That's a good idea. Or at least it would be if we could get my wife's cooperation."

"Even if she's trying to protect me, she'd surely be willing to confide in you. So why don't you go ahead and ask her?"

"Because I'm pretty sure my darling wife would lie to me about it."

"Lie? To you? That makes no sense as all."

Zach huffed out a sigh, his blue eyes troubled. "It makes sense if she's not trying to protect you but her career, instead."

"Wait a minute. What are you thinking? That someone's threatening her on account of her latest investigative piece?"

"Whatever the hell it is, yeah. That's exactly what I'm thinking. Wouldn't be the first time her work's gotten her on the wrong side of some very dangerous types, and it makes me damned nervous when she refuses to at least tell me whose business she's digging into."

"So you're really still thinking there's a chance that Andrea was the real target this morning, when the shooter mistook her for Jessie?" Though Ian's instincts argued against it, with no memory to back up the suspicion, he was willing to at least listen to his brother's theory.

Zach nodded. "I sure as hell do. If only I could get her to give up her crusading, settle down here on the ranch and be a full-time mom to Eden."

"We're not living in the fifties, man. What are you saying, that she should stick to shopping and planning meals with Mama?" Ian might have only met her recently, but such life choices didn't sound much like his sister-in-law's style.

Zach chuffed a humorless laugh. "Heck, no. Those two would probably kill each other, and Jessie's got too much drive and talent to be happy penning those skills up. I just want my wife, my family *safe*. We've already suffered enough with the last rabid bear she poked."

Ian hadn't heard the entire story, but what he had gleaned was enough to convince him Zach had every reason to fear for Jessie's safety as she went after corruption at the highest levels. But it was just as easy to imagine how such a spirited woman would react to her husband's demand.

Zach shook his head, clearly stewing over his frustrations and his need to keep his family safe. "I'd bet that fine filly and a whole lot more that threat was directed at Jessie, and she doesn't want me worrying about it. It's just the kind of thing that stubborn woman would do— try to take matters into her own hands."

As much as Ian hated to get in the middle of their marriage, he had to say, "I understand your theory, might even give it credence, but this note showing up on the same day someone tried to ambush me is damned suspicious."

"You've definitely got a point there," Zach said, "and I'll do my best to get the truth out of Jessie about what she's been up to. But it's bound to be a touchy subject since she's been swearing she won't talk—for everybody's safety."

"I can see why that would worry you. Wait, there she is now." Ian nodded toward Jessie, who was jogging their way, despite the high-heeled boots she wore with her jeans and a rolled-sleeved blouse.

Zach hurried to meet her, Ian right behind him.

"What's the matter? You look upset," Zach asked. "Is Eden all right?"

Jessie stopped and shook her head as she caught her breath. "Eden's fine. Nobody's hurt. It's just—"

"I'll leave the two of you." Ian stepped away, wanting to give the couple privacy. He was already wondering how upset Jessie would be with him for ratting her out to Zach about the threat.

But Jessie was raising her hands. "Don't go, Ian. This concerns you, too. It's Andrea. I just called her because one of the maids found a pair of headphones under the bed in the guest suite, but when I reached Andrea, she was so upset she could barely get the words out."

Alarm jolted through him. "Why? What's happened? Is it her head?"

"Not her head, her heart. You see, her fiancé was none too happy when she told him about what happened between the two of you."

"About the shooting, you mean?" Zach said. "I under-stand that, but if she wants to come back, I can guaran-tee him we'll be stepping up security around this place big-time."

But that wasn't what Jessie was referring to, Ian saw as their gazes locked. And so did Zach, apparently.

"This is about your crazy idea you could steal her away from him," he said.

"Or that kiss we shared down in the ravine," Ian ad-mitted, remembering the way their contact had ignited, making him lose sight of everything else. "Because being with her—it brings it all back. For both of us, I'm sure of it."

"Well, whatever it was," Jessie said, swinging an ac-cusatory look his way, "you've gone and gotten her not only dumped, but fired. Did you have any idea her fi-ancé was her boss, too?"

"Yeah, but I—I'll talk to him if that's what she wants," Ian said, "make him understand that it was all my fault."

"Too late for that now. I reminded her how the doc-tor at the E.R. told her she needed to be sure to rest, but she said she's packing up her things now and heading straight back to California. She says she'll drive as far as she can and then get a motel room."

As Ian fished his phone from his back pocket, Zach said, "That doesn't make a lick of sense. She'll run out of daylight long before she runs outta empty prairie if she heads toward the interstate."

"I tried to tell her."

"What's her number, Jessie?" asked Ian. "I never got it from her."

Jessie pulled out her own cell and showed him the

number on her list of recent calls. "You can try," she said, "but she didn't pick up when I called her back. I called the main number for the center, too, but all I got was some after-hours recording. I'm really worried about her, Ian. She didn't sound at all like the smart, together woman we saw when she was out here."

But Ian's attention was fully on his phone as he tried calling Andrea. After the call rolled over to voice mail, he tried again with the same results. This time, he left a message. "Don't you dare leave town until I see you," he warned. "I'm on my way to the center. Call me when you get this."

When he disconnected, Jessie shook her head at him. "You can't go running after her, Ian. It'll just escalate—"

"I'm going," he told both her and his brother. "The question is, which one of you is lending me your keys?"

Aware that she would have very tight quarters at the center, Andrea had sold off or given away most of her possessions before moving here from California. Yet in the months she'd been here, the few belongings she'd brought with her had somehow expanded to more than she would ever be able to cram inside her little blue Honda. She could pack far more efficiently, she knew, if she weren't half blinded by tears and having to stop what she was doing so often to blow her nose. Her head was pounding, too, in spite of the mild painkiller she had taken.

But it was worry that was exacting the harshest toll, the worry that her refusal to do as Julian wanted would come back to haunt her. Still, the idea that he would call her patriotism into question and threaten her career, even hinting that she might be putting herself in real danger unless she did his bidding had in the end done nothing but convince her she had to get away from this no matter the cost.

Unwilling to risk talking to the all-too-perceptive Cassidy, Andrea decided to leave the center's psychiatric nurse a note instructing her to take whatever she wanted and give away the rest. Adding to the hasty message, Andrea included an explanation for her own sudden departure, a lie about an emergency back home involving a nonexistent aunt's recovery from surgery.

Instead, Andrea would go to her friend Samantha's place, if Sam wouldn't mind her couch surfing for a week or two. Andrea told herself it didn't matter. She'd sleep on a park bench if she had to, whatever it took to put as many miles as possible between herself and Julian.

Was it possible he'd really go after her license as he'd threatened? But whether or not he followed through was out of her hands, she told herself as she wiped away more stinging tears. The only part she could control was her refusal to spy on Ian.

After blotting her red eyes, she sneaked another box of her belongings to the car. With the last few books she couldn't part with stashed beneath a seat, Andrea climbed into the car, relief spreading through her that she'd managed to get this far without detection. As she cranked the engine, though, her phone vibrated once more in her pocket.

Sorry that she had taken Jessie's earlier call while she was so upset, Andrea had switched off the ringer. She regretted her babbling even more when she saw Ian's name on the caller ID window, and her phone's call log told her she had missed seven calls from the same num-

ber. There were several voice mails, too, including one
from Julian.

She chose to listen to that message, maybe out of
the desperate hope that he was calling to explain himself at last. Instead, her eyes shot wide as his recorded
voice said, "Bail on me now, and I swear you'll regret
it, 'Andie,'" an ugly sneer dripping through Ian's nickname for her—a nickname she had never used or mentioned to her former boss. "But if you go and warn him,
if you say one damned word to him about this, I swear
to you I'll see you in a federal prison for giving aid and
comfort to the enemy."

The enemy? Could he possibly mean Ian? Her hands
were shaking and her stomach knotting as she powered
off the phone completely and sped out of the parking
lot, the acid tang of panic on her tongue.

Did Julian really have the kind of power, the authority, he implied? Or were his words no more than a last-
ditch effort to control her?

And what about Ian? Could he really be the traitor
Julian implied? She tried to fathom it, to picture the man
she'd ridden with this morning willingly providing his
captors with intelligence. Impossible, she told herself,
thinking of Ian's scars, of the suffering so painful he
couldn't bring himself to remember the details.

Whatever he'd done to survive, she told herself she
didn't blame him or doubt his honor or his courage for
a moment. She'd learned too much about the ways prisoners in captivity were broken to believe that even the
strongest, most loyal person alive could long withstand
the physical and psychological manipulation, the darkness, the starvation, the loneliness and deprivation. The
things she'd heard in sessions with other former captives

had given her nightmares, dreams so horrifying they'd had her crying out.

Nausea churning in her stomach, she fueled up at the nearest station and grabbed snacks and a bottled iced tea for what she knew would be one very long drive. More than a thousand miles, she remembered from her initial journey out here. She would have a rough time making it in one marathon session even if she were in tip-top condition. Instead, it was late afternoon already, feeling even later with the skies a leaden gray, and she was so emotionally raw that she ached with every breath. She was sore, too, from the riding, and there was a tender lump where she had opened up her forehead. All in all, she needed a warm bath and a soft bed, not a cross-country journey and a broken heart.

Just outside of town, she reached the fork in the road that forced her to make a choice. Straight on would connect her to the southbound state road that would eventually take her to the interstate she'd follow all the way to California. If she turned right instead, following the arrow with a small sign reading Spur Creek 35, Rusted Spur 70, she could be at the Rayford Ranch in less than an hour's time…could be there long enough to warn Ian—a warning Julian would have no chance of tracing through her cell phone or computer—before heading south to pick up the interstate from there and get on her way.

Behind her, a driver in a primer-gray pickup honked and glared behind dark sunglasses, alerting her to the fact that she'd come to a full stop in the middle of the road. After waving the man past her with an apologetic smile, Andrea finally made up her mind.

For Ian's sake, for old time's sake, she simply had to take the chance.

Speeding along the rural road, she struggled to calm the pounding in her chest and focus on her breathing, on the gentle rise and fall of grasslands that seemed to stretch into forever. But since her ride with Ian, she saw them differently, her gaze seeking out clues to hidden places, places that might hide either great beauty or grave dangers.

Other than the occasional distant shed, the changing fence lines and the different types of cattle, there was little to mark her progress, and there wouldn't be, she knew, until she crossed the narrow bridge that spanned Spur Creek at the halfway point. The two-lane road was rutted and emptier than the last two times she'd come this way, and she saw far more hawks, jackrabbits and coyotes than signs of other humans.

Which was why, sometime later, she was so quick to notice the pair of headlights shining in her rearview. Headlights from a huge grill coming up behind her little Honda far too fast.

"What on God's green earth do you think you're doing takin' off in my truck like that?" Zach shouted at Ian over the cell phone's speaker. "I told you I just had to grab my wallet and I'd take you."

"Sorry, but I couldn't wait," Ian said as the big Ford roared along the ranch road. "I'll return the truck as soon as—"

"You do realize it'd make Sheriff Canter's day to lock you up for driving with no license."

"He'll have to catch me first, and it's one damned big county," Ian said. Though Canter's jurisdiction extended as far as Marston, he normally stuck closer to sleepy Rusted Spur, which had been the county seat for decades before the now-much-larger town had been established.

"Last I heard, they've opened up a satellite office in Marston—with a half-dozen deputies on patrol there. Any one of 'em would score big with the boss man by hauling in a Rayford."

"What're they gonna do?" Ian scoffed. "Prosecute a dead man?"

"Maybe not, but they can damn sure throw his stubborn ass in jail for truck theft."

"Relax, Zach. I'm just borrowing your baby. And I swear I'll return it without a single scratch or dent." As if to contradict the point, Ian took the Marston turnoff too fast, tires squealing in protest as the vehicle fishtailed around the corner. As he wrestled the pickup back under control, he heard a faint protest from his brother from the floorboard, where the phone had fallen.

"You'll be the one scratched and dented," came the tinny voice, "if you don't drive any better than the last time I remember."

"Last you remember, I was sixteen," Ian told him. "I've had a little more experience since then. Now, if you'll quit distracting me, I want to give the road my full attention."

"Just see that you do, bro. I don't want you hurt," Zach said, as his angry bluster gave way to something deeper. "And call me when you find her. All right? Then, whatever you do, try to remember that she's built a whole life since she was with you—a life you've managed to totally knock off the rails in just a few days."

"Thanks for the pep talk." A moment later, Ian's sarcasm eased into sincerity. "I will call you. Promise. And believe me, I'll do my damnedest not to scare her off this time."

The more details he remembered from their time together, the more determined he was to right the wrong that had spread like poison through his life when he'd been foolish enough to let her leave it. Sure, he'd had his job, a career he'd always thought he was damned good at, and he'd loved being a part of something that he had truly believed mattered. But with the ambush, that confidence, too, had crumbled, leaving him with nothing more than fractured memories of how fortunate, how fulfilled and whole, he'd felt when he was with her.

Thunder rumbled in the distance, hinting at the reason for the purplish gloom on the horizon. Though ordinarily, he would welcome the moisture, which would bring better grazing for the family's cattle, Ian hoped the storm would slide off in another direction or at least wait until after he found Andrea and talked her out of leaving.

Once Zach wished him luck and ended the call, Ian flipped on the pickup's headlights. Within a few miles, a light patter started, and by the time he reached the Spur Creek bridge, he was cursing the steady rain and flipping on the wipers.

His aggravation nearly made him miss the break in the narrow bridge's railing, driving past before it registered. Someone must have had a wreck there or even gone over since he'd last come through here. He was half surprised he hadn't read about it in the local paper.

Maybe because it hadn't happened prior to the last edition, some instinct told him. The same instinct that had him pulling to the gravel shoulder and turning to look back over his shoulder. But from this angle there was no way he could see the water.

You're wasting time, imagining things that aren't there. From what Jessie had told him, every second he delayed was taking Andrea farther and farther away from Marston, away from him and Texas.

Unable to bear the thought, he put the truck back into gear and sped off. As he did, the rain redoubled, every drop of it raising the level of the creek.

Chapter 8

Andrea came to with a gasp, sputtering as the cold water reached her mouth and nostrils. Reflex had her craning her neck and pushing herself away from what would drown her, struggling to escape whatever held her down. Adrenaline flooding through her, she succeeded only in gouging her own flesh with her ragged fingernails. She was going to die here, right now, her final moments illuminated by the dashboard lights.

A thought cut through her panicked scrabble. *Seat belt.* That was right. She was in her car—now lying on its side beneath the bridge railing she had crashed through, as far as she could make out. In the creek itself, judging from the water pouring into her car, rising high enough that she could only breathe by straining.

You're okay. Nothing feels broken, she assured herself, though she felt sick from the pounding in her head. *It's only panic that will kill you.*

Repeating the last part like a mantra, she found and clicked the belt latch and cried out with joy when it released. Untangling herself from the shoulder harness, she splashed frantically in an attempt to raise herself above the water level. But how would she get out, with the driver's side door pinned against the creek bottom?

Why, oh why hadn't she bought one of those escape tools for the glove box, the kind guaranteed to break out the windshield with a tap or two? Without one, her frantic attempts to punch or kick her way through the windshield were useless. And with the passenger-side door above her, she faced an awkward struggle trying to get to the latch. When she could finally reach it, she lacked the strength, or anything to brace against with her legs, to force open the door more than an inch or so.

As the dash lights flickered, she wedged a foot against the side of a seat for better leverage and screamed as the car lurched, tilting farther toward its roof. "Don't tip, don't tip, don't tip!" she begged, bracing herself in a standing position to keep her head and shoulders above the swiftly rising water.

From outside the car, she felt the rush of the current, heard its chatter as it jostled the vehicle and swept past. There were more ominous noises, too: the grinding scrape of the driver's side on the pebbles of the creek bed, the ticking of the engine and the groan of metal. Knowing that any shift in her weight could be what toppled the car, Andrea felt the water leaching the warmth from her body and understood that if she did nothing, she would surely die.

With her phone lost somewhere and undoubtedly ruined, there was no way to call for help and no time, either. There was only her strength and her courage, courage that nearly failed her as she remembered the vehicle she'd been helpless to outrace or outmaneuver, the powerful truck that had smashed into the Honda's rear tire and made her lose control.

Was the driver somewhere nearby, on the bridge or by the creek's bank? Was he waiting not to help but to kill her instead if she'd survived? Shuddering with fear and cold, she told herself that by simply waiting here to drown, she would be doing his job for him.

The dash lights gave a final flicker and then plunged her into near-darkness, making up her mind.

Bracing herself, she fought to find the focus that had once made her a fierce competitor. She might be cold and battered, her strength fading with each passing second, but she'd be damned if she let whatever government goon Julian had sent win this round and then go after Ian.

Summoning a last-ditch burst of will, she powered the door until it stood above her, open. She hesitated for a moment longer, praying for all she was worth, before jumping up to thrust an elbow out of the door.

As she began to hoist herself, however, the car abruptly shifted.

"No!" she cried, frantic to get up and get clear.

But nothing could stop the momentum that had the Honda splashing down like a dead roach on its back.

Ian didn't make it a half mile down the road before he was slammed with doubt and guilt—was he really so damned selfish he would drive right past a possible wreck? A three-point turn made him feel better. He'd go back far enough to assure himself that it was nothing and then turn around again, delaying his journey less than a minute.

Except it wasn't nothing, but instead a sight that slammed his heart into overdrive. Some twenty feet below, a dark car—in the rain, it was impossible to make out the color—lay on its side in the creek, partly submerged in the waters that swirled around it. For an instant, he took the car for Jessie's blue Prius before reminding himself that she was home and safe on the ranch.

But Andrea isn't, and her car is dark blue.

He gripped the thought like an exposed wire, the shocking certainty coursing through him, mind and body. Just as he wondered if she had survived the crash, he saw the car's door rising, lifted by someone trapped inside...

He screamed her name, turning to run down to the bank when his attention was attracted by a splashing thud. When he looked again, he saw the car's wheels pointing upward, the doors and windows totally submerged. And no sign at all of Andrea.

Rain soaking into his clothes, he raced to reach her, the steep bank giving way beneath his feet to send him sliding on his ass. But that didn't matter, no more than the current's surprising power when he dove in. It pushed him past the car the first time, forcing him to swim to shore and then make a second try from upstream before he was able to latch on to the undercarriage and position himself on the lee side of the vehicle.

Sucking in a deep breath, he dove under, feeling his way when he could see nothing...nothing until his fingers tangled in her hair.

Forced to come up for air once more, he made a second dive and encountered Andrea, her body partway through a door that refused to open wide enough to allow her lower half to get through. She thrashed and fought, jerking back reflexively when he grasped her wrist, but his attempts to pull her through the narrow gap were futile, with the door wedged against the slick rocks lining the bottom.

She's going to drown. The thought raced through

his bloodstream to the frantic beating of his heart. He couldn't let it happen, refused to lose her like this.

Bracing his feet against the frame, he yanked the door with all his might. With Andrea pushing from the other side, it gave, opening a few more inches before it dug into the bottom, sticking as though cast in concrete.

The gap proved just enough, but as she came free at last, her body spasmed and went limp. Pushing off the bottom, he hauled her to the surface, then dragged her to where the bank widened and flattened out about ten yards downstream. Half crawling out, he pulled her behind him and opened her unresisting mouth, positioning her head to let the water pour out.

It wasn't enough, and her flesh was so damned chilled, the rainwater so much cooler than the mild early evening, so he tipped her onto her back and started mouth-to-mouth, his mind casting up a frantic prayer: *Breathe, please breathe.* The steps from an old first-aid class resurfaced in his memory: four rescue breaths followed by a check for a pulse at her carotid. Desperate for a sign of life, he pressed his fingers into her neck—and felt nothing but the racing rhythm of his own pounding heat.

Hoping like hell he was remembering the technique correctly, he moved to start CPR, his eyes and throat burning with an emotion that he didn't dare give in to. He couldn't think about it, couldn't doubt or hesitate a second.

Before he got in a single compression, Andrea's arms jerked, and she began coughing noisily. He turned her onto her side, where she heaved up more water, then helped her as she pushed herself back from the mess.

"Andrea, talk to me. Are you hurting anywhere? Are your neck and back—"

She held up a hand, still coughing, her body shivering violently. Her teeth chattered so hard he heard their staccato clicking.

"My phone's back in the truck," he said. "I need to call for help and see if I can find some towels or maybe a blanket for you."

"N-no call. No 911."

Breathing, speaking—now all I need is for you to start talking sense. "You need a hospital and proper warming. Your lungs could still have water in—"

"No." Her gaze found his and held it, her eyes clear and her expression urgent. "You c-call an ambulance, and I'm as good—as good as d-dead already. This w-wasn't any a-accident." She rolled onto all fours and started trying to crawl up the embankment, a scramble that felt like a knife's thrust to his heart.

Confused as she was, there was no way he could leave her alone to go and call for help, and she damned well didn't look or act like someone with a spinal injury. So instead he said, "Here, let me help you, and we'll go back to the truck and turn the heat on high."

He half supported and half carried her to the road above, finally getting her into the front seat of Zach's truck. After finding a dry towel behind the rear seat and one of his brother's old barn jackets, he helped her into the sleeves and latched her seat belt before coming around and hauling his own chilled and dripping body into the driver's seat.

For a minute, they sat panting, both of them in shock as heat blasted through the vents. But when Ian reached forward to scoop up his phone from the floorboard, Andrea's lashes fluttered, and her eyes shot wide.

"No! I mean it, Ian. A b-big truck, or maybe it was an SUV." She was interrupted by a coughing fit, only to continue soon after. "I'm not exactly sure what it was, only that it seemed huge, the way it came roaring up behind me, chasing me for several miles. I c-couldn't get away, and I was scared to death of what might happen if I tried to pull over. Then he bumped my tire and—"

"You said *he*. Did you see a man?"

She shook her head. "I was too intent on keeping my wheels on the road to really make out anybody. But one hard bump, and I completely lost control and hit the guardrail. Next thing I knew, I was coming to with creek water pouring into my car."

"You were knocked out, too? Then you definitely need the ER. I'll drive you there myself, though. It'll be a lot faster that way."

He flipped the windshield wipers on high, but when he reached for the gearshift, she grabbed his wrist with a hand as cold as death. "We can't. I can't—or next time, I'll be dead."

His mind leaped back to the gunshots fired this morning. "Wait? Are you telling me it's all really been about you? That the sniper on the ranch this morning was related to someone running you off the road. Why?"

Her eyes widened, her face going even paler as she shook her head. "I—I have no idea. I only know this was no accident. And when he first came up, I saw what looked like a gun barrel hanging out the window. That's how I knew that pulling over to wave him past w-would only g-get me killed." A shudder ran through her entire body. "Just like it'll get me killed if he finds out I've survived this."

He sensed there was more to it, something she was too afraid to tell him. And sitting here wasn't doing a thing to get her warm and dry, so he made the best decision he could.

"Okay, Andrea, I'm taking you back to the house and getting you cleaned up and put to bed, on the condition you'll explain this later. And I swear to you, you're going to see a doctor—"

"No. Please, no. If anybody finds out and it gets back…"

Praying he was making the right decision, Ian said, "Just home then, for now, and I'll keep you safe, Andie."

She gave no answer, but instead burrowed deeper into Zach's barn jacket.

Within minutes, she was fast asleep—or unconscious. He wasn't sure which. Feeling in over his head, he called his brother and explained what he knew, right down to Andrea's terror of anyone finding out about it.

"Maybe I should be heading in the opposite direction, for the ER," Ian said, glancing over at her pale face. "If I did the wrong thing, and she ends up…" The word *dying* caught in his throat.

"There's a retired doctor from Amarillo who's recently moved back to the family homestead outside of Rusted Spur. Let me make a call, see what it would take to get him here to check her out."

"Sounds like a plan, bro. Thanks, and see you in twenty."

Once Ian ended the call, he pushed his speed a little higher, driving as fast as he dared considering the rainy conditions.

But as he neared the turnoff for the ranch, his hurry—along with, he suspected, the fact that he was driving Zach's truck—drew the wrong attention…attention that came in the form of flashing red lights in the rearview mirror and the long wail of the sheriff's siren.

Chapter 9

As Ian bailed out of the truck, Zach was right there, his voice a low rumble. "Why the hell would you bring that son of a bitch here?"

Still muddy from the rescue, Ian shoved his damp hair from his eyes and glanced at Canter, who was climbing out of his SUV. "Didn't exactly have a choice," Ian told his brother. "He lit me up and pulled me over while I was haulin' ass to get here. Was all I could do to talk him into giving me an escort home instead of to jail."

"Last thing we need is this yahoo in the thick of things," Zach said before looking over his shoulder as Jessie came running outside, heedless of the rain.

Considering that the accident had happened on Canter's turf, Ian figured they would have ended up having to deal with the lawman one way or another, but Andrea was going to freak if she happened to see him. So far she hadn't reawakened, even when he'd shaken her to let her know they were home. "You reach that retired doctor?"

Zach nodded. "He's on his way, and Mama says you should take Andrea straight up to the guest suite, so she and Althea can keep Eden out of everybody's hair."

Jessie opened the passenger-side door, where Ian, Zach and Sheriff Canter all crowded behind her.

"Andrea, can you hear me?" Jessie was asking her. "Can you open your eyes or squeeze my hand?"

"Better let me take her up," Zach said.

Ian slipped past him and announced, "I've got this," before lifting Andrea carefully out of the front seat.

As he hurried to the front door, she moaned and murmured, "No hospital. Too many people."

"We're not at the hospital. We're home," he assured her. "I'm taking you to your room and putting you to bed."

Once he'd gotten her upstairs, Ian sat her on the bed's edge, where he moved to take off her shoes only to see she'd already lost them somewhere. "Better get her out of these wet clothes."

"Right." Zach spared Canter, who'd come up with them, an uncomfortable look. "How 'bout if we leave this part to Ian and Jessie, and you and I can head back down and keep a lookout for the doc."

"You promised to explain all this as soon as you got her here," Canter reminded Ian.

"That I did. And I will, as soon as Andrea's taken care of. And you'll get the chance to talk to her, too, but not before she's ready."

"Just see you keep that promise, or I swear to you, I'll—"

"For once in your life, Canter, can you hold off on the bluster?" Zach demanded. "It's bad enough you're lying in wait outside the ranch grounds for a chance to pull over and harass us—"

"Now just hold it right there, mister. You high-and-mighty Rayfords aren't the only ones who pass by on that road, and I'm doin' your brother a damned favor, takin' the circumstances into account and not arresting him for—"

The argument might have escalated if Jessie hadn't
come into the room at that point with a short, round-
bellied man with thinning gray hair and wire-rimmed
round glasses at her side. Still wearing a rain-spotted
jacket and khaki pants, he carried an old-fashioned-
looking medical bag at his side.

"This is Dr. Rosenfield," Jessie said. "Doctor, this
is Andrea. Thank you so much for coming here to—"

Rosenfield nodded a greeting and cut in. "I'll need
everyone out of the room." He set his bag on the bed and
opened it. "Everyone but you, that is, Miss—'?"

"I'm Zach's wife, Jessie," she said, "and of course, I'll
stay and help. The rest of you, downstairs. You, too, Ian."

The others left, but Ian hesitated in the doorway.

Glancing his way, Jessie promised, "The minute we
know anything, I promise you'll be the first to hear."

Zach grabbed at his arm and pulled him from the
room, then gently closed the bedroom door behind them.
"Come on, bro. Let's go downstairs and get out of the
man's way. Or better yet, let's find you some dry clothes
before Mama sees all that mud. I'm sure the sheriff can
at least wait for you to do that. Can't you, George?"

To Ian's surprise, Canter looked almost sympathetic
as he nodded. "Go take care of yourself, sure, as long
as you're not too long about it."

Ian returned to the family room in record time, more
out of anxiety over Andrea than any worries over the
sheriff's request, but Zach informed him the doctor
hadn't yet come downstairs. Though Zach had filled in
Canter on the basics, the sheriff asked Ian a number of

questions about what had led up to Andrea's rescue and what she'd said once he had gotten her to shore.

"I understand she seemed worried about whatever had caused her to lose control," Canter said from the oversize leather sofa across from its twin, where the two brothers were sitting. Unlike his mother's fussy formal living room, this area had been decorated with men in mind—big men, clearly at home with the huge fireplace, the mounted longhorn bull's head and the weathered saloon doors that could be opened by remote to reveal an enormous wide-screen TV.

"Not whatever. *Who*ever," Ian corrected, remembering their conversation. "She was very definite about it. Told me a big pickup or an SUV, maybe, came up from behind and bumped her. Said she saw a gun sticking out the window before it bumped her."

Canter frowned, seeming to consider before he shook his head. "I know she was pretty stirred up about that whole incident this morning, too. You think it's possible she got things twisted all around and mixed up, in her condition?"

Rising from his seat, Ian paced the room, his clean boots carrying him from a spotted cowhide to the tobacco-colored wood floor. "You're saying she dreamed up this second attack? Next thing I know, you'll be telling me this morning's shooting was just thunder."

"No, I wouldn't say that. I found fresh tire tracks out there where you said, for one thing. No shell casings, but that only proves he had brains enough to go ahead and pick 'em up."

"But you're not convinced that Andrea was attacked this evening?"

"She looked pretty out of it to me," Canter said. "You

can't expect too much sense out of anyone in that kind of condition. Hell, you yourself were babbling all kinds of craziness that first day after your brother picked you up and brought you back home."

Ian ground his teeth but couldn't deny it. He'd been half out of his mind, so dehydrated and overheated that no one had gotten any sense out of him for days. But the sheriff hadn't heard Andrea as she'd described another vehicle knocking her car right through the guardrail. Whether or not the sheriff wanted to believe it, Ian was convinced someone had meant to kill her.

At the sound of footsteps on the east wing staircase, where the guest suites were located, all three men went to the landing. His mother, who had been setting up Eden with a movie in the playroom, came out as well, worry lining her thin face. Though she hadn't seemed to like Andrea to begin with, it had taken her only a day or two to warm up to her polite and thoughtful house-guest, remarking—after slanting a pointed look toward Jessie—about how it was so nice to finally have a young lady around the house who seemed to enjoyed listening to the more senior generation.

"Will Andrea be all right, Harold?" she asked the man who had once been her former classmate.

He sighed and said, "She's not in the kind of shape that would warrant an airlift, not that they'd fly in this weather anyway. But I can tell you if she were my wife or my daughter, I'd put her in the car and take her to the hospital myself, to rule out a serious head injury and monitor her lungs for infection, since she inhaled so much creek water. Her core temperature needs to come up, too. Poor girl's teeth are chattering nonstop."

"Then I'm taking her to the Marston ER," Ian announced, with Zach and their mother both chiming in with their agreement.

The doctor shook his head, his jowls wobbling a bit. "I wish you luck with that, young man, because she's digging in her heels and swearing she won't go."

"We'll see about that," Ian said, already heading for the stairs.

Before he reached the suite, he heard the water running. He stopped to knock at the bedroom door and then went in when there was no answer. "Andrea? Jessie?" he called, seeing neither of them, but the bathroom door was standing open, offering him a clear view of the partly fogged mirror.

He froze, transfixed by the hazy image of Andrea, her back to him as she stood nude beside the bathtub, her skin pale and her long limbs shaky as Jessie helped her step into the steaming water. He knew he should turn away, should respect Andrea's privacy, but he couldn't make himself move, couldn't do anything but stare as memories from their time together rose like whorls of mist...

Memories of a chilly night in a friend's borrowed condo on Lake Tahoe, where they'd relaxed in the hot tub and stared up at blazing stars. A night where the possibilities had seemed so limitless and his love for her so vast that his proposal had slipped out before he'd had the chance to think through how his career would affect her...

At least not until she'd looked up at him, her damp eyes gleaming, and whispered, "You know about my mother, don't you? Know what my father's lies cost my family. So just promise me, Ian, that you'll always tell me the truth. Promise me that, and I swear we'll work through whatever else this life throws at us."

His heart had been so full that night, his desire to lay claim to her so all-consuming, that he'd told her what she needed to hear, beginning their engagement with a lie. He'd make it right, he told himself, explain what he was allowed to as soon as she'd been cleared by the agents assigned to background check potential spouses, and he would make their time together worth whatever sacrifices they were making for his country.

"There you go. Careful, now," Jessie said to Andrea as she reached to shut off the water. "It isn't too hot, is it?"

"T-too hot? Is that even possible?" Weak and shaky as it was, the sound of Andrea's voice filled him with relief.

Jessie snorted. "Are you kidding? Ian'll skin me alive if I end up boiling you like a Maine lobster."

"It's not too hot," Andrea assured her before she was interrupted by a fit of coughing. "I—I'm awake now, really. So there's no need for you to babysit me."

"Sorry, kiddo," Jessie told her as she rose to grab a towel off the counter, "but you heard what the doc—" Her eyes widened in surprise as her gaze met Ian's in the mirror.

His face burned in response, as though he'd been caught peeping into windows.

"Excuse me, Jessie. I—I just thought I'd come and check on— I wanted to see about getting her over to the ER."

Jessie turned to look at him directly before she did a double take in the direction of the mirror. When she rolled her eyes at him, he sighed and threw his hands up, feigning innocence even though he knew he was busted.

To the sound of splashing, Andrea called, "Ian, there's

no need for that. I'll be fine. I just need to warm up with a bath and tea or something. That's all." She coughed again.

He took a step forward. "But you could have a serious concussion, and your lungs—"

"I'll give *you* a serious concussion if you don't get out of this bathroom right this minute," she said.

Glancing directly at her for the first time, he saw her peeking over the outsize tub's edge, trying to hide herself from view.

"Or better yet," Andrea continued, "I might see if Jessie's up for loaning me Gretel to stand guard."

"Don't put me in the middle of this," Jessie said. "Didn't I tell you before you ought to listen to the doctor?"

"I'm not— I can't—" Andrea choked out, forgetting about covering herself as her hands moved to her face. "If he finds out I'm alive—"

"If *who* does?" Jessie asked her.

Andrea shook her head. "I—I don't know. I only know that someone clearly wants me dead."

"Or someone's trying to get to me by hurting you," Ian said, "but the thing is, Andrea, I'm afraid your secret's out already. After you conked out in the front seat, the sheriff pulled us over. There was no way I could get out of telling him what happened, no way to keep him from following us here to question—"

"Oh, no." There was a splash as she stood abruptly, clearly beyond caring whether he saw her glistening, pale body. But before either he or Jessie could reach her again, she sank back down, her eyes fluttering and rolling back in her head.

"Andie!" he shouted, charging past Jessie and leaning down to grasp Andrea beneath the arms to keep her from submerging.

Instead of giving in to the fainting spell, she shook it off moments later and pushed his hands away. "I—I'm fine," she said. "I stood up too quickly, that's all."

"If you're so fine," he asked her, "then why are those tears I see rolling down your face?"

Andrea struggled against the fear that whoever had been sent to silence her forever was going to strike again. But almost worse was the way she'd lost control of her life, lost everything that she'd thought had mattered, within the space of a few hours.

Too weak to continue fighting the issue, she let Jessie and Ian help her from the tub, then dry and dress her in a pair of clean sweats Jessie found for her. Afterward, she was vaguely aware of Ian carrying her downstairs and telling Sheriff Canter his questions would have to wait until the next morning or whenever she was strong enough to talk.

She drifted off again, and the remainder of the evening was a blur of time spent in the truck and another exam at the hospital before the doctor decided to admit her overnight for observation.

Each time she opened her eyes, Ian was right there, standing vigil so she could rest. When the doctor asked him to step out during her examination, he politely but firmly let them know that he was going nowhere. Now, as she looked up from the hospital bed, she spotted him beside the window, peering out into the night.

"What time is it?" she asked, her voice thick with sleep and whatever had been in the shot they'd given her.

Her guardian turned, half of his impossibly handsome face lit by the parking lot security lights outside and the light spilling from the room's bathroom, the door of which had been left cracked open. "About one or so. How're you feeling?"

She took a moment to assess, and found the pain in her head had faded to a dull ache. "Mostly guilty, right this minute. Except for when the nurse comes in to check my vitals, I've been sleeping like the dead while you've been keeping guard all this time. You must be exhausted."

"I wanted you to feel safe. That's the only thing that matters."

Warmth spilled into her chest, a brand of gratitude she had no name for. But with it came the understanding of how dangerous it was, feeling this way toward him, how it could end up getting one or both of them killed. "Sit down, at least, please. Come and sit beside me."

He strode across the room and pulled one of two chairs close but couldn't seem to settle. "Here, let's get you some water. The nurse brought some fresh a little bit ago."

Once she'd taken a few sips to appease him, he raked his fingers through his short, dark hair. "It should have damned well been me in the hospital, me in the water. Because I know it has to be my fault, the shooting, all of it."

She suspected he was right but was too frightened to admit it. If she told Ian everything, she had no doubt he'd make a beeline straight for Julian's office—and in confronting him, possibly ensure his own death or incarceration.

"Have you remembered something more?" she asked

carefully. "Something that would help explain why these attacks are happening?"

What looked like pain twisted through his chiseled features. He rose from the chair and paced, clearly unable to contain the wild energy crackling through him.

"I remember enough that it's eating me alive," he said, "everyone imagining I'm some kind of hero. When I must have—I had to have given them the coordinates. Who else could have led them to that listening post?"

Clued in by the way he'd phrased his statement, she narrowed her eyes in concentration. "You don't actually remember, do you? You don't know this for certain?"

He stopped pacing to spear her with a look. "I know enough to tell you I wouldn't be standing here today if I hadn't—if I hadn't betrayed my countrymen. You've heard there was a bombing, haven't you? I found online where it made the news less than two weeks after I was captured, an incident where five members of the US intelligence community died in a secret location in the Afghan border region."

"You *don't* know you did this," she said, making it a statement this time. "You're just assuming, exactly as you're assuming that whoever meant to kill me was doing it to hurt you."

"What? You're asking me to believe that a woman who works her tail off to help anyone who needs it has racked up the kind of enemies who would do something like this?"

"Hey, I could be complicated," she said drily. "Is it really so hard to imagine?"

He laughed. "Yeah, as a matter of fact. You were always putting yourself in others' shoes, seeing the good in everybody."

"Yeah, everybody," she said, pain reverberating through her at the memory of Julian's betrayal.

"Except for liars," he reminded her. "You reminded me of that the day we—the day you ended it between us."

"So you remember breaking up now?"

"Unfortunately, yeah, which is why, from here on in, I swear I'm going to be completely honest with you. Because whatever else I am, whether it's a traitor or a hero, I'm no longer an agent of the CIA."

"Honesty's a good thing," she said, guilt pinging inside her chest at the thought of the secrets she was keeping. "But, Ian, we're not going back. We can't unlive any of the things that've happened since then, no matter how it might seem." *And no matter how it makes me feel, having you watch over me.* But until she understood what was really going on, it was too dangerous to let him think there was any hope of a relationship.

"Jessie told me you were let go from the center. She told me this guy you were seeing—your boss, I guess— broke up with you because of what you told him about me."

"I don't want to get into that now. I won't."

"So you aren't my psychologist anymore, and you aren't another man's fiancée."

"Let's say I'm your friend, Ian. Can't we just leave it at that?"

He considered for a long time, his blue eyes searching her face until he finally nodded. "For now," he said. "But I should warn you, for your own safety, you might not even want to be that close."

She opened her mouth to argue but realized he was likely right. Aside from the physical risk of another, more successful attack, she was aware she would be risking her heart, too, to a man who might well be guilty of what he thought of as a betrayal of his country. Though she would go to the mat arguing the unfairness of blaming any victim of torture for divulging secrets, she knew he would be publicly vilified—possibly even prosecuted— if his role in American deaths became known. Could she bear to watch it happen, to see a man she would always care about destroyed?

"I'll help you get back to California," he said, "get you back on your feet with a new car and a place to stay."

She felt herself flush. "You can't be serious. You can't—"

"I can, and I'm going to. It's the least I can do, considering."

When she shook her head, his voice grew firmer. "Listen to me, Andie. If it's the money you're worried about, forget it. Please. Or if it makes you feel better, pay me back someday, when you're some fancy head-shrinker with your own office in La Jolla."

She laughed at that, at the very idea that she would be the type to set up shop in an upscale community where she'd spend all day helping the rich learn to deal with the burdens of their privilege. She was instead the kind of psychologist who'd be lucky to pay off her debts and earn a modest living, the kind who'd measure her success not in CDs and stock options but in the number of wounded souls she helped avoid the despair and suicide that had taken her mother from her.

What would any of that mean, though, if I turned my back on Ian? What if his guilt turns to self-loathing, if one day he picks up a gun or sees how quickly, how easily, a lasso can be turned into a noose to end his pain?

Her heart staggered with the thought, the smile dying

on her lips. She couldn't let it happen, couldn't grieve his death a second time, no matter what it cost her personally. "Thank you for the offer, for saving my life back by the creek and for staying here to help me feel safe. But I'm not going anywhere, nowhere except the ranch if you'll still have me there as a friend. Because I absolutely mean to help you remember everything."

"I'll do my best to keep you safe, hire security, whatever it takes," he vowed. "But I can't promise you won't be in danger."

"*You're* in danger, Ian. Maybe all of us are—at least until you figure out whatever it is someone wants to stay forgotten."

Chapter 10

Andrea was awakened early the next morning when someone set a tray on the bedside table and slipped from the room without a word. Nose wrinkling at the unappetizing smells from what must be her breakfast, Andrea blinked at Ian, who sat sprawled in the bedside chair, his hat tipped over his face. Sound asleep, she realized, recognizing the soft rumble that ended his every exhalation. He'd earned his rest for certain, though, since he'd remained awake and on guard throughout the long night.

But he had little time to sleep before, with a sharp rap at the door, a tall man in a khaki uniform strode in holding a hat that didn't quite block her view of the sidearm strapped to his hip. As she lowered the limp, cool piece of toast she had been nibbling, he said, "Good mornin', Miss Warrington. I'm—"

"Sheriff Canter," Ian said, coming to his feet and offering his hand so quickly that she wondered if he'd really been asleep.

The two men shook hands, each seeming to swell with testosterone as he sized up the other.

"You get the car pulled out of the creek?" Ian asked.

Canter gave a curt nod. "Had a couple of the deputies working out there half the night. Finally got some cables on it and had a wrecker drag it out this morning. No sign of bullet holes, they tell me."

"He never fired his weapon," Andrea said, nightmare images flickering through her brain like the chattering reel from an old horror movie. "When I saw the barrel, I thought he was pulling up to shoot, but instead he bumped my passenger-side rear tire. That's when my car went spinning through the guardrail and—"

"And what?" Canter asked her. "Did you see this fellow afterward, when you were down there in the creek?"

She shook her head, reaching for memories that rolled in all directions like a broken string of pearls. She could grasp a bead at a time, but the strand refused to come together. "I remember being wet, that's all. Wet and cold. My head hurt. I was trying to get out, and then the car flipped upside down, the whole world filling up with water. The next thing I know, I was lying on the bank and coughing, and Ian was there somehow. I guess he—"

Canter's sharp gaze found Ian's, suspicion rising thick as smoke. "You're saying Rayford was right there?"

Ian made a scoffing sound. "You get that badge of yours out of a cereal box, man?"

"Don't be ridiculous," Andrea told the sheriff. "He was helping me, of course. He was still dripping from pulling me out, and that same morning, we were together when someone fired at us."

Canter scowled. "Settle down, the both of you. Nobody's accusing anybody. I'm just gathering the facts. Now, if you don't mind—" he looked to Ian "—I'd like to ask the young lady a few questions in private."

"There's no need," she told him. "I won't be telling you anything I haven't already told—"

"Rayford might be a big name in these parts, but

there's no way I'm lettin' one of the boys influence the course of my investigation."

"Boys," Ian echoed, looking as though he wanted to spit at the sheriff's feet.

"All right, then. Grown men now, but it's still department policy to record each witness's recollections separately."

Ian gave a terse nod. "I'll step outside and grab a cup of coffee, but, you know, Sheriff, you could've just started with that last part instead of trotting out this bad blood you've got going with my brother. Save the both of us some aggravation."

Canter's only answer was an expectant silence that sent anxiety rippling through Andrea's stomach. Once he got her alone, would he attempt to twist her words to make some kind of trouble for Ian, or would he consider her part of the enemy camp and somehow make things worse for her?

After Sheriff Canter left about twenty minutes later, Ian came in carrying a cup of coffee. "You'd tell me, wouldn't you, if he didn't treat you right? Because I'm not about to let that tin-plated blowhard get away with—"

"Relax, Ian. It was just fine," she assured him. "He asked me about the accident and what I remembered about the shooting in the ravine yesterday morning, and he was as cordial and professional about it as you could have asked for."

Well, mostly, anyway, she mentally amended. While Canter had seemed genuinely concerned about her personal safety—and angered by the thought of an outbreak of violence on his turf—he made no attempt to hide his disdain for the Rayford brothers, warning her she'd be better off steering well clear of either of them.

"Before that money came in, those two couldn't stay far enough away from Rusted Spur," he'd said when she had called him on it. "But now that the old man's gone and the place is worth a fortune, they're all over it like fleas on a hound dog, tellin' that mama of theirs who to talk to, what to think and exactly how to spend her money."

Andrea could have argued that, as far as she could see, Nancy Rayford was anything but abused and that her sons' concern for her seemed genuine, especially in light of her past issues with prescription pills. Instead, she had simply thanked the sheriff for his concern and let him go on his way, to investigate or just pretend to, depending on his mood.

"You're sure it was all right?" Ian asked. "You look a little worried."

"I have a headache, that's all."

"You need some more coffee?" he asked.

"Not if it's as burnt as yours smells."

"You're right. This vending machine stuff's pretty toxic," he said, "but there's a café just down the road. I can have them box you up a cinnamon roll, too, while I'm at it. I'd bet that ranch it'll be a hell of a lot better than whatever's on your tray."

"I didn't go to school for umpteen years to take a sucker bet like that one, but don't worry on my account. There's no way I could eat now."

"You're feeling sick?"

"Not sick, exactly. It's the situation, that's all. But why don't you go get that roll and coffee. You probably could use it after spending all night babysitting the invalid."

"You're not an invalid, and I wasn't just doing it for your sake. There's no way I could've gone home and slept a wink, knowing that whoever put you here was out there somewhere."

She grimaced at the reminder, still scarcely able to believe that someone wanted her dead. Though the facts all pointed to it, the concept was simply too huge to wrap her mind around. What had happened to the orderly and quiet life she had been living?

Yesterday happened to it, some rational corner of her mind whispered. *And so did Ian Rayford.*

There was a quick knock, and a floor nurse, a forty-ish redhead with a harried look about her, stepped into the room. "There's a gentleman outside. I asked him to come back a little later, since the doctor's making rounds now, but he insisted I let you know—"

"Who is he?" Andrea asked, clutching the top sheet more tightly.

By the time the nurse got out the name *Julian Ross*, Andrea was shaking her head, saying, "Tell him not to bother. I don't want to see him."

A humorless smile pulled back the corners of Ian's mouth. "I'll go get rid of him. No problem."

"No!" Andrea said, thinking that Ian sounded far too eager for a confrontation. "Please don't go. I need you to stay right here."

A few minutes later, the nurse returned, gushing over a huge bouquet of yellow roses. "Aren't they gorgeous?" she said. "There have to be a least three dozen."

"Looks like overkill to me," Ian muttered. "Like someone's compensating."

In no mood for male posturing, Andrea flashed an annoyed look his way, then plucked the envelope from the greenery. Crumpling it unread a moment later, she waved off the extravagant arrangement, not caring when the note tumbled to the floor beneath her bed. How could she believe anything Julian said anyway?

"Throw them away, will you?" she asked the nurse, pushing away the gorgeous flowers. "Or, no, on second thought, take them to someone else. Surely you have another patient who could use some cheering? Someone here on his or her own?"

"There is one older lady," the nurse answered, her expression softening. "She's buried everyone, her friends, her daughter and her husband. Poor thing."

"Then tell her the flowers are to remind her that love outlives the human body, as long as she holds the memories close to her heart."

"That's a lovely thought," the nurse said, staring at her with open admiration.

Even harder to take was the pride that Andrea saw in Ian's blue eyes, pride that made her think how very odd it was that she found words of hope to offer an old woman on a day when her own life and her future had never felt more hopeless, when she could see no future beyond the promise she'd made to help this man restore his memory.

The doctor came in next, a different one than she'd seen the night before. An attractive, dark-skinned woman who wore a white coat over a pretty, scooped-neck blue dress, she gave a foreign-sounding name that Andrea didn't catch the first time.

Flipping over the hospital ID clipped to her lapel, she pointed and repeated, "Dr. Pooja Kapur," her accent making the syllables roll off her tongue in a manner Andrea could never duplicate. "I am filling in for Dr. Collins this week. I hope this is acceptable."

Since Andrea knew neither one, it made no difference to her. Nor was she particularly surprised when Dr. Kapur asked Ian to step outside so she could complete her examination in private.

"Go ahead," Andrea urged him. "Get yourself some decent coffee, anyway."

Ian shook his head. "Think I'll hang close," he said, "in case any unwelcome visitors take another crack at stopping by."

Certain he meant Julian, she nodded, breathing a silent prayer that the two would never meet.

Dr. Kapur pulled out a stethoscope to check Andrea's lungs and heart, then asked a few general questions about how she was feeling. If some of them seemed oddly phrased, Andrea didn't think much of it, attributing the woman's way of speaking to a foreign upbringing and education.

"I'm still pretty achy and exhausted," Andrea said in answer to a question.

"This is how a person in your position should expect to feel," Dr. Kapur said with a curt nod, "unless you fail to cooperate, in which case you will no longer feel any more unpleasantness…or anything at all."

Andrea blinked hard. "I beg your pardon?" Surely, she'd misunderstood the woman.

The woman stared directly into her face, her nearly black eyes unblinking. "Should you wish everyone involved good health, you must do exactly as I tell you."

Sucking in a sharp breath, Andrea glanced to the door Ian had just exited, but it remained stubbornly closed.

"That man, yes," said the supposed Dr. Kapur. "He

has one chance, only one to live to be the big hero. And that one chance is you. Do you understand this?"

With her heart hammering like a woodpecker at a dead tree, Andrea couldn't force her brain to process. "Are you even a doctor? Who *are* you?"

"I am the woman who will save your lives, if you stop asking ridiculous questions and listen to what I have to say."

"Y-you have my complete attention," Andrea told her, and for the next few minutes, she only listened, dread tightening her stomach with each accented word.

At the end of it, Dr. Kapur reached into her pocket and pulled out a prescription pad, along with her pen. Putting both in Andrea's hand, the woman in the white coat spoke one last time.

"You will print the password here, neatly and correctly. Otherwise, the next visitor to your bedside will undoubtedly be far less pleasant."

Their gazes remained locked as Andrea drew a shaky breath and then clicked the pen's button with her thumb.

"There is no other way," Kapur urged when she hesitated.

The taste of tears on her tongue, Andrea reached the same conclusion.

The skies had brightened to a deep autumnal blue by the time Ian walked Andrea to the truck that afternoon. According to the instructions on her discharge papers, she needed rest and relaxation but no further treatment, provided there were no changes in her condition.

"I'm restraining myself from saying 'I told you so,'" Andrea said to Ian on the way home.

"Not very convincingly." He sent a wry smile her

way. "But you heard what the doctor said last night. You could've had a serious brain injury or complications from near-drowning."

She didn't smile back. "*Could* have, but I didn't, and now I've cost you another fat hospital bill, along with a night's sleep. And probably a ticket, if Canter catches you driving around without a license again."

"I'd do it again in a heartbeat," he said as Marston's residential neighborhoods gave way to pastures dotted with goats and geese and donkeys, "so not another word about it, please."

"How about two instead, then? Thank you. For everything you've done."

"That's more than two, but I'll take 'em." He reached into a storage compartment and came up with a pair of Zach's sunglasses. "You should put these on. Don't want all this sunshine giving you a headache."

She shook her head. "If you don't mind, I'm going to lean back and rest for a while."

"Sure thing," he answered, sparing her a troubled glance. Since the doctor had left her room again, she'd been distracted and withdrawn, fending off his every attempt to draw her into conversation. At first, he'd worried that she might have gotten upsetting news about her condition, but when she'd finally been discharged hours later, the nurse reviewing her instructions had repeatedly emphasized how very lucky she had been.

Depends on your definition of luck, Andrea had answered with a smile that struck Ian as more desperate than reassuring.

It wasn't until they were nearly halfway home that she finally yawned and straightened. "Sorry I've been such rotten company."

"You couldn't have gotten much rest last night, with the nurses waking you up every couple of hours."

"More than you did, I'm sure. You must be exhausted by now, and if you've had anything to eat at all, I didn't see it."

"I'm fine." Behind the sunglasses he had donned, his eyes burned with fatigue, but it was nothing he couldn't set to rights with a couple hours' sack time and a visit to the kitchen. "And anyway, I'm not the one who crashed my car and nearly drowned, not to mention whatever went on between you and your boss."

Grimacing, she shook her head. "I might be the shrink here, as you'd put it, but I should really have my head examined for ever getting involved with my supervisor in the first place. Talk about putting all your eggs into one basket."

Ian chose his words with great care, reminding himself how his return had complicated her life, unraveling what she'd made of it in the two years since they'd parted. "So it didn't go over well, I take it, when you told him why you couldn't keep counseling me?"

"You know what? It's over now, and I'm finished with him. Finished with Warriors-4-Life, too, as long as he's a part of it."

"That place meant a lot to you, didn't it?" he said, hearing the regret in her voice.

She sighed. "I'm really going to miss it, not so much the place as all the people. We were a tight-knit group, and the soldiers there are such an inspiration. They keep trying for a new life, fighting their way back even when their families have given up on them and employers are afraid to take a chance on—"

"Head cases like me," Ian mused.

"They aren't *head cases*, Ian, or damaged goods, or whatever labels you've come up with to punish yourself and judge others like you. You're all just people, people who need a hand up after someone's knocked them down. It's what you're doing for me, isn't it? You don't think any less of me for it, do you?"

"Of course not, but that's different," he told her. "You were physically injured, and anyway, men are supposed to be—" His father's face forked through his brain like lightning. Dark with fury, with the spittle flying as he shouted, *Don't give me any of your sniveling, or by God, I'll teach you how a real man bears up.*

A leather belt swung through the darkness. Behind the wheel, he flinched, hearing the crack of that strap against tender flesh. Burning with remembered shame as, in his desperation to keep from crying out, he had felt his six-year-old bladder give way.

"Supposed to be what?" she asked. "Carved from stone or forged from metal?"

"My old man damned sure was," said Ian. "He wouldn't have given the enemy the satisfaction of..."

From the recesses of his mind, Ian heard a grown man's voice cry, *"I'll tell you what you want. I'll tell you anything, I swear it."*

Had it been his own, in the moment his resistance had crumpled? That moment he'd cost five others their lives?

"Of what, Ian?" Andrea pressed. "Being a flesh-and-blood human, instead of some celluloid character from an old John Wayne movie?"

"Come to think of it," Ian said, "it wouldn't be the first time that foul-tempered son of a bitch steered me wrong."

"Then maybe you should try showing yourself a

measure of the compassion you've shown me," she suggested. "The same compassion I suspect you'd show to anyone but yourself."

As something shifted in his thinking, he thought how well suited this woman was to the profession she had chosen. How incredibly generous she was, to reach out through her fresher pain to try to ease his own.

They passed a little band of horses, dun and brown and gray heads that lifted from the grass to mark their progress.

"I'm sorry, Andie," he said, "sorry for messing things up for you at Warriors-4-Life." *But I'll never be sorry that I kissed you, only that I was such an idiot to think, even for a minute, that a woman like you mattered less than my career.*

She crossed her arms to rub them. "My fault. I never should've imagined I could— Let's just forget it, okay? I can't talk about this. Slow down. This is it, right?"

Leaning forward against the shoulder belt, she peered out toward the bend of Spur Creek he'd pulled her from. She was staring toward the rocks, furrows digging deep into her forehead.

"I thought it would be deeper," she said. "I remember the water pouring in, so much water that I couldn't breathe."

With no traffic behind them, he slowed the truck to a crawl. "Yesterday, it was. Water levels come up fast with a hard rain, but it doesn't take too long to drain off."

They passed an area of disturbed earth, rutted with tire marks, probably from where her poor old Honda had been pulled out and then towed away. At the center of the bridge, they passed a section strung with orange netting and a warning sign, the place where she'd crashed through the railing.

"We could've both drowned when you jumped in to free me. Could have both been in the morgue now."

"But we're here and we're alive, so how about we make it count for something?"

Not seeming to hear him, Andrea shuddered and covered her mouth to hide her muted cry. Reaching over, he squeezed the fingers of her free hand, and he wanted to tell her how damned sorry he was for somehow bringing things down on her head. But words failed him, as they often did, and all he could think of for the remainder of their journey was how he was going to do whatever it took to make sure no one ever threatened her again.

Once they arrived at the ranch, he took care to deflect his family's well-meaning concern when they came inside—well, everyone but Eden, who took one of Andrea's hands and solemnly laid it onto the back of the larger of her two Australian shepherds. "When I get scared or sad, I just pet my puppies. Lionheart—that's this one—gives the best hugs, but Sweetheart's extra good at kissing faces. Would you like to borrow one... just for today?"

Andrea smiled and squatted down, wincing only a little, a reminder of her soreness. As she stroked the young dogs' heads, first one and then the other, she said, "That's so generous of you, but both of them are so sweet, I wouldn't know how to choose. So how about I come back out and rub both tummies, once I've had a good sleep."

"And Gretel's, too?" Eden asked, pointing toward the Rottweiler, who sat politely beside Jessie. "She likes tummy rubs the best."

"Then Gretel, too," Andrea said before returning her attention to the adults and thanking Ian's mother, brother and Jessie for allowing her to be their guest again. "You're very kind to have me back."

"Of course, dear. You're very welcome to stay as long as you like," said Ian's mother, sounding as if she genuinely meant it.

"I've moved a few things into your closet," Jessie chimed in. "The pants might be a bit short for you, but they'll get you through the next few days till one of us can take you shopping."

"Sounds perfect. Thanks," she said, but her gaze was straying toward the stairwell, a hint his family took that, above all else, she needed rest and privacy.

Ian helped her settle in, bringing her fresh toiletries to get her started and asking her to make a list of anything else she would need. "Whatever you think of, please don't hesitate. I know what it's like to lose everything you own."

"I guess you would," she said with a wan smile. "But you've already done so much. And I don't want to be a charity case."

"You're not a charity. You're my friend, right? We agreed on it," he said. "And my one real shot at figuring out what it is someone doesn't want you helping me to remember."

Her worried eyes avoided his, making him wonder, was there something she knew or guessed but hadn't told him? Or was she only frightened and trying not to show it?

Instead of giving her more space, he took a half step forward and pulled her into his arms. Beneath her warm flesh, her body was as stiff as wire, so he stroked her back and spoke to her as if she were a frightened colt. "We'll get this fixed. I swear it," he said. "Until then, keeping you safe is my number-one priority."

Instead of melting into his arms as he'd hoped, she pulled away to study his face. "But who will keep you safe, Ian? Who will stop the bullets the next time they come flying?"

"We have people on it, so don't you worry about that. Just concentrate on getting stronger so you can work a little of your magic on my head. All right?"

She hesitated a moment and then nodded, her long lashes clumped with moisture. As upset as she looked, it seemed wrong to notice how beautiful she was, how much her every touch made him ache for more.

Fighting the impulse to kiss away her worry, to make each of them forget everything except the other's body, he headed for the door.

"Wait," she said. "There is one more thing I'm going to need, if it's not too big of an issue. I have to log in to my work account and make sure all the clients I've been seeing are properly taken care of."

"Sure thing. I'll loan you my laptop. You're welcome to keep it as long as you're staying here."

"Thanks, but won't you miss it?"

He shook his head. "Since Zach insisted on getting me that new smartphone, I've been using if for just about everything. And if I need something bigger, I'll just borrow Mama's—all she uses the thing for is playing online word games anyway."

After bringing Andrea the laptop, he headed downstairs to the kitchen, where he caught up with his brother while raiding the refrigerator for the leftover fried chicken, potato salad and baked beans he had missed the night before.

"Keep that up, and you'll be too stuffed for the pot roast I smell cooking," Zach warned as he watched Ian practically inhaling his first plateful. "She'll be baking yeast rolls to go with it."

Ian looked up from his chicken leg. "If you're plotting to eat my share, don't count on it, or I may just gnaw your arm off. Didn't want to leave Andrea unguarded too long, so I skipped lunch today. And breakfast."

"It's a miracle you didn't eat an orderly or something, the way you've been going through food lately, buzz saw," Zach said.

"Buzz saw," Ian said. "I kind of like that. But I'll sure miss hearing you call me bonehead."

"Don't count on it, bro." Zach's wry smile faded as he got down to more serious matters. "Just wanted to let you know Virgil's set a couple of our best hands working up around the barn for the rest of the week. He's asked them to keep a close eye out for any strangers and report back to him or me immediately. I've put in a few phone calls, too. We need a head of ranch security, and we need somebody good."

"On a permanent basis, you mean? Not just until this SOB's caught?"

His brother nodded. "That's what I'm thinking. The family was high profile enough before this gas discovery, and then your return hit the news. And wherever people know there's money, they start looking for a way to separate you from it. Everything from elaborate cons—you wouldn't believe the calls and emails I've been fielding—right down to kidnappings."

"You're worried about Eden."

"I'm worried about all of us, but, yeah. I'd be a fool not to realize my five-year-old daughter's vulnerable, especially now that she's attending public school. She loves it there, loves her friends and her teacher, and I don't want to have to twist Jessie's arm into homeschooling her just because I'm afraid."

Ian put down the chicken bone and wiped his mouth with a napkin. "I was right before. I should leave and take Andrea with me somewhere I can keep us both—"

"We've already had this conversation, and I can tell you, running off isn't the answer. Especially when I'm still not convinced this isn't somehow tied to Jessie's work."

"Not to downplay the risks involved in her career, but you're beating a dead horse, Zach. This guy who knocked Andrea's car over the bridge couldn't have mistaken her for your wife this time."

"You don't think, in a rainstorm, he might mix up—?"

"You're grasping at straws, man," Ian said. "Have you asked her about the note yet?"

Zach sighed. "Not much point in doing that unless I'm prepared to believe her answer. Maybe if I looked for it myself…"

Ian stared as if his brother had sprouted horns. And people called *him* paranoid. "That woman's the best thing that ever happened to you, and you're going to *spy* on her?"

"I went so damned long without a family, any family," Zach said, shaking his head in frustration. "The things our old man did made us—made me—so closed off, so guarded that it's a wonder anyone ever bothered cracking through to find her way in. But now that I finally have everything I really need, there's no way I'll risk losing it. No way I'll take that chance."

In that moment, Ian's brother was a stranger to him, a man who, for all his toughness, would go to any extremes for those he loved. But Ian couldn't fault his brother for his willingness to risk anything he thought might secure his family...

Not when Ian still had the sealed, crumpled note he'd picked up off the floor in Andrea's hospital room and stuffed into his pocket. Though he suspected that reading it would be a terrible idea, he hadn't been able to bring himself to dump it in the trash can either, as he'd first intended.

But whether or not he or his brother had begun to plumb the depths of craziness when it came to the women they loved, Ian wouldn't let Zach shoulder the entire burden alone.

"I'll tell you what," Ian offered. "Why don't you let me take over the job of hiring security for the ranch."

"There's no need for that, not when you're still getting your feet back under you, recovering from—from what you went through, over there."

"I've been eating your groceries and playing the lone cowboy long enough. It's time I started pulling my weight around here, and security's my area of expertise. I'll handle any strange emails you get, too."

"I still think we need somebody full-time."

"Then let me do the vetting and take care of the hiring. I have some pretty good contacts in that arena."

Zach shook his head, his eyes betraying his uncertainty. "It's not that I don't appreciate the offer, man, but you've only been back a few weeks. And you still—

we've heard you late at night. Heard you shouting out with those nightmares."

"Hell," said Ian, raking his fingers through his hair. "I'm sorry about that. Why didn't you say something? I'm not—I'm not scaring Eden, am I?"

"A little bit, a couple times, but we got her settled right down."

Ian grimaced, his face heating, certain that his brother was downplaying his kid's reaction so as not to hurt his feelings. "Sorry, Zach. And what about Mom? Has she heard me, too?"

Zach hesitated before admitting, "Listen, man, she's so glad to have you back, she'd never say a word about it. It's really no big deal. Forget I brought it up, will you?"

"I will," Ian promised, "but only if you'll start treating me like a brother and a partner instead of a grenade somebody's pulled the pin on."

Zach extended his right hand, and the two shook on the deal. Later that evening, Ian packed a couple of boxes and moved over to the guest wing, down the hall from Andrea's bedroom. He told himself he was doing it for Eden's and his mother's sakes, and to be available should their guest need anything during her recovery.

But down deep, he suspected that the closer he was to the woman he would never stop loving, the less of an issue the nightmares would prove to be.

Chapter 11

After two days spent "resting" in her room, where she chewed antacids like candy to combat the anxiety chewing through her, Andrea knew that if she didn't get out of her own head, she was bound to have a meltdown—or end up back in the emergency department, this time with a bleeding ulcer.

Terrified by Dr. Kapur's implied threats if she didn't record every detail of Ian's progress, Andrea filed new logs. But instead of writing the truth—that she could barely speak to Ian for the fear and guilt coiling around her middle like a python—she had logged a fictional account of how recent events, namely the shooting and her accident, had distracted him from his work on the root causes of his post-traumatic stress.

As plausible as her logs sounded, Andrea doubted they would hold off those reading them for long. They were clearly after something in particular, she thought, some piece of information they were so desperate for her to bring to light that they would threaten, even try to kill both her and Ian to gain her cooperation. She seriously doubted that whatever they were after would be found in the logs she'd already recorded, since she'd never had the chance to make notes about his revelations the morning of the shooting...

The morning of the day my entire life went down the tubes.

Was it something to do with his CIA work or his time among the terrorists that Julian and Dr. Kapur were really after? And once Andrea did help Ian recover the memory and gave it over for the pair to see, would that be the end of this waking nightmare as the "doctor" had implied?

But as desperately as Andrea prayed the woman would be as good as her word, Andrea feared it was more likely she and Ian would both be silenced in order to keep confidential whatever volatile secret these people were hiding. Or was it possible that this was all about a public prosecution, making Ian a scapegoat for Americans killed because his superiors had failed to move their listening post after his capture as they should have?

She was losing her mind, trying to figure out which or to come up with some alternate scheme that wouldn't end up causing even more trouble.

When Ian brought a tray with lunch that afternoon, he frowned in the direction of the food still sitting on the guest room's small desk.

"You haven't even had your breakfast," he said, nodding. "And you barely touched last night's dinner, either. Are you feeling sick?"

"Not so much sick as sad, I guess. And worried about what comes next."

"Take it from me, you'll feel a lot better once you get some of Miss Althea's chicken salad in your stomach—have more energy, think more clearly. And a little shot of vitamin D definitely wouldn't hurt you, either."

Puzzled by the comment, she frowned. "Vitamin D?"

He nodded. "Sunshine, in the open air. It's a gorgeous afternoon, so how about a walk or, better yet, another riding lesson?"

"I don't know, Ian. I'm still kind of sore, and what if—if the shooter—"

"Oh, come on. I'll take it easy on you, promise. We'll stick to the corral, since Virgil has a couple of our best hands working around the paddock area to keep an eye on things. They'll do, at least until I find the right guy to take over ranch security full-time."

"You're looking for someone?"

"I've made some calls, but it's not the easiest thing on earth to lure someone qualified to a ranch that's hours from civilization."

Her lips pursed as she considered for a moment. "What if I told you I might know of someone, somebody with a background in military security? Raised in ranching country in Wyoming, too, I think, so he might fit it quite well."

"And this guy's looking for a job?"

"I'm sure of it."

"Wait a minute." Ian's eyes narrowed. "This is another of your patients, isn't it? One of your psych cases from the center."

She stared at him, astonished that he would take such a view of someone who'd suffered in the war as he had. Not exactly the same way he had, but they'd both made terrible sacrifices in the service of their country.

"If you want to miss a chance to hire a qualified candidate, that's your loss." She allowed a hint of disapproval to drip through her voice because, whether or not Ian realized it, in refusing to consider her suggestion, he was casting judgment on his own wholeness and self-worth, just as he had when he had spoken of *head cases* earlier.

A look of discomfort passed over his face, and she thought he might say more on the subject, something that would allow her an opening to draw him into conversation. *Why? So you can secretly report it?*

Instead, he shook it off and changed the subject. "How 'bout we meet outside the barn, by the hitching post in forty minutes? Will that give you enough time to finish your lunch and get yourself together?"

She looked down at the borrowed robe she was still wearing, abruptly conscious that she hadn't even brushed her hair this morning. "Sounds good," she agreed. "I guess it is time I pull myself up by the bootstraps."

He smiled. "Now you're talking like a real Texan. I'll have you chowing down on chicken-fried steak and saying *y'all* and *fixin' to* in no time."

"Heaven help us all." She faked a shudder at the thought.

Once he was gone, she forced herself to eat the fruit and half a sandwich, which she washed down with some sweet tea. Afterward, she washed up, brushed her teeth and pulled her hair into a long, sleek ponytail. She opted to wear the outfit someone had laundered for her, the same jeans and blouse she had been wearing that afternoon her car had left the road. Though there were a couple of faded stains, at least they fit well—and served as a reminder that she must soon rejoin the living and purchase herself a few changes of clothing.

Once she joined him outside, Ian smiled at her, with Eden's two Australian shepherds wagging and grinning at his side. "Looking good," he said, leading the same mounts they'd ridden on their previous outing to the hitching post. "Nice to see you back among the living."

"Thanks," she said, dropping a pair of borrowed sunglasses down to cover her eyes. "You're not looking so bad yourself, cowboy. Every day, you look like you've put back on a couple more pounds." Maybe it was the brilliance of the blue sky, the warmth of the September sunshine and the crispness of the air, or maybe he'd been right about the magical properties of Althea's chicken salad, but she couldn't help notice how well he wore the extra muscle mass.

Out of nowhere, her mouth watered at the thought of unbuttoning the deep blue work shirt he was wearing to check out his abs and pecs. Not that she'd be doing any such thing, under the present circumstances, but that didn't stop her imagination from dragging him into the hayloft. What on earth was wrong with her?

He mimicked a fork-to-mouth motion and winked at her as he explained. "It's all in the elbow action."

A bright peal of laughter slipped out of her own mouth, unexpected after days of gloom. "Well, you're looking more like your old self these days." The same gorgeous hunk of self that had practically started her drooling that first day when he had stopped to help her. "Probably feeling a whole lot better, too."

"Hang on just a minute," he said before heading back inside the barn and quickly returning with her riding helmet, along with a wooden box containing a variety of brushes, combs and hoof picks.

He taught Andrea how to groom Princess and clean her hooves, something she took to with no problem. When they got to the saddling, Andrea found it somewhat tougher, and it took several attempts for her to master the correct knot and get the cinch tight enough that the saddle wouldn't slip.

"We'll make a rancher of you yet," he said approvingly once she'd finally passed muster.

"Maybe I can write a grant to get riding therapy added at the youth center when I go back to San Diego."

At her reminder that their situation was only temporary, his smile faded. But it was only fair, she told herself, to keep him rooted in reality. He needed home and family to support his move to a full recovery. And she needed, more than anything, to put this painful chapter of her life behind her.

As she strapped on her helmet, he bridled both horses and led Princess to the mounting block. Andrea had noticed before that he didn't have to use it, but with her body still stiff and sore from the wreck, she decided this wouldn't be the day to try to climb aboard on her own.

Once in the saddle, she looked around and noticed a couple of cowboys working under the hood of a dented, rust-brown pickup not far beyond the paddock area. One had tossed aside his jacket and was working in a muscle T-shirt. Both wore boots and hats and enough testosterone to make her friend Cassidy's freckles jump right off her face.

But Andrea's gaze didn't linger, instead going to Ian's sharp blue eyes as he appraised her.

"Hang on," he said. "Jessie must've been out riding since we last went. Stirrups are too short."

In an oddly intimate adjustment, he had her move back each foot so he could raise the stirrups to adjust them for her longer legs. As he worked, his forearm brushed her thigh, an accidental touch that sent awareness rippling through her, followed by an aching need. *Touch me there again, one last time before I...*

As if he'd read her thoughts, he tensed, and a silence settled over them, a palpable strain magnified by every look that passed between them and each averted eye.

Does he already know I've handed over the password? Has he figured out I'm being threatened?

Her heart skipped a beat when Ian laid one callused hand on her calf, and the sigh that slipped from his mouth warmed the flesh beneath the denim. Or maybe that was only her imagination. But she was certain that the worry she saw in his expression was as real as the tingling of her leg and the flutter of her pulse.

"I've got a confession, Andie. I've done something I shouldn't have, and I'm scared to death you won't forgive me."

Her eyes widened. "W-wait. Forgive *you*? As kind as you've been? Are you kidding? Not to mention that you saved my life."

"Guess I do have my finer moments, but picking up that sealed card, the one you plucked out of those flowers and then dropped on the floor, wasn't one of them. I'm sorry."

"Wait. You mean the card from Julian? The one that came in the roses?"

He nodded, regret darkening his handsome face. "I only meant to toss it for you, dump it in the trash there. But I got to worrying a little, thinking he might've written something—I don't know, but you seemed so upset, and I still hadn't gotten over that moment I spotted your car in the water."

"So you took the note and read it," she said, fear rippling through her as she wondered if Julian had written something that would alert Ian to the danger he was in and possibly make things worse for them both.

"It was crazy, stupid. The kind of idiot move my brother—never mind that. I just wanted to clear the air between us and apologize for getting in your private business. Andrea—are you all right? I swear your face just went gray."

"I—I'm fine," she said, remembering to breathe again. Because, clearly, Ian was feeling guilty, not furious, as he would surely be had he had any idea that she was being coerced to share his secrets. "It's just— I'm surprised, that's all."

He looked up into her eyes. "And disappointed, I hope. Because I'm disappointed in myself."

"What did the note say, Ian? Tell me that, and I promise you're forgiven."

He turned from her but went only a few steps to mount his palomino horse in one smooth motion so that they were looking at each other almost eye to eye. Urging his horse a little closer, he dipped two fingers into the left pocket of his checked shirt to produce the note. "Here you go."

She took it from him, then drew a deep breath before unfolding it and reading.

Please come back to me. Let's talk this over and make things right.

She turned it over, looking for more, for the apology or Julian's promise to put a stop to the threats and violence. But there was nothing else, nothing at all.

Without meeting Ian's gaze, she jammed the note into her back pocket and nudged the mare's side, wanting nothing more than to distance herself from the reminder that, for all her education, she was no better than her mother at avoiding men with dangerous secrets.

Ian cleared his throat, then started giving her instructions, at times demonstrating the positioning he wanted as he made a circuit of the corral. Distracted as she was, she wasn't sure how much she got out of the lesson, other than to notice his easy athleticism in the saddle and the streaming white banner of his horse's snowy mane and tail.

For the next forty minutes or so, she did her best to follow his directions. As they worked, the conversation was stiff and formal, both of them sticking to the subject at hand. Eventually, though, she shifted in the saddle, trying to relieve the ache in muscles she'd forgotten she possessed.

"Looks like you've had about enough fun for one day," Ian noted.

"It *was* fun." *Or at least, it should have been.* "I really do appreciate the lesson. And just so you know, I meant what I said earlier about the note. I'm not upset. It's not important."

"It's important to me," he said, regret shadowing his square jaw. "Important enough to get me thinking about the man I used to be. And about the man I want to be, if I'm ever to deserve you."

She looked up sharply. "What on earth makes you believe that I deserve *you*?" If she did, she'd find the courage to tell him that because of her, someone was likely poring through her case notes even now.

He nudged his gelding's side. Closing in, he reached out to claim her hand. "Because I don't remember everything, but I damned sure remember you."

You remember someone else, someone a lot braver, someone who hasn't struggled to escape a car while the waters rose to swallow her alive. The woman who'd emerged brought with her a new understanding of how fragile life was. Of how willing these people—whoever they really were—would be to kill if they were crossed.

"Why are you shaking, Andrea?" he asked her.

"I'm ready to get down. That's all," she said. "I'm exhausted."

By the time he dismounted and moved to help her, she was already on her feet and walking the mare back toward the barn.

"What's really wrong?" Ian pressed, leading his own mount beside her. "Ever since the hospital, you've been withdrawn and miserable."

Heat rose to her face. "Seriously, Ian, how would you expect me to behave under the circumstances?"

"It's more than that, I know it. There's something you haven't told me."

"I'm scared, that's all, scared to stand too close to a window. Being outdoors in the open—it's pretty overwhelming."

He pulled open the sliding door to the barn and gestured for her to walk Princess inside. As he followed, leading Sundance, he said, "Tell me more about this man you mentioned from the center. The one with the security background. You really think he's qualified, or are you just feeling sorry for him because he needs a job?"

She frowned over her shoulder. "Pity's never been part of my therapy, Ian. For example, I don't feel sorry for you right now, just annoyed that you would ask that."

"And you're sure he's ready for this? He's not like…"

He thumped his fingertips against his sternum. "Still all messed up?"

"I can't discuss his personal details, but suffice to say I wouldn't have recommended him unless I thought he was well qualified and capable. Your safety and your family's matter too much to me."

"All right, then. Have him email the ranch a résumé. I'll write the information down for you when we go back in."

She studied him. "You aren't just doing this to try to make it up to me for reading my note, are you?"

"You want the correct answer or the true one?" he asked, a smile ghosting through eyes the color of a field of spring bluebonnets in the sunlight.

"In that case," she said, "I withdraw the question. Because in some instances, it's better not to know for sure."

As Ian unsaddled and put away the horses, he did his best to engage Andrea in conversation. But no matter how he tried, she was so quiet that he wondered if he'd been wrong thinking there was something she was keeping from him.

"I shouldn't have pushed you so hard," he said as he closed Sundance's stall door and dusted wisps of the sweet-smelling hay he'd given each horse off the front of his shirt. "Riding was a lot of physical activity for someone—someone who was almost..." The shock of it twisted through him: how cold she'd been lying on that sandy bank, how stark-white her complexion. Combined with the bluish tint of her lips and her soaked body's corpse-like limpness, the horror of the memory was forever branded on his brain.

"I'll be fine," she assured him. "After all, Princess was the one who carried me, not the other way around."

Unable to escape the memory, he said, "I've seen dead men before—women, children, animals—all the ugliest scenes that terrorism has to offer. But nothing's ever kicked me in the gut like thinking I'd lost you on the bank of Spur Creek. Even after I did mouth-to-mouth—"

She looked up, her face stricken. "You gave me mouth-to-mouth?"

"You weren't breathing, Andrea. And I was about to start on CPR when I couldn't find a pulse. That's when you came out of it, when you came back and it felt like—something like my own heart being restarted. *Kick*-started, like an old motorcycle with a rusty engine."

She shivered, hugging herself. "That must have been so—what am I saying? I know how it hit you. I understand exactly because I felt something inside me come alive again, too, the day that I found out you'd come back from the dead."

"Even though you'd left me and found someone else?"

It grew so quiet inside the barn that he made out the sound of hammering from somewhere outside and what he recognized as the happy, growly chuffs of the two young shepherds playing in the paddock area. There was another sound, as well, the lumbering thump of his own heartbeat, a sound that grew swifter every moment he looked into her eyes.

But he couldn't tear his gaze away, couldn't do any more than stare in fascination as she studied him, too, thoughts darting swift as swallows in the expanding darkness of her pupils. It was one of the things that he loved best about her, that sense of so much going on behind each look and every word. Maybe, as an old friend from the agency had told him after he and Andrea had parted, men with secrets like theirs were better off sticking with uncomplicated women. But he'd never wanted anyone too naive to see through his lies...

Had never wanted anyone who didn't think before she answered the important questions.

"Julian helped me through my grief for you," she finally answered. "He was good to me and kind, and we shared a passion for helping traumatized veterans—something I became intensely involved with after hearing of your...after I received that knock at the door."

"I'm sorry for what you were put through on my account."

"Don't be, because that's not my point. The thing is, Ian, Julian might've been the man I turned to. But he wasn't, he's never been, the man I needed."

His pulse booming in his ears, Ian closed the remaining space between them, his lean, work-hardened arms enfolding the sweet softness of her body. This time, when they kissed, he forced himself to hold back, to begin a wordless conversation based not on his hopeless desire to go back in time but on a wish to start anew. Only this time, he swore to himself, he'd do whatever it took to build a real relationship instead of another shimmering mirage.

He trailed kisses to the tender spot beneath her ear, making her shiver when he gently nipped the delicate flesh.

Her breathing deepening, she tipped back her head and whispered, "You, yes. Always you, except...except, Ian, there is something. Something I've been meaning to...tell..."

A word dissolved into a groan as he cupped her breast

with his hand, as he pressed her up against one of the beams that separated the stalls. Right now, he didn't need or want words. He only wanted her, needed her with a fever-bright intensity that made every other consideration fall away.

Andrea's glazed eyes and parted lips told him she was swept up in the same warm current, a current that put him in mind of turquoise waters, green palms and a certain blue bikini forever imprinted on his mind.

"Later. Tell me later." His voice grew hoarse as he leaned in and their bodies came together, their movements an ebb and flow as natural and as ancient as the tropical tides.

"Ian," she murmured, her hand dropping low to squeeze the hardness making his jeans so damned uncomfortable. Moments later, she seemed to regain control of herself. "We really can't— We shouldn't. Not here, at least. And not before I talk to you about what I—what I've done."

He covered her mouth with his own, swallowing her protest. He couldn't process words now, not while he was burning body and soul with the need to lose himself in the sensation, to lose himself in her.

"Come with me," he said, gripping her by the wrist and taking a step toward his brother's office. When she hesitated, he said, "Please, Andie. Before a bunch of damned talk gets in the way of what you know we're both feeling, what we both want and need."

Her beautiful hazel eyes locked on to his, a denial written in them. But when he lifted her hand to his mouth, when he turned her wrist just far enough to taste the flesh that covered the delicate tracery of blue veins, he felt her frantic pulse slow, felt the moment when whatever resistance remained in her gave way.

Inside the barn office, he turned the lock on the door and prayed to everything that was holy that wherever his brother was, he would stay away a good long while.

For a long time, he and Andrea kissed right there, beside the door, his hands rediscovering the hills and plains, the secret valleys of the remembered country of her body, his mouth feasting hungrily on hers. Her fingers were busy, too, unbuttoning his shirt and running through his sparse, dark chest hair, sliding her palms over work-sculpted muscle and driving him into a frenzy.

He helped her pull off her shirt, too, tossing it onto the floor in front of the oversize desk. As he reached to unhook her bra, he thought of sweeping that desk clear in a single, reckless moment, of laying her back atop its broad expanse and taking her right there. But he was distracted by the irresistible glory of her freed breasts, by an impulse so strong that he pushed her against the door to suckle first one and then the other.

"We—can't—someone will hear…" Her words dissolved into a moan. "Oh, Ian, how I've missed…"

The protests ended, and she reached for the buckle of his belt, undoing it and the top button of his jeans. Starting the zipper's downward journey, until his rock-hard erection was free of the constricting pressure.

Somehow, they made it to the sofa, a trail of clothing marking their haphazard progress. As they stood beside it, she began kissing her way down his body, his awareness of the heat of her mouth and the sharpness of her nails as they lightly scored his flesh so all-consuming that he barely registered her soft words. "Have to make it up to you. All of it, you have to forgive…"

The first brush of her lips against his heated shaft was nearly enough to set him off. But as what she'd said sank in, he put a hand on her shoulder and drew her to her feet to look into her eyes, the lashes dark and spiky with her tears.

Though it nearly killed him to resist, he groaned, "You have nothing—nothing at all to make up to me, darling."

"But, Ian, I was sent here. Julian made me come. He wanted me to spy on—"

"Guess I should pay him a visit then, to thank the son of a bitch for sending you to me."

"He wanted your—"

"Shh, Andie. I don't give a damn what he wanted, not when I'm right here wanting you more than I've ever wanted anything or anybody in my life." Taking her by the hand, he guided her onto the sofa, sat down beside her hip.

She looked up into his face and her breath hitched. She froze like a fawn when the wolf passes nearby.

His hand glided over one of her soft breasts, his fingers lingering to toy with her hard nipple. Sliding to his knees, he followed with his mouth, tempting and teasing until he heard her sigh slip free.

And then he was kissing his way up the column of her neck, drawing soft murmurs of pleasure from her. Beside her ear, he whispered, "And I want you, Andie, want to look at you, to watch your face the very moment that I slide inside you…like this."

His hand found and stroked her damp heat, his fingers dipping inside her, pumping her until she arched and gasped.

"I'm going to watch you lose control," he said, placing a knee between her creamy thighs, his excitement an exquisite torment. "Watch you come to pieces while I—"

"Now, please. I need you now, Ian." Her eyes captured his, the worry in them shifting into pure feminine desire.

He drank in the sight of her, so beautiful, so helpless with want, so completely his as he would always be hers. And then in a single long thrust, he buried himself inside her, lost himself in a rising spiral of sensation that built and built and built until she finally, fully brought him home.

Spent and satisfied some time later, he held her on the sofa, kissing the soft hair at her temple and feeling as content and relaxed as he had in the days before they'd parted. So content that he drifted off, forgetting for the moment where he was...

Until, some minutes later, the ventilation system kicked out a whiff of straw, a trace—perhaps imagined—that somehow found its way past the homey scents of horse and leather, of wholesome hay and grain. The acrid smell of fear came next, jerking him awake. He was reminded of deep shadow, deeper shame, and the deep voice he'd heard crying out beside him—a voice pleading for mercy, not for Ian, but himself.

Ian was back there again, right there, he realized as his tormentor raised a meaty fist, the end of the chain wrapped around it.

Startling to alertness, the woman beside him rolled over, staring as he scrambled off the sofa and started grabbing for his clothing. "What is it? What's wrong? Ian, can you hear me?"

His heart pounding silver nails of adrenaline through his system, he jammed a leg into his jeans. Unable to answer, to think past anything but the need to escape the tangled images ripping their way through nerve and muscle, biting into bone. They were jumbled together, shards from childhood and keen-edged blades from that place, that reeking hole beneath the floorboards, where slivers of light reached down to touch the filthy straw.

Andrea rose like a hallucination, speaking in a voice that floated across the continents and oceans. "Ian, listen to me. You're having a flashback, remembering something from the past. But you're safe now. You're with me here, in Texas. You're home, and we're okay."

He snatched up his shirt, looking around for an exit. Would there be a guard just outside, waiting for him to make a break, another excuse to lay into him? Would he have to kill again, wrapping the chain around the thick neck, pulling and pulling until he heard the crunch of cartilage?

"Can I touch you, Ian? Would that be all right with you?"

He elbowed his way roughly past the image of his Andie. The hallucination stumbled, looking both hurt and bewildered before she pulled herself together. "What is it, Ian? What's going through your mind now? What are you *remembering*?"

One splinter pierced his reality, shattering everything he thought he had known. His heart pounded and his gaze snapped to the memory of the only woman he had ever allowed himself to love. "I wasn't—wasn't there alone. A-another man—another American. He watched it. Watched me."

Two patches of color stained her cheeks, some emotion burning hot inside her. She sounded almost real as she asked, "Watched what, Ian? Watched your *torture* back there? Back before you came home?"

Ian tried to force himself back into that memory, but it was like trying to shove his entire body through a tiny pinhole. He could peek through sometimes, if the light was just right and he had the correct angle, but there was no way, no way in the damned world, he was ever going to squeeze himself into that space.

Squeezed...space. So damned dark back there, with the smell of musty straw burning in his nostrils. A deep voice, big and booming—the old man's voice, his old man's face, with the chain in his hand now.

Any minute he'll be coming back.

"Ian? Are you with me?" Andrea asked, and he noticed she was pulling up her own jeans, her top half clothed already and her now-loose hair wildly tousled.

"What?" he asked, blinking at her before his head jerked toward the low rumble of approaching voices. Male voices, sounding more casual than alarming, but Ian wanted to curse them anyway for intruding before he'd quite remembered where he was.

"Is that your brother I hear?" Andrea asked. "That's Zach out there, isn't it?"

Ian stared at her, trying to make sense of what she was saying. As the voices grew nearer, she hurried to unlock the door just before it opened.

His brother stopped in the open doorway, with a graying, goateed man visible behind him. Zach didn't come inside, his sharp gaze flicking from Andrea to Ian, his look of surprise melting into one of comprehension. There was no judgment in Zach's eyes, only the hint of a smile as he said, "Sorry to interrupt. I'll just take Doc Spencer to see to that lame heifer first and brew us up some coffee later."

They were standing in Ian's way, blocking his only

exit, he realized, as reality once more spun on its axis. His vision dimmed, memory creeping on spiders' legs out of the darkness, its needle-sharp fangs dripping with a venom that burned like fire as he thought of being trapped here, trapped by the stranger in the doorway who wore his father's face.

Charging the door, he shoved his way past the first man and barely missed the second as the man jerked out of Ian's path. Ignoring their startled exclamations and the woman crying out his name, he headed full bore toward the outer barn door, the guards' furious Pashto curses ringing in his ears...

He fled the men, fled the bullets he expected to take him down at any second and raced out into the daylight, into freedom. Staring around wildly, he spotted an unsaddled horse grazing in the distance and started toward it—

Before abruptly changing course and sprinting toward an old brown truck.

"Ian!" Zach shouted, but his brother didn't answer.

Panic pounding through her, Andrea grasped his arm to stop him as he started toward the open barn door. While the vet stared after them in shock, she told Zach, "Wait. Something's set him off— He's remembering. Remembering too much."

"You stay back, too, Andrea. He looks pretty damned riled up, and I don't want you getting— No, Ian!" Zach raced outside, where Ian was running for the old pickup the two hands had been working on. The rusty hood was down now, the cowboys nowhere in sight.

She ran out after Zach, but Ian was already in the cab, cranking up the engine. For a moment, she didn't think it would catch, but an instant later, the engine rumbled to life, and he lurched off, tires shooting pea-sized gravel in their wake.

"I'll go after him, make him stop." Zach ripped the keys from his pocket and sprinted for his own truck.

Andrea was hot on his heels. "No, Zach. If you chase him while he's still trapped in the flashback, he won't get the chance to think things through. He'll just react and end up racing you to get away. Someone will get hurt."

Zach stopped short and looked after the receding truck, his handsome face contorted with anguish and frustration. "Are you sure you know what you're doing? What if we let him go now and he just keeps on driving—or worse yet, splatters his damn fool brains over the roadside when he rolls into a ditch or something."

"I can't be sure," she admitted, unshed tears making her vision shimmer, "no one can, and I'll admit that a big part of me wants to chase him down with you and drag him straight home, hog-tied and yelling his head off if that's what it takes. But my training and experience both tell me he'll wind down soon, get a grip on himself and come back once he's had a chance to process the memory that's upset him."

"What memory? Is it—what they did to him?"

"I'm not sure exactly, but it's definitely tied in with the torture." She recalled being with him, every worry driven from her mind by the kissing, touching, the way he'd looked into her eyes as he had moved inside her. She remembered, too, that moment when his body had jolted, every muscle tensing as he'd pushed himself away. He'd said something about another person, some other *American* who'd watched him *there*, which must mean the place where he'd been held and tortured. But what had

Ian meant exactly? Had an American taken part in what had been done to Ian, or had he been a fellow prisoner, doomed to suffer the same torments?

Whatever the truth was, its impact on Ian had been so immediate, so profound, an insight struck her like a bolt from the blue. This had to be it, what Julian had wanted from her all along, what he and Dr. Kapur wanted. And what they would stop at nothing to keep Ian from telling anyone, especially a reporter like his sister-in-law, Jessie.

To prevent that from happening, Andrea felt sure they would do whatever damage control they deemed necessary...

Damage control that might very well include the murders of anyone who knew the truth.

"If there's anything you'd like me to do," the veterinarian said, sounding genuinely concerned, "or anyone I should call for you—the sheriff, maybe?"

"No, that's fine," Zach said. "We've got this covered. And even if we didn't, Sheriff Canter is the last person on the planet I'd ever ask for help."

"Then, I'll just go in and see about that heifer you've got penned up, shall I? You said it's the left foreleg she's favoring, didn't you?"

"That's right, and thanks, Doctor. She's in the last box stall on the left."

The veterinarian went inside, leaving Andrea and Zach to watch the receding cloud of dust that marked Ian's progress. As the truck vanished from view, Zach shook his head and swore. "I ought to beat that brother of mine senseless for taking off like that, scaring people half to death—and again, without the license."

"I understand you're worried," she said, "and I know it has to be frustrating. But he is making progress, remembering more each passing day. Learning to handle it, to self-regulate the reactions—that's slower to come, but I promise, it *will* come."

"If he doesn't destroy himself first, you mean?" Zach's fear for his brother bled straight through his gruffness. There was love, too, in the mix, a deep though mostly unspoken bond between two men shaped by the same upbringing. A difficult upbringing, marred by their father's violence.

"I swear to you, he's not going to do that, not as long as I have breath and strength to stop it." The professional in her knew that it was reckless, irresponsible to make such a promise. But she wasn't speaking as a psychologist any longer, just as a woman. A woman whose body ached for Ian…and whose heart had no idea how to let him go.

"But there's still someone out there, isn't there? I mean, that car of yours didn't end up in Spur Creek all on its own, now did it?"

"Someone hit me," she repeated, "someone who wanted me either good and scared or stone dead."

"Then we'd better damned well hope that Ian doesn't end up running into that person before he figures this out and drags himself back home."

As the hours passed with no sign of Ian, she regretted her rash statement, along with the advice she'd given Zach that pursuing Ian would have been a very bad idea. She came to regret it even more when Zach found Ian's cell phone on the floor near his office sofa, where it must have fallen while they'd been…

The thought had regret knifing through her. Had it been the heat and intensity of their lovemaking that had somehow triggered a memory Ian clearly hadn't been prepared to deal with?

Without the smartphone, with its GPS, there was no way to track him down if need be, as she had thought at first. And no way to prevent him from somehow finding the means to keep going, leaving all of them as bereft as they'd been at the first reports of his death.

The first, but not necessarily the last.

What if she'd been wrong, if he'd really run the truck off the road as Zach had suggested? With every second that ticked past, her anxiety wound tighter, leaving her trembling with imagined scenarios where the driver who'd run her off the bridge burst out of nowhere, shooting from his window at Ian. Or what if Ian had instead regressed to the fugue state he'd been in when he'd first been found. She pictured him pulling over along some lonely stretch of roadside, leaving the door of the pickup open and walking blindly across country, continuing the odyssey he'd begun months before.

Needing the family's company as badly as they seemed to need her reassurances, she joined them that evening at the dinner table. With the exception of Eden, who was happily oblivious as she alternately shoveled potatoes, pork and peas into her mouth and chattered about a drama involving an escaped hamster in her kindergarten class, everyone else did little more than pick at their meals, each of the adults struggling with worries about what might have happened.

As Andrea watched them, she wondered if Zach's mother, his brother and Jessie were all struggling against the same fear that gripped her: the worry that somehow, some way, death had reached an icy hand through the encroaching prairie darkness and reclaimed the man who had once miraculously escaped its grip.

Chapter 12

A garish twilight glow crouched along the dark horizon when it finally came to Ian that there was no outrunning memory. No outracing it, either, especially not in a rattletrap old pickup that was already running on fumes. He had a dim memory of pulling off to the side of one of the rutted dirt roads that crisscrossed the ranch in an attempt to pull himself together. But it clearly hadn't worked, for he was traveling down a paved road now, a narrow two-lane highway, moving toward that bloody splash to the west...

Or could it be the east? Rising on a pulse of panic, the question had him wondering if he'd lost not only his sense of direction but also more time than he'd imagined, if he might be looking at dawn's lights instead of dusk.

Breathing hard, he clenched the wheel more tightly and pulled over, staring into the dimming light until a few emerging stars convinced him it was just past sunset after all.

The first order of business, he realized, was to figure out where the hell he was and get to the nearest gas station, or he would end up adding the need to call for a ride home to the growing tally of his failures.

Though he knew he should at least set Andrea's and

his family's minds at ease, it came as almost a relief when he checked his pocket and found he didn't have the cell phone with him. At least that reassured him that Zach wouldn't be jumping down his throat at any moment, demanding an explanation for what had tripped him off. Ian's gut twisted at the thought of how the memories ran together, with both his torturers and the American whose voice he'd heard, all bearing his old man's face.

Even worse than the thought of looking like a lunatic in front of his family was the idea of trying to explain the way he'd run out on Andrea after making love to her. It came to him in a rush how sad and anxious she'd looked, in the moments before he had finally seduced her, how she'd begged for the chance to "make it up" to him…

To make up the fact that—he reached back through the smoky haze of spent lust and adrenaline, struggling to remember exactly what she'd told him. Something about being sent to him, forced by the fiancé who had been her boss, as well.

He spun it around in his brain, wondering if, despite her show of reluctance, she could have been placed in his path in the hopes that pillow talk would loosen his tongue, coaxing him to reveal whatever the hell it was that this Julian and whomever he was working for were after.

They want the American, the American who watched, Ian thought, cold chills ripping through him at the hazy memory of the man who'd begged to be spared his own beatings. But as unsettling as that thought was, the suspicion that Andrea might have been coerced to sleep with him, forced against her will, turned the blood pumping through his body to ice water in an instant.

Was it possible she could have faked the cries of ecstasy, the quivering clench of her innermost muscles? Or had her reaction been no more than a physical response, one that had left her dealing with despair and shame afterward?

He ground his teeth, telling himself it couldn't be true and noticing a brighter section of the darkening sky, a glow that had him putting the truck back into gear and heading toward what he suspected must be Marston, since tiny Rusted Spur didn't have enough in the way of stores and businesses to create much light pollution.

Before he made it far enough to confirm or disprove his hunch, the truck's engine sputtered once before giving up the ghost. Rolling to the stony shoulder, Ian tried in vain to restart it before climbing out of the cab, hoping like hell he'd find a gas can in the truck's bed.

He dug through tools, old flashlights and a length of rope to find a spouted red container in the pickup's rusty toolbox. But he cursed in frustration to realize his wallet was nowhere to be found. Of course, he thought, since he'd never seen the need to carry it around the ranch.

With no other choice, he chose the flashlight with the brightest beam and started walking anyway, hoping he could prevail on someone's kindness toward a stranger in need. And praying he would be fortunate enough to come across a Good Samaritan rather than the sniper who had already tried once to shoot him—and nearly murdered Andrea on another lonely road.

An hour after dinner, Jessie was down on the floor of Eden's bedroom with her daughter, the two of them building weirdly imaginative, though oddly angular "dinosaurs" from LEGO blocks. Though Zach's mother would have wrinkled her nose at their "unladylike play," Jessie and her daughter were having a blast making their creations roar before launching them into epic battles. Both of them laughed like loons whenever a tail or claw or head went flying. Barely able to restrain themselves from joining in, Sweetheart and Lionheart played the part of enthusiastic spectators, barking and wagging hairy rumps.

Unable to resist the impulse, Jessie flipped over Eden, freshly bathed and in her pj's, and tickled her until the little girl squealed. Jessie suspected it was a huge mistake to do so this close to bedtime, but she needed the release as badly as she needed to draw breath.

Ian's disappearance, worrisome as it was, only added to the stress that had been weighing on her lately—stress and guilt about the secrets she was keeping, the discoveries she'd made. She'd wanted to talk some more to Andrea, maybe even confide about what she'd stumbled across a few days earlier while helping her mother-in-law install a software update on the computer the older woman mostly used for online word games. Jessie was still in shock over the email Nancy Rayford, a computer novice, had inadvertently left open, a message that had instantly caught Jessie's eye when the name of a target of her investigation jumped out at her.

But there had been no chance to get Andrea's take on the situation. With the exception of this evening, she'd mostly kept to her room since her return, looking so drawn and pale the one time Jessie had gone up to check on her that she hadn't had the heart to bother the woman with her troubles.

A tap at the door interrupted the impromptu wrestling match, and Zach came in.

"Daddy!" shouted Eden, springing up and running to him as if she hadn't just seen him a half hour earlier. "Read me another chapter, please. Me'n the puppies want to hear the one about the funny cow dogs."

He scooped her up for a hug, but the tightness around his eyes and his single glance at Jessie sent anxiety throbbing through her body.

Is it Ian? Is there bad news?

"I'll tell you what, Eden," he said, his deep voice taking on the tones he used to gentle a frightened young horse or soothe an injured calf. Big and powerful a man as he was, he never used his size or strength to command respect, but there was a core of strength there that made nearly everyone, from the ranch's dogs and horses to the roughest-natured cowboys, obey him without question. "If you'll pick up your toys while your mom and I go and talk for a while, I promise you, I'll come and do just that a little later."

"*Two* chapters," said Eden, whose unerring child's instinct told her she was in a position to bargain. "Two chapters, and bedtime fifteen minutes later?"

"Pick up your blocks, and we'll see about the rest," he said, the somberness of his words making Jessie's stomach flutter.

"Listen to your dad," she said.

Eden glanced from one parent to the other. "Okay, Daddy. I'll do it." She smooched his stubbled cheek. "And then you won't have to be a grumpy face anymore."

"Thanks, Glitterbug. You're the best," he said, bending to put her down. "I'll be back in a little bit."

He held the door open for Jessie and then closed it behind the two of them once they'd stepped into the hallway.

"What is it? Is it Ian?" she whispered urgently.

Zach only shook his head and nodded in the direction of their bedroom. Hurrying to keep up with his long strides, she felt an ominous weight squeeze the air from her lungs, certain that the news was as dire as any of their fears.

Inside their room, she glanced anxiously at the dark windows. Away from the ranch's security lighting, the blackness would be almost complete, the distant stars and thin sliver of moon offering only the barest scintilla of relief. "If you're scaring me like this for nothing…"

"I can tell you this much—Ian hasn't wrecked the truck somewhere on the road to Rusted Spur or Marston. About a half hour after he left, I sent Virgil off in one direction and those cow-patties-for-brains hands who left the keys in the truck's ignition in another to check the roads—and Marston's beer joints, too, as long as they were at it."

"I thought you said Ian's not a drinker."

"He's not—or hasn't been since the two of us stirred up so much trouble back when we were looking for ways to punish the old man…not that that ever worked out so well for either of us."

She caressed his forearm lightly, her heart twisting at the thought of the violence that had defined his early years. It made her proud, too, of Zach's efforts to be a far different type of father than the sorry example who had blighted both brothers' childhoods.

The question was, was she willing to allow the late John Rayford's sins to open up a fresh new set of wounds with the publication of her story? But the thought of hiding the man's low character, of letting her target get away with outrageous behavior didn't sit well with her, either. Nor could she bear the idea of letting Zach try to remake her into the kind of woman she would never be, even if he did so in the name of love.

"Just wanted to rule out the drinking," Zach explained, "because whatever he's remembered—if you'd only seen the look on his face. It was like he was still back there. It was the kind of pain a man might do any crazy thing to numb."

She nodded, feeling terrible for Ian. "Sometimes I wonder if he'd be better off keeping those demons buried."

"We both know that's no good, either, because buried or not, those damned memories have been eating him alive."

"He's been a little better since Andrea, don't you think?"

"Better, yeah—or just more focused on her than his own problems. From what I've seen, it's not entirely one-sided, either."

She smiled, once again touching him lightly. "So you're just now noticing that?"

He shrugged and stalked in the direction of the bed he'd had built for them, a bed that she sometimes joked could only be owned by a cattle rancher or a king. Between its massive proportions and its dark headboard shaped to resemble the spreading, hand-carved horns of a bull, it might have been ridiculous if Zach weren't able to deliver on the virility it promised.

But boy howdy, did her husband ever deliver, in more ways than even he might guess.

"I'm too busy thinking about cattle prices, cowboy grudges and natural gas leases to notice that kind of thing."

"In other words, you're a man."

He shrugged. "A man who also has to keep an eye out for whatever mischief you and that daughter of yours are getting up to."

"Oh, so she's mine when she annoys you?" Jessie said, lightly but delicately. For biologically, Eden was related to Jessie, through her own twin sister, and not Zach—not that he'd ever treated her as anything less than a natural daughter.

"And mine whenever she's an angel," he said. "Ask my mother if you don't believe me."

She snorted, relieved that she hadn't said the wrong thing after all, but as they sat down on the bed's edge, she couldn't help noticing that his smile was strained and his touch distracted when he patted her hand.

Apprehension fluttered in her stomach, but she told herself he had no idea what secrets she was keeping. "So where do you think Ian's gone?"

He shook his head. "I'm out of ideas, but he couldn't be too far. He left his wallet behind, for one thing, and Jimmy says there wasn't much fuel in that old gas guzzler."

"Ian's made his way home once. He will again." Despite her reassuring words, worries wriggled beneath the surface like mosquito larvae in a stagnant puddle.

"I imagine he will when he's ready," Zach said, his gaze cooling. "But I didn't bring you in here just to talk about that."

"What is it then? You're making me nervous."

His scowl did nothing to reassure her. "I need you to finally come clean with me about how this new story of yours affects us as a family."

"I told you, it's nothing to worry about," she said, nervousness pulling the lie from her, though she knew that in the long run, it was only going to make things worse.

"Then what about this—what I found hidden in your office?"

When he pulled a small packet of folded papers from his back pocket and slapped them down on the bed between them, her jittery stomach threatened a full-scale rebellion. As guilty and regretful as she felt, she jumped to her feet to face him, the first words uttered coming out completely wrong.

"My office is my private workspace, so what on earth have you been doing in there, snooping through my research files?"

He unfolded the pages and laid them down, one after the other. And Jessie held her breath as he displayed the four notes she'd found these past three weeks, tucked beneath the blade of her car's windshield wiper or, once, left on her front seat, though she could have sworn she'd left the car locked when she went inside the school to speak to Eden's teacher. After the fourth sheet, Zach stopped, staring at her as he waited for her explanation.

Which meant, she hoped and prayed, that he didn't have the printout she'd made of his mother's incriminating email. Didn't have his finger on the trigger of a weapon that would wound.

Or kill, Jessie thought, laying her hand protectively over her roiling stomach. And wondering if Zach could have been right when he'd suggested that the attacks on Andrea and Ian both traced back to a secret she had no right to keep.

Chapter 13

The darker the sky outside her bedroom window grew, the blacker Andrea's suspicions became. *He's not coming back. He's walking.* She pictured him blindly stumbling, tripping over rocks and grassy tussocks, saw him tumbling down the side of a ravine and splitting his head. Or maybe he would suffer the same fate he'd saved her from after falling into a creek, drowning between a pair of sandy banks. The thought sent panic churning through her, flooding her brain with vivid memories of the moment her car had rolled over, filling with water so quickly she'd barely had time to snatch a breath of air and hold it.

Heart thumping, she paced the room, remembering his eyes, his voice, his heated touch. What if death was even now cooling those hands, that mouth, the whole of his magnificently sculpted body? If something she had done or said had provoked the flashback that drove him from his home?

Done...or said.

She stopped short, thinking of the way Ian had looked at her when she'd tried to explain to him what Julian had forced her to do. *Guess I should pay him a visit then, to thank the son of a bitch for sending you to me.*

Was it possible he might recover from his shock enough to do so? That he would go, not to *thank* Julian as he'd said, in his eagerness to soothe her aching conscience, but to confront him about what was going on?

If Ian suddenly showed up at the center, demanding explanations or hurling accusations, would he, too, suffer an accident, just as she had? Or would he once again go missing, never to return?

Furious with herself for not having thought of it earlier, Andrea left her room and trotted down the staircase in the hope of finding Zach—or anyone she could convince to loan her a vehicle or drive her. Downstairs, the house was quiet and dark, other than a few dim lights that had been left on, which had to mean that everyone else had gone upstairs, as least for now.

Her teeth worrying her lower lip, Andrea remembered spotting a rack hanging in the mudroom, with a number of key rings dangling from its copper hooks. But was she really so ungrateful a guest, after everything the Rayfords had done for her, to take a set of keys without permission and steal a vehicle?

Her heart thumped at the thought of it, but with her mind full of Ian, there was little room for uncertainty and no room at all to worry over whatever consequences she might suffer. For there was absolutely nothing worse than the thought of losing the man she loved—the man she could only now admit had always and would forever own a piece of her heart.

Standing near the back door, she was lifting a key ring when she heard a jingling sound behind her. Pulse racing, she whipped around, only to see close to a hundred pounds of vigilant Rottweiler standing in the doorway, her deep brown gaze fixed and her broad head lowered.

"Nice doggie. Good Gretel." Andrea used the same soothing tone she reserved for troubled clients, but she suspected that the well-trained animal scented her nervousness like a raw and bloody steak. Andrea waited for the curled lip or the growl that would indicate the dog was about to punish her transgression, probably in a manner that would involve another visit to the hospital.

Instead, the Rottweiler looked over her shoulder, where Jessie was standing in the shadows.

"What are you doing with my car keys?" she asked.

"Oh, you surprised me...." Andrea stalled while her mind raced to come up with a halfway plausible explanation. "I was thinking that the other day, when we went out to lunch, my lip balm might've rolled out of my purse. I didn't want to bother you about it, but I thought I'd go and check under the seat."

"You're worried about *lip balm*? When you lost the whole purse and everything you own in Spur Creek?"

Gretel's low growl barely registered. Did the animal somehow sense the lie, or was she mirroring Jessie's skepticism instead?

"It was recovered—the purse, I mean. Dripping wet with most everything inside it ruined, but..." Andrea let the story wind down as Jessie stepped into the light, her eyes damp and her face blotchy. "What's wrong?"

Jessie wiped at her eyes. "Other than your lying to me, you mean? Nothing."

"Now who's lying? It's not Ian, isn't? You haven't heard anything?"

"It's not Ian. It's Zach. I just had... We were discussing—" Jessie heaved a sigh. "I thought I was sparing him, sparing all of them by keeping my investigation into North Texas campaign fund-raising tactics to myself. But all I've done is screw things up. Zach's already livid that I've dug into his mother's donations—he thinks I'm doing it for spite and not because I care that some sleazy local politician's milking her for whatever he can extort. And once Zach finds out the rest, he'll—"

She dug a tissue from her pocket and turned away to blow her nose.

The car keys still in her hand, Andrea stepped closer to lay a hand on Jessie's shaking shoulder.

"I'm such a colossal screwup," Jessie said. "I just wanted to— I thought I could use my investigative skills to solve one family issue, not create a dozen more."

"If it makes you feel any better," Andrea told her, "you aren't the only one to foul up. I was about to take off with your car."

"Why would you do that?" Jessie looked more confused than angry. "I'm going out on a limb here, but I don't see you as the type to take a joyride in my Prius."

"I had an idea, a crazy idea, maybe, about where Ian could be heading."

"Where?"

Andrea drew in a deep breath. "Back to Marston, at the center where I worked. And I think he could be heading straight for trouble."

"But it's an hour away. Shouldn't we just call the satellite office over there and have them send a deputy to head off trouble?"

"No," Andrea said firmly, convinced Ian would run at the first sign of a patrol car. And heaven only knew where he might go after that. "But if you'll lend me your phone, I'll try calling a friend of mine who works there and have her keep an eye out for any trouble."

"I don't understand. Why would Ian go there in the

first place? I mean, that's the reason we had you come here to work with him, since he refused to leave the ranch for counseling."

"This isn't about counseling, but it could take a lot of explanation. And I'm afraid we don't have that kind of time, not if I'm going to keep Ian from making the worst mistake of his life." *Or maybe even the last.*

Jessie stared another moment before making her decision. "Then let me grab my purse and leave a note for Zach, and we'll talk on the way. But first, give me those car keys. And don't you dare try to take off before I come back."

She gave a quiet command in German, then left the Rottweiler watching Andrea with an intent expression.

Grimacing, Andrea called after her, "Wouldn't dream of leaving."

Gretel seemed to smile at her, exposing a row of shark-like teeth.

Ian took it as a good sign when the headlights coming from behind slowed instead of speeding up and gunning for him. An older, red Corolla pulled up and the driver put down the passenger-side window. "Saw your truck back there. Need a lift into town?"

Ian took in the clean-shaven face of a male in his late thirties, a sandy-haired man who was giving him the same cautious appraisal, probably hoping he hadn't just offered a ride to some psycho killer. Nodding, Ian said, "Thanks. I'd sure appreciate it."

After stowing the gas can behind the front seat, Ian climbed in next to the driver and buckled up.

"I'm Connor." The driver reached over to shake his hand. "Connor Timmerman."

"Good to meet you. Ian Rayford, and I feel like the biggest idiot in the Panhandle for running dry way out here."

"Wait. You're *him*, Captain Rayford, right? Yeah, of course. I recognize you."

Ian winced as it dawned on him that with all the publicity Jessie's story had generated, he was probably as close to a celebrity as it came around these parts. Though he'd declined the scores of requests for on-camera interviews that followed, it hadn't prevented anyone from digging up whatever old photos they could find. "That's me, yeah." *Unfortunately.*

"Awesome. I was just talking to some guys about you."

Ian tensed. "What guys? Who was talking about me?"

Timmerman shrugged. "Just some of the veterans I work with. You're an inspiration to them, man. They would absolutely love to meet you."

"Veterans... Wait. You're not the same Connor that Andrea Warrington mentioned to me, are you? Over at Warriors-4-Life?"

"One and the same. Big fan of Andrea's," Timmerman admitted before his smile faltered. "I understand she was working with you at the ranch for a short time before she decided to leave the center."

"She *quit*?"

"That's what we're hearing, and I can tell you, it's a real blow, losing her. Hard to believe she'd bug out on her clients, on all of us, without a word of explanation. I tried calling her a couple times, but her voice mail box is full."

"She's back at the ranch," Ian said, "recovering from a wreck she had the night of the storm."

"She was in an accident? Is she all right?" Too distracted by the news to drive, Timmerman left the car in Park.

Judging the man's surprise and concern to be sincere, Ian said, "The car was totaled, but her injuries weren't serious. She's already back on her feet. It was no accident, though."

"No accident? What do you mean?"

"I mean, a larger vehicle ran up on her and forced her over the Spur Creek bridge. She damn near drowned before I happened on the scene and pulled her out. And if I ever get my hands on the bastard responsible—"

"Does Julian know all this? Julian Ross, our director?"

"Absolutely, he does. He came to visit when she was under observation at the hospital." Wondering what else he might get out of Timmerman, Ian didn't mention that Andrea had refused to see Ross.

"I can't believe it. Why on earth wouldn't he have told us, unless—"

"Unless what?" Ian asked when Timmerman abruptly cut himself off.

"He's seemed kind of *off* lately, and he got pretty short with the staff when we tried to press him about why Andrea would leave. You have to understand. Julian's a good administrator and a real rainmaker when it comes to funding, but Andrea's the one most of the clients and the staff would throw themselves on a grenade for. She's the heart and soul of that place."

Ian let the words sink in, judged them to be genuine. "Yet Ross wouldn't give you any explanation?"

Timmerman shook his head. "He just said it was a personal matter and ordered us to drop it, giving us this no-bull army glare that made everybody back down."

Ian perked up. "So the man's ex-military?"

Timmerman snorted. "Retired army colonel, yeah, though he doesn't like to talk about it."

Ian ran it through his mind. When he finally spoke again, his voice was grim. "Sounds like there are a lot of things this boss of yours doesn't like to talk about. So how about you and I forget the gas station trip and go try and get some answers out of Colonel Ross now instead?"

Convincing Timmerman took a lot more talk, but the counselor started driving anyway, turning onto a road on Marston's outskirts rather than continuing toward downtown. But by the time he turned into the drive of a low brick building fronted by a Warriors-4-Life sign, Timmerman was shaking his head and sounding more uncertain than ever.

"I don't know about this, Rayford. I consider Andrea a good friend. I mean, she was the one who convinced me they really needed a counselor with my combat experience to give the program credibility, but still…"

"Don't you want to know why Ross fired her, then? Because that's what Andrea told my sister-in-law happened, just before her car was forced off that bridge."

As the car glided to a stop, Timmerman jerked his head to stare at Ian. "You aren't suggesting that Julian had anything to do with that, are you? Because whatever the deal is between him and Andrea—and the whole staff's figured by now there was something going on between them—I don't peg him as the type to fly off the handle and do something crazy. He's just—he's more methodical, you know? More measured in the way he deals with issues."

"Is that your personal or your professional opinion?"

"Both. You have to understand, I work with a lot a

seriously volatile people, people who have hell on earth bubbling up inside them looking for a place to boil over."

"People like me, you mean."

"I don't know you, Captain Rayford, and you have to understand, I'm not passing judgment on you. I'm the last person in the world who would, considering what I've been through personally. But, yeah, from what I've read and seen about your situation, I'd be damned surprised if you didn't have some issues."

"But Julian Ross doesn't? That's what you're trying to say to me?"

"I'm sure he does. Doesn't everybody? But not the kind that involve the kind of craziness you're talking."

"I appreciate your take on this." Ian reached for the door handle. "But if you don't mind, I'll need to get some answers for myself."

They both climbed out of the car, and Ian hesitated. "Before we head inside, can you tell me which vehicle is Ross's?"

Timmerman scanned the parking lot, which was lit by a pair of security lights. A moment later, he shook his head. "That's odd. I don't see his Explorer. He must've run in to town to pick up something. But don't worry. I can't imagine he'll be gone long."

"Then I'll be waiting for the colonel by the time he makes it back. Can you take me to his office?"

Timmerman nodded. "That'll work. He's sure to stop in there to check for messages, and I do have a key. But still, I can't just— I have a lot of clients counting on me here, especially without Andrea around to counsel them."

"Don't worry. There's no need for you to be involved in this. I won't mention that you let me in."

"These questions you're here to ask my boss," the counselor asked as he studied Ian intently, "can you promise me that's all you're here for? Nobody's going to get hurt, are they?"

"Someone already has been," said Ian darkly as he thought of Andrea. "But I'll give you my word, I'll do my best to keep things safe and civil."

"And afterward, you'll fill me in?"

"I'll definitely find a way to do that. For one thing, I'll still need a ride to grab some gas—and maybe to borrow twenty bucks, if you can spare it, since I lit out without my wallet." As much as Ian hated to admit it, he figured such a request deserved some explanation. "Damned flashback got the better of me."

A look of understanding crossed the older man's face, and once again, he offered a firm handshake. "You've got it, Captain. For Andrea."

"For Andrea," Ian echoed.

Jessie glanced over from behind the wheel of her car. "So tell me, Andrea, why are we heading out now? And I still don't understand why we you were so dead set against taking the dog."

"Because that's not a dog. It's a T. rex in a dog suit," Andrea argued. "I'm already nervous enough."

Jessie shook her head. "What the heck is going on with you?"

"I could ask you the same thing," Andrea said, concerned about how troubled Jessie had seemed. Whatever was really going on between her and Zach must have been pretty serious to strain a marriage that looked so solid.

"You first," Jessie said. "It's only fair, since I'm taking off to drive you without a word to Zach, which, I guarantee you, is going to cause an issue."

"So why do it, then?" Andrea asked. "You could've let me borrow your car."

"You've got to be kidding. After what you did to the last one you drove?"

Andrea smiled though it was clear to her that Jessie had wanted out of the house. "You did say you left him a note though, right?"

"Yeah, right on his pillow, where he should see it after he's gotten Eden down for the night. But trust me, he'll still be furious. So spill it, Andrea."

"Let me make that call first to my friend at the center?"

"Only if you promise you'll answer my questions when you're done."

Once Andrea agreed, Jessie pulled her cell phone from her purse and handed it to Andrea. Soon, she managed to connect with Cassidy at the center.

"I need you to do me a big favor," Andrea told her. "No questions, no arguments—just take my word that it's important, and I promise you, I'll introduce you to some of the most gorgeous cowboys you've ever laid your eyes on."

Jessie jerked a curious glance her way, but Andrea shrugged it off. "Okay, now. I need you to head straight out to be parking lot. You may want to take a flashlight with you."

"These better be some seriously prime cuts of beef you're talking about," Cassidy grumbled. "I just got out of the shower, and I'm a dripping mess. And maybe you can tell me, what the heck happened with you, anyway? One minute, you're off doing some one-on-one with a client, and next thing I know, you're gone—poof, and Julian's shooting the atomic death glare every time your name's brought up."

"I'll explain everything later. I promise. But for now, you need to tell me, do you see an old brown pickup in the parking lot?" Andrea described the truck Ian had been driving as best she could but didn't know whether to be relieved or disappointed when Cassidy didn't find it.

"No."

"What about Julian? Is he there?"

"His Explorer's gone, in case you were wanting to come by to pick up something you left."

"Great. I'm on my way, but I need you to call me back at this number if you see any sign of either Julian or Ian Rayford."

"Ian Rayford? The guy you were counseling? I don't understand. Why would he be here, and what's this have to do with Julian?"

"Just promise you'll call me, and I'll be there as fast as I can."

Andrea ended the call and laid the phone in the car's center console.

When Jessie glanced over at her this time, the soft glow of the dash lights highlighted her impatience. "Okay, now explain, with no more stalling. I'm not going to be put off a second longer—unless you're a big fan of long walks."

Andrea nodded, dragging in a deep breath. "The truth is, my being on hand and available to work with Ian was no coincidence. Someone appears to have gone to a lot of trouble to put me in place before Ian's return."

"I *knew* it." Jessie popped the steering wheel with

one hand. "I've been saying the same thing to Zach from the start, how it seemed awfully convenient. He just said we shouldn't waste too much energy questioning good fortune."

"It did seem odd to me, too, but I was so shell-shocked after hearing about Ian's return that I wasn't seeing the forest for the trees."

"I imagine it's been as overwhelming for you as it has for Zach and his mom," Jessie said.

Andrea shook her head. "I should've known something was up when Julian insisted that I come out here to counsel Ian in the first place. When I told him I didn't think it was a good idea because I'd been in a relationship with Ian, Julian already knew all about it. He said the only thing that mattered was getting Ian to open up, and I might be the key to his healing."

"He might've had that part right. Ian didn't exactly rush across the room and kiss the daylights out of the last couple of psychologists the government sent to look under the hood. My mother-in-law's still in shock over it. Though you have to understand, the woman practically passes out over the kissing scenes in Eden's princess movies."

Andrea made a face at the memory. "I thought I was going to pass out from embarrassment myself that day, considering how hard I was working to convince her I was a professional."

Jessie laughed. "You convinced her you were Eve offering the serpent's apple, trying to lure her poor boy from the garden. But she got over it pretty quickly. Nancy really likes you."

"I like her, too, though I can imagine she's not the easiest person in the world to live with."

"You could certainly say that, but then, rumor has it, I'm no pushover myself."

Andrea's smile was fleeting. "I was so caught up in my own emotions, I still didn't understand there was something going on with Julian, at least not until I went back after the shooting and refused to keep working professionally with Ian. We'd been too close, and it was obvious he wasn't able to keep his feelings for me in the past."

Jessie glanced over as they turned onto the state highway. "He wasn't the only one having that problem, was he?"

"He wasn't." Andrea recalled riding her bike in one of California's inland deserts, a desiccated, brown landscape she'd revisited days later only to find it filled with vibrant blossoms in the wake of a spring rain. With her training and her books, she'd thought she understood something of the human psyche, so how was it she hadn't comprehended that emotions could lie as dormant as those withered plants, that all the love she'd ever felt could burst forth no matter how she fought it? "Or he isn't, I should say, because I've... I'll always care for Ian. Love him, even when I have no right to."

"Why would you say a thing like that?"

"For one thing, Ian's memory's not right. He's nowhere near right, not yet. And as a psychologist, I should be able to divorce myself from my feelings, keep everything professional—"

"Professional ethics, rules in general, can't stand up to fate, Andrea. And anyone with eyes can see that you two belong together."

"*Fate?* I've heard too many people use it as a handy excuse for caving to their own selfish desires." Her father, for one, Andrea remembered, thinking of how he'd explained his serial marriage habit as something that was *simply meant to be*.

"You have a point there. But what you have with Ian, it's not just fate, it's love, isn't it? The kind of love a person's lucky to find once in a lifetime."

Andrea sighed. "I thought I loved Julian. I did. Maybe in a different way, but—"

"That must have been one tough conversation when you told him."

"I would've understood if he'd been so jealous he'd wanted to lash out at me. But his reaction was a mix of that and something scarier, something I couldn't—I kept it secret because I was so scared and ashamed."

Jessie looked over at her, her voice tightening. "What did he do to you? If he hurt you, I swear we'll find some way to make him pay."

"He didn't hurt me," Andrea said. "Not physically, at any rate. But he threatened to have me charged with unethical conduct, to ruin my career, if I didn't—if I wouldn't keep acting as his spy."

"His *spy*?" Jessie shook her head. "I don't understand, unless—who is this Julian, and what does he really want with Ian?"

It came as a relief when Andrea told her what she knew of Julian's military background, and how she suspected that the government might have a hand in what appeared to be a plot to acquire intelligence about what had really happened during the months Ian was in captivity. She detailed the threats he had used against her, followed by the visit from the mysterious Dr. Kapur.

"What I can't understand," Jessie said, "is why they'd come after you on the road like they did? Killing you wouldn't have gotten them what you're saying they were after."

"I'm a little shaky on that part myself," Andrea admitted. "Best I can come up with, they were trying to keep me quiet after I refused Julian that afternoon. Either that, or it was meant to scare me into helping them, only the warning got out of hand."

"Maybe, if they put some hothead on it. Unless—you don't think it was Julian himself, do you?"

"Before I would have said no way, but now—now I wonder if I ever really knew him. He played me for such a fool. I can't believe I bought that compassionate, dedicated act he was selling."

"Don't beat yourself up. It sounds to me almost like these people went out of their way to find out what made you tick and came up with the kind of man that would be guaranteed to attract you."

A chill swept over Andrea, and she nodded in agreement. "They caught me at a vulnerable time, too, while I was grieving what everyone thought was Ian's death."

"Not everyone, I'm betting. Julian and whoever's running the show—the army, I'm guessing—must've suspected he was alive and headed home months before any of us had any inkling. They knew it and said nothing, while they plotted out this operation when they couldn't find him."

Andrea hesitated, uncertain whether she should say more, especially to a reporter, who had both the power and the inclination to spill dangerous secrets. Finally, she said, "Can I tell you something with the understanding that all this is off-the-record?"

Jessie thought about it for a minute before nodding.

"You've got it. But only because I care a lot more about my family than any story."

"*Your* family," Andrea echoed.

"Yeah, mine," Jessie said, comprehension dawning in her face as she nodded. "They're my family now, too, and as important as my career is to me, they're what really matters in the end."

Hearing the sincerity in her voice, Andrea told her, "Ian isn't army. He never really has been."

After Andrea explained it, Jessie gave a low whistle. "Wow. Talk about a bombshell, especially with the military participating in my whole heroic soldier story. But it explains a lot, too. This long-range plot has spy secrets written all over it."

"What scares me to death," said Andrea, "is worrying over whether spy secrets might become *deadly* secrets if Ian shows up and starts demanding answers out of Julian."

Engulfed in the darkness of Julian's office, Ian flicked the fading yellow beam of his flashlight over photo after photo hanging on the ivory walls. Most showed a fit-looking man in his midforties with dark eyes and a military bearing. In some of the shots, Julian Ross wore tailored, dark suits as he glad-handed the presenters of oversize checks. In others, he was more casually dressed as he cheered on a group of young men participating in what looked like an outdoor team-building exercise.

Show photos, Ian figured, meant to convince the world he was a real-life humanitarian rather than the kind of man who would force a woman he had claimed to love into an impossible situation. Determined to find out what Ross was really after, Ian pulled papers from the file cabinet, scanning before scattering them as he proceeded.

His cursory sweep turned up nothing of interest, only the logs, files and handwritten notes he would expect to find. After sitting in the wheeled, leather desk chair and switching on a small lamp, Ian methodically pulled out the contents from one drawer after another, caring only about finding whatever leverage he need to get answers—and shut this SOB down.

Hidden beneath the false bottom of the top, left-side drawer, he found not the evidence he'd been looking for, but a different form of leverage. Carefully, he lifted the .38 automatic he recognized as an antique collector's model.

Before he had the chance to see if it was loaded and operational, he heard swift-approaching footsteps in the hallways. Rather than getting up and hiding, Ian opted to stay seated, concealing both hands and the gun beneath the level of the desk.

As the door opened, the same man from the photos stood there staring at him, another pistol in his right hand…

But unlike the century-old Colt he'd found, Ian would bet his bottom dollar that the gleaming new SIG Sauer Julian Ross was holding was in perfect working order, with a bullet in the chamber.

Chapter 14

"Captain Rayford," Julian said as he casually approached his desk. Except there was nothing casual about the way he held the pistol, not pointing it at Ian but slanting it slightly downward, where he could raise it in a hurry. "What a pleasure it is to finally meet you."

"Wish I could say the same," Ian told him, not moving from behind the desk or showing his hands, either. "But I'm hardly ever pleased when I encounter a man holding a gun."

"Just as I'm rarely pleased when I run across someone going through my desk drawers," Julian countered, his Southern accent as smooth and deep as well-aged whiskey. "Would you mind showing me your hands? Then perhaps we can dispense with all this hardware and talk this through like gentlemen."

I doubt that very much, thought Ian, trying to figure out what Andrea might have seen in this old man. Sure, he appeared to be in good shape, with intense brown eyes and a full head of hair, as far as Ian could tell in the dim light beyond the desktop lamp's range, but there was something that rang false about him, something that had unease churning in Ian's stomach.

Allowing that a man in his midforties wasn't exactly

geriatric and he would probably hate any man who had ever touched Andrea, Ian laid both hands on the desktop. But he left the antique gun pinned against the seat by his own thigh, where he could quickly grab and fire it if need be—provided the old pistol was operational. "There you go. Now how about yours?"

Ross went one step further than Ian had dared to hope, clearing his gun's chamber and ejecting the magazine before laying it on top of the clutter of strewn papers. Raising his palms, he said, "There you go. So tell me, Captain, what brings you here to see me?"

"Are you sure you're not a shrink, too, *Colonel*? Because you've got the moves down pat."

Ross laughed. "I'm not, I assure you. But I've spent enough years administering mental health services that I suppose I've picked up a few of their tricks."

"I don't want to be soothed. I want to understand this. What do you want out of me? And why did you feel the need to threaten Andrea to get it?"

"Threaten Andrea?" Julian's jaw unhinged, his gray-brown brows rising in an almost theatrical display of shock. His accent growing even more pronounced, he asked, "Why on earth— What are you talking about, Captain?"

"Your fiancée told me all about it, how you threatened to destroy her career if she didn't do your bidding."

Ross moved forward to the edge of his seat and slapped a hand down on the desktop. "Destroy her career? She's all but done that herself with these outrageous lies."

"You'd better damn well watch who you're accusing."

"Who *I'm* accusing? I don't know what that woman's playing at. For one thing, she's no fiancée of mine. I'd never get involved with a subordinate. It's completely unbecoming."

"Maybe in the military it would be a problem, but out in the civilian world—"

"And I've never threatened anyone." Ross's face grew redder with each word. "My reputation—the people here—mean everything to me."

As angry as the man's words were making Ian, Ross's Southern accent was burrowing even deeper under his skin. Or maybe it wasn't the accent, exactly, but the timbre of his voice, the way he strung his words together. "You brought her flowers at the hospital, tried to go and see her."

"Of course I did. I felt bad that we'd parted on bad terms. I was hoping we could smooth things over…for her clients' sakes, not mine."

Ian shook his head. "A man doesn't bring three-dozen long-stem roses to an employee—"

"We really need her back here." Ross shook his head. "But if she honestly believes the things she's saying, then she's even more unstable than I feared."

"What the hell? You two—you were getting married. She told me."

"Have you ever seen any evidence of this? A ring, perhaps, or another individual who mentioned this *engagement*?"

Ian turned it over in his mind and shook his head. "I don't need proof. I have her word."

"The word of a woman who's been terminated from her position here for increasingly erratic behavior?"

"That's insane. If she was so erratic, why would you send her to see me?"

Ross winced and sighed. "Because I was asked to do

what I could for you by a former superior—and because she truly is an excellent psychologist when she's taking her own medications."

"And here I expected you'd try to make out like I'm the crazy one." A wild energy crackled through Ian, making him feel like leaping across the desk and putting this liar in a chokehold.

The older man shook his head, his expression filling with what looked like real regret. "You should know that people with psychiatric issues aren't crazy. When correctly treated, they can lead fulfilling, useful lives, have productive careers, be loving family members."

Beads of perspiration broke out on Ian's forehead. The accent threw him off, but that voice, those words… or was it something in the man's face that seemed so familiar. Had he met the army officer through the agency during his days working in D.C.? Or had it been somewhere abroad? "Andrea's not crazy. But you sure as hell are if you expect me to believe—"

"A tendency toward delusional behavior under extreme stress is often passed down through families, you know. Did she ever mention her mother's suicide?"

"Yeah, after her father was exposed and the family publicly—"

"Psychotic depression, triggered by the unfounded belief that the father had taken on *shadow families*. None of it was real, of course. There's no evidence at all he was some sort of bigamist. No archived stories in the hometown paper. Look it up yourself. It's all—"

Ian snatched up the antique gun, rising from his seat to glower down at Ross. A trickle of hot sweat rolled down the channel formed by his spine. "Your technique's giving you away, the way you're weaving a complicated web of lies to sell your story. Anything to confuse the target enough that he'll dismiss his own perceptions and grasp on to your version."

Ross remained seated, looking into Ian's face instead of at the gun. "What are you suggesting?"

"That you're not working for the army. For all I know, you never were. You've been forcing Andrea to feed you information about what happened to me so you can pass it on to—"

"You do want these people punished, don't you, not only for your suffering but for the bombing of our listening post in—"

"You're part of the intelligence community, aren't you? CIA, NSA or maybe FBI."

"Take a step back from this—this paranoia. Have a seat, and put the gun down. It isn't loaded anyway. Check it for yourself."

Ian pointed it at Ross's head, his hand steady but his anger and confusion growing. Because his theory *did* sound crazy, even to his own ears, and Ross's calm demeanor was so damned reassuring, his smooth Southern voice both calming and disturbingly familiar.

Another drop of sweat broke free from just beneath the hairline, but as the stinging moisture ran into his eyes, Ian didn't make a move to wipe it away. He couldn't, with the kindness on Ross's face morphing into the remembered cruelty of Ian's father. With the memories jumbling his senses, raising the reek of rotting meat and old blood, the shadows of silhouetted figures...the sounds of clinking chain and desperate pleas.

Let me go! I'll tell you! I'll tell you anything you want! Just don't—I can't take another minute!

Desperate words, spoken by a desperate American,

a captive stripped of all defenses, of his accent—one of many learned with the assistance of a dialect coach the agency had contracted—to the expert disguises he so often employed.

Ian's mind was swirling, churning, the cone of light from the desktop lamp burning into his brain. The gun in his hand rose, seemingly of its own volition, his finger squeezing the Colt's trigger.

As they stood in the center's parking lot, Andrea turned to Jessie. "If I'm not back within ten minutes, I want you to call 911."

"To report what?"

"Anything, as long as it'll bring a lot of lights and sirens in a hurry."

"Just what're you expecting to find?"

Andrea shook her head. "I don't know for certain, but the last time I was here, Julian surprised me. He'd loaned his Explorer to one of the counselors, so who knows if he's really here?"

"If you think this guy is dangerous, maybe I should come in with you."

"What I'm really scared of is Ian confronting him, so I'll be safer if you wait here and try to hold him off if he shows up. But if it comes down to it, Jessie," Andrea warned, "don't stand in Ian's way."

"You aren't thinking he'd be dangerous? To me, I mean?"

"I know he would never willingly hurt you, but you didn't see him earlier, in the grips of that flashback. It's possible he's confused."

"Like he was when Zach first brought him home?

You don't think he's back in that state, do you? Or, worse yet, violent?"

"I don't know what to think. To tell you the truth, I'm grasping at straws to even imagine he'll come back here. For all I know, I've dragged you out tonight, gotten you into more hot water with Zach, and all for nothing."

"Don't you worry about my marriage. I'll find a way to make things right with Zach—for our sake and our children's."

Andrea froze in place. "Your *children's*? You aren't saying that you're…"

Jessie nodded. "Almost three months, but I've been afraid he'll seize on it as an excuse to try to stop me from my work."

"You'll figure it out, the two of you, as long as you keep loving one another."

Jessie said nothing for a moment. "Just get inside and make sure everything's okay."

Andrea gave her a spontaneous hug before trotting to a side door, where Cassidy was waiting to let her inside, her red ringlets dampening the shoulders of a sweatshirt that swamped her pint-size body.

"He's here," Cassidy warned, her voice low and her eyes wide. "Julian, I mean. I guess Michael has his Explorer again, but I spotted Julian heading for his office. If you're looking to avoid him while you check your room, I can keep watch for— Hey, where are you going?"

"I need to make sure Ian isn't with him," said Andrea, her longer strides quickly outpacing the younger woman's. "Finding him is too important to pussyfoot around."

"I'm not so sure Julian's going to be happy to see you back. The way he was acting earlier when we asked about you—"

"I'm miles beyond giving a damn what makes Julian Ross happy."

Cassidy staggered to a stop, sounding uncertain as she called, "Andrea, please."

Andrea broke into a run, her pulse thrumming an urgent warning. But the intuition that had her in its grips came too late, for as Andrea approached the door to Julian's office, a crack of gunfire broke the evening stillness—the sound of a bullet as it pierced wood, then ripped a white-hot channel across her upper arm before it slammed into the wall behind her.

An SUV pulled into a space, and a smaller man with a short beard climbed out and headed inside. From what Jessie could make out from where she was crouched behind her Prius, the guy looked too young to be Ross, but she checked out the vehicle anyway and found it was a dark gray Explorer.

Reasoning that Julian must have loaned out his SUV again, Jessie wondered if it was possible that this same vehicle had been used to knock Andrea's car off the Spur Creek bridge? Walking all the way around it, Jessie used her smartphone's flashlight to check for any dents or paint damage.

Finding nothing other than a thin layer of road film, she let out a deep breath just as her phone began to vibrate in her hand. She groaned, heart thumping as a photo featuring Zach's handsome grin popped up to identify him as the caller.

"Betcha any money you're not smiling now," she murmured, since she'd already ignored several calls from his phone. Bracing herself for the chewing out she knew she deserved, she put her thumb over the green button to answer.

Instead, she flinched, startled by what sounded like a backfire or a single clap of thunder. Except, she realized, it had come from the direction of the building.

And her every instinct screamed at her to duck and dial for help.

The blast rang in Ian's ears. The smell of gunpowder filled his lungs, and from the hallway just outside, a shrill scream had his blood freezing in his veins.

Had the shot he'd deliberately aimed high found an unintended victim? An innocent woman, whose blood was on his hands?

Seized with horror, he barely reacted in time to avoid Ross's leap across the desk toward him, a move that sent the lamp tumbling to the floor. Glass shattered, plunging the room into darkness as Ross shouted, "Drop it, Rayford! Drop the weapon—before somebody gets hurt!"

Heart pummeling his chest wall, Ian heard the clatter of other desktop items falling to the floor—or was it Ross fumbling to reload his own weapon? Uncertain whether he might be shot at any second, Ian took what little cover he could find behind the filing cabinet, the antique pistol hot as a glowing coal in his hand. Or maybe it was only his guilt as he wondered if some poor woman was bleeding, dying—or maybe even dead already in the hallway.

"Toss the gun and lie facedown on the floor!" Ross ordered, his voice deep and commanding.

"I know that voice. I know *you*." Though Ian knew he would do better to keep his words from giving away his position, adrenaline tore the memory from his mouth.

The memory of a man who'd bargained for his own freedom after being forced to witness Ian's beatings. Willing to do anything to save himself, his fellow agent, who had looked very different with the darker hair and thick gray beard he'd worn to blend in for his overseas work, had given up information that had cost five Americans their lives. Lives Ian had had on his own conscience, certain that he had been the guilty party. "It's over now, you traitor. I'm not taking the blame for their deaths anymore."

"Put the gun down now," Ross repeated. "You're having a psychotic episode." Raising his voice, he shouted in the direction of the door, "We'll need restraints! Connor, Michael, anybody! Get Cassidy in here right now with something to calm this man down!"

Realizing that Ross was going to try using the same tactic he'd attempted to discredit Andrea, Ian crept forward, intent on jumping the man, subduing him until his own memories could be verified. But the door opened, spilling light from the hallway into the dark room.

Andrea leaned around the door's edge. "Ian, put the gun down! Before someone else gets hurt!"

His gaze locked on her blood-soaked upper right sleeve, where she tried to stanch the flow by clamping her left hand over the wound. As the realization that he'd shot her hit Ian like a closed fist, Ross slammed him down backward, sending the antique pistol spinning from Ian's grasp.

He landed hard on his back, his breath violently forced from his lungs as Ross came down on top of him. Ian flipped the older man off him but was soon distracted by his own struggle to draw breath. The harder that he fought to fill his lungs, the more painfully they spasmed.

In his peripheral vision, he caught sight of the old Colt where it had come to rest underneath the desk. But he could no more reach the gun than he could sprout wings, not laid out as he was, unable to do so much as cough.

For one adrenaline-charged moment, Ian imagined his rib cage crushed by the fall and pictured himself turning blue, then dying where he lay, with Andrea looking on in horror. He heard her screaming, saw her pushing past Ross to get closer to him. As Ian's gaze connected with hers, his breath returned in a dizzying rush.

With the sudden flow of oxygen, a roaring noise filled his brain, one quickly drowned out by a jumble of urgent-sounding voices, male and female, Pashto and English. Andrea was pulled away, and the terrorist's vicious threats dissolved into a nightmare haze, leaving behind a reality that was just as disconcerting.

He fought to sit up, to get away from several people who surrounded him while Julian Ross yelled, "The shot. Give him the needle," Ross urged, "before he hurts anyone else."

Strong hands held him down, and Ian saw that one of the two men was Connor Timmerman, who had seemed so damned friendly when he'd picked him up along the roadside, who *sounded* friendly even now, as he said, "Don't try to get up, buddy. Don't fight this, and you'll be safe."

But Ian didn't feel safe, not when he spotted a petite red-haired woman holding a hypodermic needle, her gaze flicking uncertainly from Julian Ross to him.

"What are you waiting for?" Ross demanded. "Give him the damned drugs."

"I don't need meds." Ian's gaze sought Andrea's. "I

just need you to listen. Please, Andrea. Tell them how he's threatened you, how he's tried to force you to spy on me for him."

Her face was white as paper, her bloody arm dripping onto the carpet.

"I'm so sorry I hurt you," he said, darkness fizzing through his vision, "but you can't let them do this. Can't let Ross get away with—"

"I know you didn't mean it," she said, her face drawn and pale as she shook her head. "I know you'd never intentionally hurt me or anyone."

Ian turned to glare at Ross. "*You* told me it wasn't loaded, you lying sack of—"

"You can see, he's highly agitated." Ross told the woman with the needle. "A danger to himself and others."

Ian bucked against Timmerman's grasp, fighting to catch Andrea's eye. "It was him, Andie. He was captured with me and held in that same cell. Only instead of beating him, too, they forced him to watch my torture until he broke down, until he was willing to tell them anything to keep from getting a taste of it himself."

Ross surged forward, shaking his head. "The shot now, Cassidy. Don't you know classic paranoid delusions when you hear them?"

"Ian," Andrea said. "Please stop fighting."

"It was him. I swear it," Ian repeated. "Haven't you ever wondered why he brought you all here, where he could watch and wait once he was tipped off that I'd escaped?"

Ross swore, his face reddening, but Cassidy ignored him to stare a question in Andrea's direction. But Andrea was watching Ian, her eyes wide, her mouth slightly open. In shock from pain and blood loss, he thought, or was it uncertainty he read in her face? Did his accusations sound so outrageous, or could she really be buying Ross's self-serving garbage?

Ian fought free of Timmerman's grasp, throwing the counselor into the tiny redhead. With a startled cry, she fell, the needle rolling from her hand.

"Stay down!" Timmerman shouted at Ian as he and a younger man with a short, dark beard made a grab for Ian's arms.

Scrambling to his feet, Ian ignored Andrea, who was helping Cassidy up, to point at Ross. "This man's name is Davis Parnell, and he's a traitor to his country! He's a missing CIA agent, a master manipulator, and he'll say anything, hurt anyone to save his own—"

"Give it back! You're not allowed to do that!" Cassidy told Andrea.

"Let me. He won't hurt me," she said, and it was then Ian realized that Andrea had picked up the fallen hypodermic needle. The needle loaded with enough drugs to ensure that he woke up in a freaking psych ward in restraints.

At the thought of being tied down, panic pounded through him. He'd die before he let them chain him in that dark hole, where rats crawled through the musty straw...the smell that took him back to a child's spiraling terror at being bound with ropes and left alone inside a pitch-black feed room, a punishment for some childish transgression.

As he flung off the bearded man, Ian saw out of the corner of his eye Ross's hand dipping into the pocket of his jacket. Certain he was going for the gun, Ian opened his mouth to shout a warning, but Andrea stepped in, the hypo in her bloody hand.

"Time to sleep now, Ian," she said, those long-lashed hazel eyes he loved shimmering with tears. "Time for you to lie down, where I can keep you safe."

Inside of Ian, something fractured, broken beyond repair by her betrayal, but he couldn't bring himself to shove her away. Couldn't do anything but stand like a dead man as she ignored Cassidy, who was warning that Andrea could lose her license by dispensing medication, to push the needle toward the inside of his arm.

Chapter 15

Andrea's heart broke at the look in Ian's eyes, the look that told him he believed she had turned against him. There was more working as well, for she'd recognized the signs of flashback in his glazed look only seconds earlier as the past and present came together in one perfect, deadly storm.

In this state, he was dangerous, as he'd already proved with the gunshot that had creased the outer layers of her upper arm. Sure, the shallow cut stung like a thousand wasp stings, but it was nothing compared to what he could do if he blindly swung his fists or made a sudden grab for her throat.

Press the plunger, and he'll be safe. He'll go down and sleep, and Julian will take his hand off that gun I know he's holding, the gun he'll use if it's what it takes to end this now.

A flash of insight raised the fine hairs behind her neck. *No wonder he's been so desperate to make me his eyes and ears at the ranch. All along, he's been trying to figure out whether he'll have to kill Ian to protect his own secrets.* Now that she knew that nothing short of death would ever keep Ian quiet, Andrea was terrified that Julian would find some excuse to pull the trigger—and silence the threat forever.

"There you are," she said, turning her body so the others wouldn't see that she was only pretending to inject the drugs into Ian's arm. As the plastic slid harmlessly past his inner elbow, light flickered through his blue eyes, followed by a dawning comprehension. "Rest now, Ian, and you'll feel so much clearer when you wake up. Everything will make sense, and *everyone* here will have a chance to calm down."

Careful to keep the hypo out of the view of those behind her, she clasped his arm, willing him to understand that this subterfuge was for his safety—and hers as well, considering that Julian must have already tried to kill her at least once, on the bridge.

Ian pressed his lips into a grim line, nodding his agreement but clearly none too pleased with the idea. "I think— I'm just so tired. Everything's so mixed up."

"Let Michael and Connor help you, then. Let them help you to lie down."

Rebellion sparked in his eyes, a quick grimace that told her his mind was fighting the idea of lying prone and helpless.

"In the chair, then," she suggested, leading him back toward Julian's desk. "Just sit and lay your head down."

As they moved in that direction, Connor righted the fallen chair and wheeled it back into place.

"Sorry if I hurt you, man," Ian told him. "I didn't want any of you hurt. I just couldn't—couldn't let him—"

Connor helped him into the chair. "I understand. I've been there. We're all on your side here."

As Ian slumped forward onto the desk, Andrea's attention was drawn by movement of the one man who definitely wasn't in Ian's corner. "Where exactly are you going?" she asked as she moved between Julian and the office door. In her uninjured left hand, she kept the needle behind her hip, wondering if it was possible... *Even if I pull it off, you'll still have time to put a bullet in me—and possibly everyone else in this room.*

"Someone should check on the clients in the game room," he said. "They were gathering to watch a movie, but if any of them heard that gunshot..."

As ploys went it was a good one, Andrea decided, a reminder that Ian wasn't the only person on the premises whose PTSD might trigger flashbacks. But if Julian escaped this room, she knew there was a good chance he'd head to the parking lot and take off to stay one step ahead of Ian's accusations.

"My gosh, Julian," Cassidy scolded. "Don't you see her standing there, bleeding like crazy?" Marching toward him, she caught his sleeve. "Here, let me have that jacket. It's got a big rip in it already, and we need something to wrap up her arm and apply pressure before she passes out."

He jerked his arm free of her grasp. "Not my jacket. I'll be right back with bandages, towels, whatever you need."

But as Andrea's gaze locked with his, they both knew he didn't give a damn about giving up a ruined sports jacket. It was the gun inside the pocket he couldn't afford to part with, the gun and wallet and whatever else he'd need to put distance between himself and the truth.

As much as she hated the idea, it would be safer to let him go, to turn over the job of capturing this traitorous coward to the authorities instead of risking her own, Ian's and her friend's lives in some desperate gambit.

But when she opened her mouth to tell this man who'd used her so cruelly, this monster willing to kill to keep from accepting responsibility for his own cowardly actions that he could leave now, the only words that came out were, "So tell me, where're you really off to in such a hurry...*Davis Parnell?*"

Even at that point, Ian thought later, things might have still turned out all right. The man calling himself Julian Ross might have simply pushed past Andrea to make a break for it, escaping, maybe, but at least no one would have died.

Instead, the sound of sirens outside caught everyone's attention, the flashing of red-and-white lights shining through the window.

Ian opened his eyes just in time to see Ross grab Andrea by the neck to pull her in front of him, his other hand coming up to point the SIG Sauer at her head.

As Cassidy screamed, Ian dropped behind the desk, groping desperately for the antique pistol—a pistol that Timmerman must have picked up earlier, for he came up with it, shouting at Ross, "Let go of her, Ross! Let's talk whatever this is through!"

Hiding behind Andrea, Ross turned the gun toward Timmerman. A split second later, Ian caught the blur of Andrea's bloody hand as she jabbed the needle hard into Ross's thigh. Ross screamed as it stabbed his leg, but jerked away from her so quickly that Ian doubted that she'd managed to get much of the drug into his muscle.

It wouldn't have mattered anyway, with adrenaline propelling those next few split seconds. As Andrea tried to jab him again, Ross grabbed her hair and swung the gun back toward her skull.

Bellowing to distract him, Ian charged, Timmerman right behind him. As Andrea twisted away and out the door, there were two loud cracks, followed by a third as Ross began to crumple, the first geyser of blood already spouting from his chest.

But he had strength and will enough to squeeze off a final shot, and he pointed the SIG Sauer at Ian.

A final shot he aimed…except not well enough.

Chapter 16

Andrea sat at the back of an ambulance, where a paramedic wrapped her arm, since she had refused transport to the hospital.

"I'm not making a third trip there this week," she told the kind-eyed woman as she improvised a sling, "not for a cut on my arm and a h-handful of torn-out hair. And especially not when—when Cassidy will never..."

Andrea dissolved into sobs, her vision filling with the image of Cassidy sprawled on the floor, her beautiful ringlets soaked with blood. Andrea knew instinctively she would never forget the stricken look on Ian's face when he knelt to check for a pulse. "I'm so sorry, but she's gone."

"If I hadn't fought him, hadn't stabbed him with that needle," Andrea had stammered.

Ian shook his head. "It was me. He meant to shoot me."

Connor, too, had looked ill as he'd stared down at the two guns he'd set down on the desktop: the one he'd picked up off the floor, meaning to defend Andrea, and the one he'd pulled from Julian's still-twitching hand before Ross had spasmed and gone still, without anyone making a move to try to help him.

As Andrea wept, Jessie came and wrapped a protective arm around her waist. Ian and Connor were still inside going over what had happened with the chief deputy, who'd taken control of the scene until Canter could arrive, but Michael stood near the ambulance, as well, his fingers repeatedly running through his short beard and his eyes glazed with shock.

Through her tears, Andrea noticed that the other staff members and most of the residents had ventured outside, some of them staring at the flashing lights of the ambulances, fire trucks and sheriff's department vehicles that had responded to the call Jessie made on hearing the first gunshot. A few of the patients were pacing wildly and one appeared to be talking and gesturing to himself.

Someone should be helping them, talking them through the strategies she, Michael and Connor had been teaching them to cope with flashbacks. Someone better equipped, but who else was there, really, with all of them in shock?

While the paramedic questioned Michael, one of the center's clients walked up, a wild-eyed man in his latter twenties, who was chain-smoking away his restless energy. "Is she really dead? Miss Cassidy?"

"She and Julian Ross both are," Jessie answered for her, the words echoing through Andrea's hollowed heart.

"Colonel Ross?" The chain-smoker, Kris Vargas, asked Andrea. "But why? What happened, Doc? Is it— it's the war again, isn't it? It's just like Ty said. It's followed—followed us back home."

As he wandered off without an answer, it occurred to Andrea that he was right, that every one of these men and women, along with Ian and Julian, had carried home a piece of the war locked inside their minds. For Ian, that memory had been overwhelming enough that his psyche could only deal with bits and pieces at a time. For Julian, it had been so unbearably shameful that he'd been willing to create a new identity and threaten or even kill to keep the secret instead of turning himself in or dealing with the psychological torment he had been exposed to.

Intellectually, she understood it. Emotionally, she knew she never would. But that didn't mean she had to allow herself to become another victim, not when there were people here who urgently needed her help.

She came to her feet, intent on answering Kris, though he had already wandered off to shout the same questions at Michael.

"You need to sit down. You're hurt," Jessie told her.

"We're all hurt. Every one of us. The question is, what do we do with our pain?"

"Andrea, you're in shock. The psychobabble can wait for someone else to—"

She wiped away her tears, swallowing back her pain. "They need me now, someone they know and trust to help them. And if I'm to make it through this night, I'll need them just as much."

Jessie looked as if she might argue, but Zach pulled up in his truck, then jumped out and ran to his wife.

He pulled her into his arms, relief and worry mingling in his expression. "What the hell's happening? Are you all right?"

"I'm fine, and so's your brother. He's inside, talking with Canter's second in command about the shooting that happened here tonight."

Zach pulled back to stare a question at his wife. "Shooting? What the hell?"

Leaving the couple to their discussion, Andrea went

to see if she could roust Michael from his shock and grief to help her. It took a few minutes, but she talked the younger counselor into refocusing on the center's mission.

"It's what Cassidy would've wanted," she told him, "what she would have found the strength to do if it had been one of us."

"You—you're right," he said, giving her a hug and pulling himself together.

For the next hour or so, the two of them kept busy, recruiting support staff to do a head count and organizing client teams to offer mutual support and redirect their individual thought patterns. Ignoring her throbbing arm and aching head, Andrea spent time, too, talking to Kris and one female patient who'd been especially close to Cassidy, helping relieve their heightened states of anxiety.

Time seemed to slow down, the lights blurring and the voices growing muffled as she worked on. She didn't see the tall man coming up behind her, didn't hear him even when he called her name. When finally, he caught her by her good arm and turned her toward him, she startled and cried out.

Then she saw that it was Ian and buried her face against his broad chest, her shoulders shaking as she leaned into his strength.

Ian stroked Andrea's back and hair, holding her tightly as she wept against his chest. As the evening wore down, a front had dropped the temperature and kicked up a cool wind. He felt her trembling with the chill—or possibly pain and exhaustion. Considering all she'd been through, he'd been amazed to find her out here in the first place, going from one group to another with her bloodstained arm in a sling. One of the most traumatic nights of her life, and she was pouring every scrap of her strength into helping those around her. But that strength was spent now, and she needed him, whether or not she would admit it.

"Come on in with me now," he said, slipping out of his own jacket to wrap it around her. "We need to get you warmed up, and anyway, Canter's swearing he'll come hunt you down if that's what it takes to get your statement."

She shook her head. "Then let him. I'm not coming in while there's still one client unaccounted for." In spite of her insistence, her voice was as brittle as the dried leaves rattling past their feet. "Ty Dawson's practically a kid, one of our most at-risk."

"Blond guy, right? I heard about it, but Timmerman and Michael are almost sure he'll be found holed up in some dark corner until things quiet down. Apparently, he's done this sort of thing before."

"He has, several times, but it's still possible he could've been drawn outside by all these lights."

"The rest of the staff has stepped up and some of the patients, too, checking room by room for any sign of this guy. Zach's in on the search, too, and Jessie's taken charge of brewing coffee in the dining area. You could go in and keep her company while she—"

"That's all great, but I'm the senior staff person now. I need to make sure everyone's safe."

"Listen to me, Andrea. You're cold, you're hurting and you're heading in now, too—unless you're looking to spend another night at Marston Regional. Because I swear I'm hauling you over to the ER to get that arm looked at if you don't at least sit down and let me get you something hot to drink."

She pulled away from him, her brow furrowing. "This is exactly what Jessie was saying about you Rayford men. Give you an inch, and you want to take over a woman's whole life. No wonder she's been reduced to hiding her work from—"

"I wouldn't *have* to take over if you knew enough to take care of yourself."

"Are you suggesting you know better than I do about how I should get through this night? Exactly what is it that gives you that expertise, the Y chromosome or the Rayford blood? Or is it your vast experience in handling your own trauma?"

Temper burned through his restraint. "You act like you forget, but I was in that room, too. I was there when Ross, Parnell—whatever you want to call the bastard—pointed that gun at me and missed. So before you start acting like you're sorry that he did, maybe you should rethink lashing out at someone who only wants to help you."

She sucked in a startled breath, gaping as though she had been slapped. "I'm not—not sorry he missed you. How c-can you even think that?"

"I don't. Of course, I don't. I'm sorry. It's only— It's been a horrible night for both of us. Let's say we don't end it by wounding one another."

She wiped at her eyes. "I'm sorry, too. I didn't mean to say such hateful things. I don't even know where that came from."

"From a place of pain. And I do know from experience. After all, I've been lashing out at everyone, acting like a jerk since I set foot on the ranch."

"Everybody understood," she said. "Even if they didn't love the behavior, they loved *you*."

"And I love you, which is why—"

"Why you're backing off right now, Ian, and leaving me alone."

"Until you do what? Fall down with exhaustion?"

"You don't understand. If I stop, I'll have to—" She ground her knuckles into her forehead. "It keeps replaying through my head, how furious it made him when I jabbed him with the needle. It was why he pulled the trigger, why poor Cassidy's lying in that—"

"Listen to me, Andie. We could stand here arguing all night about who set what off back in that office— whether it was me remembering that Ross was really Parnell, you reacting the way you did, Timmerman grabbing the gun, or Michael, who's beating himself up for freezing at the crucial moment. The fact is, there's only one guy who pulled the trigger, one man who used the master manipulator skills he developed in clandestine services to hide his shame. Parnell shot her, no one else, and he paid the price. Sad as it is, that's where this story needs to end."

"But it's *not* over. It can't be, because Cassidy is gone forever— She's *dying* forever, in an endless loop each time I stop for a moment. And I'll always know I could've changed the way it ended. One little movement, one shift in my reaction, and I might have—"

"You might have *died*, or maybe me, or one of your other friends in that room. Or all of us or maybe no one, but it really doesn't matter because things played out the way they played out, and no amount of reliving them in your head is ever going to make it different, just like it will never change what happened to me in that cell hidden in the mountains. It will never fix what snapped inside Parnell when he was forced to watch."

Andrea shoved her hands into the pockets of his jacket and made a sniffling sound. "I know I've said those same words, or something like them, to so many others. And in my head, I know you're right."

Ian stepped back to cup her face with both hands, forcing her to look into his face. "I need you to understand this, not just in your head, but in your heart before you fall into the same trap I did, blaming yourself for something totally out of your control, running it over and over in your mind how you should've been stronger, smarter, luckier or faster. How you don't deserve to be the one who walked out of there alive. Because it's not about *deserving*, Andie, and even if it were, I'd take a hundred bullets myself if I could only guarantee you'd come through this unscathed."

She pulled out the flashlight he had in his pocket, and flicked it on to look at him. "And all this time, Ian Rayford, I've imagined you were the one who needed my help…"

Shielding his eyes from the beam, he said, "Don't sell yourself short. You've helped more than you know. And now it's time for me to return the favor."

She winced and blew out a long breath. "I just need to call—C-Cassidy's family in Colorado. How will I ever tell them?"

"It's all taken care of. I helped Timmerman locate her personnel file in the office, and local law enforcement there is notifying her father and her brothers. So let's go in now, Andrea. Let's get you off your feet."

As she nodded, he felt her pain so acutely it was like a stone bruise to his own soul. He felt, too, the horrific waste of the young nurse's life, a sense of loss magnified by the grief of those who had loved Cassidy.

He put a protective hand behind Andrea's waist to guide her to the building's side doors. She trudged forward like a zombie, not seeming to see anything around her—at least not until she swung the light's beam to the left and muttered a choice word under her breath.

"That woman—do you see her? It's Dr. Kapur, from the hospital."

"Who?" Ian couldn't recall hearing the name.

"Julian sent her there to threaten me. She forced me to give up my passwords."

"When?" he asked. "How did she get past me?"

But Andrea was already making a beeline toward a woman wearing a navy suit with what looked like a laminated ID badge clipped to her lapel. Ian pegged her as federal government before they made it within ten feet of her. Had she forged an alliance with a former colleague, or was her relationship with "Julian" personal?

"Dr. Kapur," Andrea called, clearly beyond caring that she was interrupting the woman's conversation with one of the deputies.

Kapur turned toward her, jaw dropping as she took in Andrea's sling. "Miss Warrington, I hadn't heard you were hurt. Could I get you some—"

"It's *Dr.* Warrington," said Andrea, moving close enough to glare at her. "And your partner's dead. Did you know? Or maybe the right word isn't *partner* but *accomplice*?"

"If you mean Julian Ross, I've been briefed about what happened—" Kapur nodded her thanks to Chief Deputy Browning, who tipped a nod of his own before walking off to talk to one of the men he supervised.

"And I'm terribly sorry to hear about tonight's tragedy. We'd very much hoped to have him in custody before it ever came to—"

"In custody? Who *are* you?"

"Special Agent Neela Chapal," she said, the accent nowhere in evidence as she held up a laminated ID badge on a lanyard. "Federal Bureau of Investigation. I've been part of a joint task force looking into the bombing of a listening post in—"

"You *threatened* me—threatened to kill Ian if I wouldn't cooperate with Julian's—"

"I'm very sorry I allowed you to believe that." Chapal spared Ian an apologetic look and shook her head. "But what I actually said was that giving me those passwords was the way to save his life. By then, you see, we strongly suspected Ross was missing clandestine services agent Davis Parnell. We just needed to prove it without tipping him off and letting him escape again— to see what he was seeing and track how he was reacting so we could arrest him before he resorted to violence to protect his secret."

"But he did, and now—now he's killed Cassidy!" Andrea surged toward her, so upset that Ian wasn't certain what she would have done had he not caught her around the waist to stop her.

Frustrated, she turned her fury on him. "Stop it, Ian! Let go of me."

"Not until I know you're not going to end up spending tonight in jail for assaulting a federal officer."

But as the heel of her shoe connected with his shinbone, Ian began to wonder if he was the one who was going to end up bruised.

Chapter 17

Andrea had promised to come inside once she had cooled down, and Ian finally, reluctantly backed off. She saw him gritting his teeth, clearly fighting his natural inclination to take care of her, but at least he had the good sense to know she was in no mood to be managed.

The woman who had called herself Kapur too excused herself, saying she had to step inside out of the wind to phone in a report. As the chief deputy held the door for a pair of men wheeling a gurney toward a dark van, Andrea stood alone, a sick feeling in her stomach as she watched what was clearly a body being loaded through the vehicle's rear doors.

Was it Cassidy or Julian, or would both of them leave together, separated only by a pair of body bags. At the thought of it, pain sparked in Andrea's chest, a white-hot anger so consuming that she had to turn away.

In the tail of her vision, she caught a fleeting movement from between two parked vehicles, a flash of what she could've sworn was light blond hair ducking down and out of sight. Breath hitching, she jogged after the person hiding from view.

"Tyler—Ty, is that you?" she called. The wind gusted, sending dried leaves skittering across the concrete surface. Imagining she heard receding footsteps, Andrea flicked on the flashlight again and slipped between a parked pickup and an SUV bearing the markings of the Trencher County Sheriff's Office.

As she hurried after the sound, her beam swept across the dark brown Tahoe's gleaming front fender. But something about the reflection was *off* ever so slightly, something that had her stopping in her tracks.

She turned, her pulse drumming a rapid-fire warning that she shouldn't be out here alone. But that was ridiculous. With Julian dead and Kapur a legitimate government agent, Andrea told herself she no longer had anyone to fear. And Ty Dawson was no danger to her or anyone, just a troubled client in need of guidance— a boy, really, not even old enough to drink. She tried to move forward, telling herself she'd lose his trail if she didn't hurry, but some instinct kept her rooted to the spot...

An instinct that sent apprehension skittering on spiders' legs along her backbone, whispering that it hadn't been what she'd seen reflected that had triggered her alarm at all but instead the *nature* of the surface. Taking a deep breath, she turned the flashlight's beam back toward the Tahoe's fender. Only this time she registered the slight dimpling of the metal, along with a patch of paint that didn't quite match.

As if someone had inexpertly repaired body damage in that one spot—a bad fix on a vehicle that otherwise looked pristine.

She told herself that it was nothing, that law-enforcement vehicles were probably involved in accidents quite often. Still, why would someone try to cover it on the sly instead of taking it back to the dealership or at least a paint-and-body guy who knew what he was doing?

Foreboding contracted low in her gut, an instinct that had her remembering something Jessie had said about her investigation into some *sleazy local politician*. Sheriffs were elected, weren't they? And wasn't there already some kind of bad blood between Canter and the Rayfords?

An image, sharp as a knife's edge, sliced away reality. As the night around her fell away, she saw a dusky sky made darker by the pouring rain outside of her car's window, saw the side-view mirror with the dark grill bearing down. She recalled jamming hard on the accelerator, shooting toward the bridge, but her pursuer was closing in too fast. His front fender slammed against her rear tire with a crashing crunch that flung her like a tin can into—and through—the bridge's guardrail.

She shivered, staring at the fender, suddenly dead certain that if the paint was flaked away from that faulty paint job, she'd find another splash of color underneath it—the blue of her own car.

"But why my car?" she asked herself. "What would make him want to kill me?"

A twig cracked just behind her, and a deep male voice said, "Because I've always considered myself a truck man. Those damned little foreign cars all look alike to me."

In the dining area, Ian poured a cup of coffee, as determined as he'd ever been in all his life.

On her way past with sandwiches, Jessie stopped and did a double take. Setting the tray on the nearby tabletop, she said, "Whoa, Ian. Are you all right? Because

I haven't seen a look that intense since I came downstairs right after you slugged your brother that morning at the house."

"I'm not slugging anybody, but if Andrea thinks I'm giving up on her, she's got another think coming." He dumped enough sugar in the mug to make up for the lack of cream. *If the mountain won't come to Mohammed, then Mohammed's heading to her—armed with fresh, hot caffeine.*

Frowning at him, Jessie appeared not to notice his brother walk up behind her, the Rottweiler padding at his side.

"But she's asked you for some space, right? Space to wrap her head around what's happened?"

Zach stopped, with the half sandwich only inches from his mouth.

"Yeah, she has. And before you start on me about how I'm smothering her like my brother—"

"Trust me, you don't want to do that. You don't want to scare the woman so much she runs straight back to California to get away from the bad memories."

"If she does, I'll follow her. I'll find work out there. I'll do anything—"

"Or frighten her into entering the witness-protection program to get away from a psycho stalker. And in case I'm losing you here, Ian, I mean you, the way you sound right now."

Did he really sound that unhinged when it came to Andrea? "Is it really so bad, Jessie? Knowing someone loves you so much that it's making him a little crazy?"

Zach grimaced at the question, a pained look on his eyes as he awaited Jessie's answer.

"I—I love your brother with all my heart and soul,"

Jessie said, her words tinged with sadness. "I can't remember how I ever lived without him, can't imagine how I ever would again. But it *is* scary, wondering how far love can go before it's all-consuming. Especially with— I haven't even told Zach this yet, but…"

Ian waited patiently, but Zach's restraint crumbled. "Told me what, Jessie? If your career means so much to you, please forget I ever said anything about you quitting. Let me work with you, find some way to help you make things safer for all of us, with no secrets and no holdouts. I know I've been an ass at times. I know I've been demanding. Just don't leave me, Jessie. Give me another chance to get the most important thing in my life right."

Jessie's surprise at seeing him eased into a softer emotion that sent a flush rising to her cheeks. Slipping into his embrace, she said, "Of course, I'm not going to leave you, you big lug. What with all my deadlines and keeping up with Eden, *somebody's* going to have to pitch in and take his turn changing diapers."

Zach pulled away to stare at her face. "Diapers? Eden's a long way past—"

She looked up at him, her green eyes glimmering. "I know I might've been a bit hard on you lately, but in my defense, the hormones—"

"Diapers?" Zach repeated, as if the word were foreign to him.

Ian laughed at the expression on his big brother's face. "Who's the blockhead now? She's telling you she's pregnant. Sounds like Eden's going to be a big sister pretty soon."

Jessie was nodding, smiling at him. "Lots and lots of diapers, Zach. At least, that's what the doctor said when she found the heartbeats." She held up first one and then a second finger. "Two heartbeats, two babies. But I guess you knew that twins run in my family."

Ian clapped his dumbstruck brother on the shoulder before leaving the two to a joyful celebration.

He had a woman of his own to find, support and someday very soon claim for all of their forevers.

But first, he meant to get a cup of hot coffee in her, a reminder of the one she'd brought to begin their dialogue.

As Sheriff Canter moved in closer, Andrea reflexively backed away until she stood trapped against the SUV's front door. The cut on her arm, the older bumps and bruises from her car wreck, all throbbed in time to the breakneck drumming of her heart. She fought not to look down at his hands, at least not at the one holding his drawn gun.

Canter clenched his jaw, his face looking monstrous with her flashlight illuminating his features from below. "It should've been mine, all of it. The natural gas find and the cattle, the house and all the land. *I* was the one who took care of her, you know, who saw to her all those years after those two good-for-nothing hell-raisers of hers lit out like the punks they were."

"Wh-what are you talking about?" she asked, knowing that her best chance, her only chance, was to keep him talking, make him feel that he was, perhaps for the first time, being heard. From what Ian had told her about the Rayford family's history, Andrea had no doubt, either, that two abused teenage boys, unable to get their mother to speak up on their behalf, had done what they'd had to to survive. "You took care of— You're talking about Zach and Ian's mother?"

His mouth twisted as he fought some internal battle. "Who else was there for her to call on, once the *lord of the manor* turned to roughing her up after those two losers were gone?"

Despite the icy terror ripping through her, Andrea felt a pang of sympathy for the proud and fragile Nancy Rayford. "So that was when he started hurting her, after the boys left?"

Rayford's lip curled, revealing long, white teeth, along with his disgust. "Back when I was still a deputy, I got a disturbance call from The Cattleman in Marston—'bout the fanciest restaurant in these parts. He'd been in a mood over something, had gotten sloppy drunk before the bill came. When she tried to calm him down, get him to lower his voice and stop botherin' everybody, what do you think that SOB did?"

She loosed a shuddering breath, his unfocused look telling her he didn't really want an answer. That he had been biding his time for years, waiting for a chance to tell his story.

"He doubled up one of those big fists of his and popped that tiny woman, not a hundred pounds, in the eye. She cried and carried on but wouldn't dream of pressing charges. She said later, though, how she'd liked the way I'd handled him, how I'd talked sense all respectful-like and without hurtin' his pride so much he'd feel the need to take it out on her later."

Canter closed his eyes, lost inside a memory. But when Andrea dared to take a step, the dark eyes widened, and his left hand shot out to block her escape. With his right, he pressed the barrel of his weapon against her ribs, aimed at her pounding heart.

She scarcely dared to breathe. *One wrong move, and I'll be the next one leaving in a body bag.* Leaving the center and all the people here who needed her, but it was the image of Ian's handsome face that filled her with regret for what might have been, if the two of them had only had time.

"I gave Mrs. Rayford my personal number that night," Canter said. "And afterward, she called me now and then when things were getting out of hand."

"Are things getting out of hand now, Sheriff Canter?" Andrea asked quietly. "Because I'm thinking there could be another way. A way to back this off, let everybody breathe a little like you did with him so well that first night."

Canter scowled down at her and shook his head. "You don't even look like Zach's woman at all, not really. It's just, what the hell were you doing out riding her horse anyway? And that car's the same damned color. When I followed it off the ranch road, I thought—"

"But why Jessie?" Andrea asked, the fine hairs rising behind her neck. "Why would you want to—"

"Woman's been asking questions all over the county, digging into things that're none of her damned business. Not only that, but Nancy's pretty sure the little bitch had been nosing through her emails, including one where I reminded her just how far I was willing to go to—to make sure he never beat on her again."

Andrea stared at him, remembering having heard that Zach and Ian's father had died of a heart attack about six months before Ian had gone missing. But something in Canter's phrasing, in the hard look on his handsome

face, struck her with the certainty there was far more
to the story.

"The bitch has figured it out," Canter said. "And I
see it in your face she's told you, hasn't she? She told
you all about it."

Andrea shook her head emphatically. "The only thing
Jessie said was she'd been looking at some campaign finance stuff on some North Texas politicians. But when I
asked, she said she had nothing on you. Nothing."

At his hesitation, a cold thrill chased through her nervous system. *You're thinking it though now, just how and
where you want to kill me. Because I might've bought
Jessie a reprieve, but you have to know you can't possibly let me go. Not without risking everything.*

Grabbing her by the arm, he ordered, "Open up that
back door. We're going for a little ride."

"No!" she said, "That's not necessary. Listen, Canter,
I know how to keep my mouth shut. And anyway—"

He let go of her long enough to pull open the Tahoe's
back door. Long enough for her to glimpse the steel-
mesh cage separating the SUV's rear from the front-seat
passenger. A structure meant for prisoners, who would
have no access to door handles or window controls. Who
would have no way of escaping as they were taken to
the Trencher County Jail.

But Andrea had no illusions that she would make
it that far. A man who'd spent his life patrolling this
mostly rural county was bound to know of any number of rugged tracks and cattle paths, places where a
body might lie undisturbed by anything but the buz-
zards and coyotes.

"Get on in there," he said. "Don't make this any
harder than it has to be."

Still resisting, she made a wild guess. "I think I understand. A person's loyalty should be rewarded, right? And after you got rid of John Rayford for Nancy—"

"He had a heart attack. He really did. It was his own damned fault he happened to be stuffed inside a closet gagged and handcuffed when it happened. It was the only way to keep him from killing her without taking him to jail."

"And Nancy Rayford knows about this?"

He nodded. "It was her idea to take off the hardware and the gag, give the man a little dignity in death. Spare her the embarrassment—"

"And spare *you* any kind of inquiry."

Canter's scowl deepened. "Get in now." He shoved her toward the open door, pushing her hard enough to bang the side of her head.

That was when the first rock cracked against the driver's side window. As Canter spun around, a second stone the size of a man's palm smacked into his temple, eliciting a shout of pain and rage.

Andrea didn't stop to question the miracle or wonder where the easily spooked Ty had found the courage. Seizing on the distraction, she bolted, making for the wooded area surrounding the pond. Between the trees and the darkness, she figured she might just stand a chance— at least if Sheriff Canter didn't shoot her in the back.

"Go get help, kid, right now," Ian had whispered urgently to the scared and skinny blond who'd come upon him in a panic. His stutter was so severe he'd gotten out little more than Andrea's name before half dragging Ian to the parking lot, where Ty pointed out Canter having an intense conversation with Andrea next to the Tahoe.

"Find the deputies or another counselor," Ian instructed as the two of them crouched behind a pickup, "anybody you can get out here in a hurry. If you can't get the words out, just make some noise or knock someone down, anything to get 'em chasing you. You got that?"

Ty nodded and took off, but as squirrelly as the kid seemed, Ian had no idea if he'd go for help or race off to find another bolt-hole.

Tossing aside the mug of coffee he'd been carrying, Ian crept in closer, adrenaline flooding through his system. He couldn't be sure what Canter was so angry with Andrea about, but clearly something was very wrong— something the lawman would just as soon keep to himself, judging from his furtive glances around, as if checking to see if anyone was coming.

When Ian made out the word *bitch* and then the sharpness of Andrea's refusal, it was enough to get him moving, looking for sticks or rocks, anything he might use for a distraction. He hauled off and threw two good-size stones, giving Andrea the chance she needed to take off running.

"I'll kill you!" Canter bellowed, blood trickling from his temple, as he spun and looked around wildly for mere seconds before cursing and then abruptly sprinting after Andrea instead.

Racing after him along the sidewalk, Ian could only hope the sheriff didn't turn around and fire. But he'd rather take a bullet than allow the lawman to catch up with Andrea. Canter was so out of control that Ian had no doubt of his intention to kill or hurt her or anyone who got in his way.

Canter charged forward like a maddened bull, shouting at her, "Hold it now, or I swear to you I'll—"

A security light gave Ian a glimpse of Andrea leaving the sidewalk that ringed the pond and making a beeline for a thick, dark grove of trees. But Canter clearly saw her, too, stopping to take aim at her back.

"No!" Ian bellowed, racing forward to leap at him.

Distracted by his shout, Canter whipped around and took a wild shot, close enough that Ian saw the flash and felt the bullet buzz past his ear like a wasp straight out of hell.

Before Canter could fire again, Ian struck him at chest level, taking them both down hard and knocking the gun out of Canter's right hand. As he grabbed for it, Ian pounded his face, slugging him repeatedly and rolling both of them downhill and then into the cold water.

Canter used his legs, flipping Ian over. Catching him by the throat, he shouted, "Rayford!" before driving his head beneath the shallow murk.

The water wasn't a foot deep, but it would be enough, Ian realized as he bucked and flailed to free himself of the hand gripping his neck. Fighting for the surface, he instead sucked in a muddy mouthful and heard Andrea, far too close by, screaming, "Let him up! Let him breathe!"

Why the hell wasn't she running, going to get help?

Choking and coughing, he wanted to shout at her to get out before Canter could finish him and then kill her, too. But Ian couldn't do anything but thrash more and more weakly—until a last-ditch swing connected with the side of Canter's head.

The lawman let go of Ian's throat, allowing him to come up, still coughing. Canter scrabbled for shore, crawling on hands and knees for the gun knocked from his hand earlier.

Seeing his intention, Andrea, too, lunged for the weapon. But even if she reached it first, could she really bring herself to do what it would take to stop a man intent on killing them both?

A deep snarl was the only warning either of them had before a huge black-and-tan blur leaped at Canter. The Rottweiler clamped down on the sheriff's arm, attacking with a ferocity that had him screaming as he fought to protect his face and neck—all thoughts of his weapon forgotten.

Andrea darted in to claim it, just as Jessie shouted, *"Aus! Hier!"*

Zach, standing just behind her, called, "Gretel," and the dog broke off her attack and ran back to the two of them.

Chief Deputy Browning ran up behind them, his own weapon drawn as he yelled, "Hands up, all of you! Grab that animal before I shoot it, and drop that weapon, Dr. Warrington!"

"Shoot them, Browning!" Canter shouted, bleeding from a dozen places. "Kill every one of them right now!"

The deputy swung an incredulous look in his direction as two more of his fellow officers, along with Special Agent Chapal, hurried into view.

"I've got a better idea, Sheriff," Browning told his superior, his voice as grim as the look etched on his face. "Why don't you go ahead and raise those hands where I can see 'em, at least until we get all this sorted out."

Then and only then did Ian finally release the breath he had been holding.

Chapter 18

Two months later...

A hard lump formed in Andrea's throat as she hung up the phone in the small reception-area niche she'd claimed as her temporary headquarters. Fighting back tears of frustration, she wished she had a door to close so she could pull herself together—with deep breathing, loud cursing or perhaps a headlong dive into the stash of delicious European chocolates some anónymous angel kept adding to her bottom desk drawer when she wasn't looking.

After "Julian's" office had been restored to order by contractors from the insurance company, she had made what she believed to be the sensible decision to use that more private space as she'd worked to undo the damage done by all the negative publicity, but it was hopeless. Every time she walked through the door, she was overwhelmed with nausea as the events of that horrific night replayed in her mind.

The irony hit hard that she was experiencing so many of the same symptoms as those she sought to help, from nightmares and hyperreactivity to loud noises to extreme watchfulness. Certain she ought to know better, she'd forced herself to focus on the needs of others, refusing to take time to talk to the new counselor Warriors-4-Life's umbrella organization had sent to help with what the national director was now calling "the transition."

A transition he had just confirmed would end with the Marston center's permanent closure, in spite of all the endless meetings and phone calls she'd put in trying to forestall it.

She heard the footsteps before she saw them, her stomach tensing as she recognized the sound of Ian's boots against the tile. "Hey, Andrea."

"Hi, Ian." She turned her head just enough to glance and nod at him. Any more, and she feared he would see her face and ask her what the matter was. Then she'd fall apart for certain, before she'd had the chance to speak with the staff or anyone. "Here for your appointment?"

A few days after Cassidy's memorial service, Ian had blurted an awkward proposal, begging her to join him at the ranch and put the tragedy and all of Warriors-4-Life's headaches behind her. Feeling overwhelmed and fragile, she had turned him down—on three separate occasions—before finally insisting that he needed to work on learning the difference between real love and a fixation.

If that's what it takes to convince you, then sign me up, he'd told her, and since then, he'd been coming to the center three times a week to meet with Connor. He'd stopped proposing, too, though she wasn't certain whether he'd lost interest or was simply biding his time, waiting for her to come around.

Her stomach fluttered at the thought, though she told herself it was a good thing she'd found a way to put distance between them. All too soon, that distance would be physical—and permanent, as she looked for another way to continue working with the veterans whose welfare meant so much to her.

"Just finished up my session," he told her, "and I was hoping I could lure you away from your desk for a little walk."

"I'm— I really don't have the time now."

"C'mon, Andie. Come celebrate with me. It's a gorgeous day and—"

"What exactly are we celebrating?" asked Andrea, who felt less like celebrating and more like drowning herself in the chocolate drawer with every passing moment.

"Connor thinks I'm ready to move from individual to group sessions." Ian flashed the open smile that reminded her so much of the man she'd first fallen for. Only now, there was a gravity behind it, a steadiness and patience that had convinced his brother to let him take over the management of the family's increasingly complicated finances. According to Jessie, who had stopped by a couple of times after visiting her obstetrician, he'd made amends with his mother, too, both he and his brother forgiving her for covering up the circumstances of their father's death. And she was so thrilled about the prospect of becoming a grandmother to Jessie's twins that she had made peace with her daughter-in-law, too.

Moved by accounts of Nancy Rayford's abuse, a Trencher County grand jury had refused to indict either her or former-sheriff George Canter on charges related to John Rayford's death. But that hadn't prevented the panel from indicting Canter on multiple counts of attempted homicide against both Andrea and Ian, along with additional charges of public corruption for extorting "campaign contributions" from Nancy Rayford and other citizens and using much of the money for his own personal gain.

"That's excellent news," Andrea said, coming out of her chair to give Ian a spontaneous hug. "I'm so glad to hear you're making such great progress."

He lifted her jacket from the back of her chair and held it out for her. When she hesitated, he asked, "Then why are you standing there looking at me like the saddest, most stressed-out person on the planet?"

She jammed her arms into the jacket's sleeves and started walking quickly. If she was going to lose it—and the tears were coming now, unstoppable—better she should do it outside, away from where any client, staff member or visitor might walk past and see her. For his part, Ian didn't try to stop her; nor did he call after her demanding answers to explain the emotional tsunami...

A tsunami spawned not only by the loss of the center that meant so much to her, but another reality she hadn't even begun to wrap her head around.

She walked beside the center's pond, tears streaming as she made three circuits and then five of the same place where she'd watched Canter shove Ian's face beneath the water. It was a moment she'd never forget, a memory that rose like muddy bubbles in her dreams every night. Only in her nightmares, the horror didn't end with Gretel's attack and the arrival of the deputies and special agent; instead, Andrea woke screaming at the sight of Ian's body floating facedown, his dark hair matted with algae, his strong hands limp and swollen.

Finally, she stopped, then closed her eyes and listened to the sound of approaching footsteps. The dogged, determined footsteps of a man too foolish or too stubborn to ever give up, even if she walked as far as he had to return from the dead.

Turning around, she slipped into his strong arms, those arms that had been waiting so patiently for her to finally admit she needed his strength.

"They're shutting the place down next month," she said, "claiming they need to distance the organization from the *Julian Ross legacy* before the decline in donations forces them to close other centers, too. After all the work I've done, all the people I've met with—but who am I kidding? I'm no fund-raiser, no administrator. I'm just a broken-down shrink who can't even fix herself."

He looked into her eyes, his gaze reading far beneath the surface. "There's nothing broken down at all about you. You're just tired, that's all. Exhausted from working your tail off to help everybody but yourself."

"But what good have I done, Ian? The patients whose families didn't pull them after the shooting will be split up and sent to other facilities, sure, but how far will some of them regress with the new location and new counselors?"

"You've done wonders, Andrea. Look at Ty. I know you're still working with him personally. I saw him today. He was talking up a storm and laughing—really *laughing*—while he and a few of his buddies played basketball in the gym."

She smiled, though she couldn't help worrying over how hard it was going to be for him to leave the one place where he felt safe before he was fully ready.

"And look at me," Ian said. "Thanks to your expert advice, I've got my memory back, I'm handling stress a whole lot better, and—this next part's the most important—I even made my counselor sign a note to prove it to you."

"To prove what?"

He dug into his pocket, and a plastic bag of chocolates, each piece wrapped in gold foil, fell out. As he scooped it up and stuffed it back inside, she laughed.

"*Busted*, Angel of the Bottom Desk Drawer. And thank you, from the bottom of *my* rapidly expanding bottom. Seriously, Ian, I've put on five pounds since you've started with that. *Five.*"

Dashing a hellion's grin against the talk of angels, he took a step back and spun her around by the shoulders. Once he had her turned away from him, he leaned close to her ear. "I'd say they look good on you. Damned delectable, in fact."

The warmth of his breath sent a tingle of pleasure through her, though she tried to hide the way he made her shiver. She had to focus, to remember she would soon be tucking her tail between her legs and heading off to work at whatever veteran's program would have her. But one of his hands slipped to her waist, making her desperate for distraction.

"So what about this note from Connor?" she blurted, stepping away and turning to look at him from a safer distance. "What was so important?"

A smirk slanted across Ian's handsome face, and he pulled out a sheet of paper, unfolded it with a flourish and presented it to her.

She squinted at the spiky print she recognized as Connor's, her lip quivering as she read aloud:

"In my considered professional opinion, the client, Ian Rayford, now completely and accurately distinguishes between the concepts of 'real love' and 'fixation.'"

Looking up at him, she asked, "And you honestly figured this was going to cut it?"

He shrugged and said, "Why not? I bribed him extra to throw in a couple of two-dollar words, you know, on account of you having your doctorate in head shrinking."

She snorted and then broke out laughing at his good-old-boy act—especially because she knew darned well that Ian had a couple of degrees himself, in global politics and finance.

"I was hoping it might at least break the ice that's built up the past couple of months between us." His voice sobered as he explained, "Because I can honestly tell you, you were right. I *was* fixated on a mirage, just the way you said, an image of a perfect woman who never really existed anywhere except in my imagination."

Andrea gave a shuddering sigh, pleased that he had made so much progress but aching with the realization of what stepping back as she had, letting him grow away from her, might have cost.

"But the thing is," he went on, "these past two months, I've had the opportunity to get to know the real you, the one who sees a need, realizes she can help and throws herself into it with a passion I can only envy…a passion

I'm finally truly free to pursue, since serving my country in the covert operations is no longer an option for me."

"I'm sorry that was taken from you, Ian."

He hesitated for a long while before taking her hand. "I'm not, not anymore. Because that brand of passion, that kind of life left me no room for anyone else. No room for the family I need or the very real woman I want to walk the next part of my journey with."

Her throat tightened and her vision blurred. "You understand I'm leaving, don't you? That I'll be hunting up a new position as soon as I make certain all the clients are placed and the members of this staff won't be tainted by their association with this center."

"Why should they be tainted? They weren't responsible for Parnell's actions. None of you were. All of you do great work here. The kind that really matters."

She shook her head. "Tell that to the donors and the Warriors-4-Life board."

"They're running scared, that's all. Not seeing how this bad publicity can all be turned around."

"Turned around how, Ian? I've done everything I can to convince people—and get reporters interested in covering the good we do."

"You have done all you can, but *I* haven't even started." He beamed at her, his smile warmer than the autumn sunshine. "Trust me on this, Andie. Once the reporters show up for tomorrow's press conference—"

"What press conference?"

"The one I've conned Jessie into setting up. That woman's called in more favors—she swears she'll have national network news on this, the big cable outlets, too, not to mention about a dozen influential papers."

"For what? I don't get it."

"For Captain Ian Rayford's first live press conference since his return."

She gaped in amazement, her heart twisting at the thought of him giving up the privacy he'd insisted on all along. "But you—you've told everyone you weren't going to be anybody's show pony."

"What I said was I wasn't about to let the government trot me out to sell some pack of lies to cover up *their* cover-up. But what I will do is say thank you to an organization—and a woman—who've made all the difference in my life. And why not do it in a way—one that will come with a very large check from the newly established Rayford Foundation I'll be running—that'll raise awareness of the issues PTSD-affected veterans are facing...and with any luck touch off a landslide of donations?"

Bouncing on her feet, she threw her arms around him. "Oh, my gosh, Ian! Thank you! That's incredibly generous of you."

"Not entirely," he admitted, slanting a look down at her that sent a shock of energy straight to her libido. "I do have ulterior motives..."

"What motives are those?" she asked, pretending that she couldn't guess.

"I want to keep my wife close," he said, "because the idea of a long-distance marriage doesn't work for me."

"So that's what all this is for, then? The press conference and the big donation? Just to convince me we should get hitched?"

He shook his head. "The chocolate might've been a bribe, but not this. I meant what I said. Whether or not you ever say yes to my proposal, I'm making that do-nation—all seven figures' worth—and doing the press conference, as long as Warriors-4-Life agrees to keep this center open."

"I can't imagine they'd do anything but jump at the opportunity."

"What about you, Andie? What would you say to the opportunity to live together, love together, build a family together as we both work at something that changes people's lives?"

"You're talking about commuting to and from the ranch?" As much as she wanted to believe it was possible, that there was a way to make things work between them, the idea of the hour-long commute each way was less an issue than the thought of intruding on what felt like Zach and Jessie's home and family.

He shook his head. "I mean building our own house in Marston, someplace where we can have the privacy we need to focus on our work…and each other."

"And our own growing family," she added, warmth flowing through her as she finally allowed herself to think about the doctor's appointment she'd finally had the nerve to go to just this morning—and the confirmation that his test had provided.

"Growing… Wait. You don't mean…?"

She nodded. "I figured there was probably a reason most of those five pounds I've gained seem to have grav-itated to my breasts."

"Oh, baby…" he murmured.

"Oh, yes," she told him. "*Yes* to everything…because it seems as if the coming year's going to offer a bumper crop of little Rayfords. And most of all because I love the man you always were and the man you've grown into."

"I know you shrinks are really fond of talking," he said with a wry smile, "but if you don't mind, darling, I'm itching to put those lips of yours to better use right now."

And so it was that a walk that had begun with tears ended with her laughter, followed by a kiss that tasted sweeter than the fine chocolates in his jacket...

Chocolates that were crushed and melted by the time the two of them finally made it back inside.

* * * * *

If you loved Ian's story, LONE STAR SURVIVOR, check out his brother Zach's story

LONE STAR REDEMPTION

Available now, from Colleen Thompson and Harlequin Romantic Suspense!

REQUEST YOUR FREE BOOKS!
2 FREE NOVELS PLUS 2 FREE GIFTS!

⊞ HARLEQUIN®

ROMANTIC suspense

Sparked by danger, fueled by passion

YES! Please send me 2 FREE Harlequin® Romantic Suspense novels and my 2 FREE gifts (gifts are worth about $10). After receiving them, if I don't wish to receive any more books, I can return the shipping statement marked "cancel." If I don't cancel, I will receive 4 brand-new novels every month and be billed just $4.74 per book in the U.S. or $5.24 per book in Canada. That's a savings of at least 14% off the cover price! It's quite a bargain! Shipping and handling is just 50¢ per book in the U.S. and 75¢ per book in Canada.* I understand that accepting the 2 free books and gifts places me under no obligation to buy anything. I can always return a shipment and cancel at any time. Even if I never buy another book, the two free books and gifts are mine to keep forever.

240/340 HDN F45N

Name _____ (PLEASE PRINT)

Address _____ Apt. #

City _____ State/Prov. _____ Zip/Postal Code

Signature (if under 18, a parent or guardian must sign)

Mail to the **Harlequin®** Reader Service:
IN U.S.A.: P.O. Box 1867, Buffalo, NY 14240-1867
IN CANADA: P.O. Box 609, Fort Erie, Ontario L2A 5X3

Want to try two free books from another line?
Call 1-800-873-8635 or visit www.ReaderService.com.

* Terms and prices subject to change without notice. Prices do not include applicable taxes. Sales tax applicable in N.Y. Canadian residents will be charged applicable taxes. Offer not valid in Quebec. This offer is limited to one order per household. Not valid for current subscribers to Harlequin Romantic Suspense books. All orders subject to credit approval. Credit or debit balances in a customer's account(s) may be offset by any other outstanding balance owed by or to the customer. Please allow 4 to 6 weeks for delivery. Offer available while quantities last.

Your Privacy—The Harlequin® Reader Service is committed to protecting your privacy. Our Privacy Policy is available online at www.ReaderService.com or upon request from the Harlequin Reader Service.

We make a portion of our mailing list available to reputable third parties that offer products we believe may interest you. If you prefer that we not exchange your name with third parties, or if you wish to clarify or modify your communication preferences, please visit us at www.ReaderService.com/consumerschoice or write to us at Harlequin Reader Service Preference Service, P.O. Box 9062, Buffalo, NY 14269. Include your complete name and address.

HRS13R

Calvin Sweet knew he was taking some big chances, but
taking risks always invigorated him. Coming back to his
home in Conard County was the first of the new risks. Five
years ago he'd left for the big city because the law was closing in on him.

Returning to the site where he had hung his trophies was
a huge risk, too, although he could claim he was out for a
hike in the spring mountains. There was nothing left, anyway. The law had taken it all, and the sight filled him with
both sorrow and bitterness. Anger, too. They had no right
to take away his hard work, his triumphs, his mementos.

But they had. After five years all that was left were some
remnants of cargo netting rotting in the tree limbs and the
remains of a few sawed-off nooses.

He could close his eyes and remember, and remembering
filled him with joy and a sense of his own huge power, the
power of life and death. The power to take it all away. The
power to enlighten those whose existence was so shallow.

They took it for granted. Calvin never did.

From earliest childhood he had been fascinated by spiders and their webs. He had spent hours watching as insect after insect fell victim to those silken strands, struggling mightily until they were stung and then wrapped up helplessly to await their fate. Each corpse on the web had been a trophy marking the spider's victory. No one ever escaped.

No one had escaped him, either.

He was chosen, just like a spider, to be exactly what he was.

Chosen. He liked that word. It fit both him and his victims. They were all chosen to perform the dance of death together, to plumb the reaches of human endurance. To sacrifice the ordinary for the extraordinary. So he quashed his growing need to act and focused his attention on another part of his life. He had a job now, one he needed to report to every evening. He was whistling now as he walked back down to his small ranch.

A spiderweb was beginning to take shape in his mind, one for his barn loft that no one would see, ever. It was enough that he could admire it and savor the gifts there. The impulse to hunt eased, and soon he was in control again. He liked control. He liked controlling himself and others, even as he fulfilled his purpose.

Like the spider, he was not hasty to act. It would have to be the right person at the right time, and the time was not yet right. First he had to build his web.

Don't miss UNDERCOVER HUNTER by *New York Times* bestselling author Rachel Lee, available January 2015 wherever Harlequin® Romantic Suspense books and ebooks are sold.

HRSEXP1214

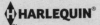

ROMANTIC suspense

Heart-racing romance, high-stakes suspense!

HIGH-STAKES PLAYBOY
by *New York Times* bestselling author
Cindy Dees

Available January 2015

Who will get this Prescott bachelor first— the girl or the killer?

To help his brothers, marine pilot Archer Prescott goes undercover to find out who's sabotaging their movie set. But the die-hard bachelor isn't ready for what he finds in the High Sierras: his doe-eyed girl-next-door camerawoman is the prime suspect.

Marley Stringer isn't as innocent as she seems. As Marley turns irresistible and the aerial "accidents" turn deadly, Archer begins to wonder who's more dangerous—the perfect woman who threatens his heart...or the desperate killer who threatens his life.

Don't miss the first exciting installment from Cindy Dees's *The Prescott Bachelors* series:

HIGH-STAKES BACHELOR

Available wherever Harlequin® Romantic Suspense books and ebooks are sold.

ROMANTIC suspense

Heart-racing romance, high-stakes suspense!

BAYOU HERO
by *USA TODAY* bestselling author
Marilyn Pappano

Available January 2015

One family's scandal is responsible for a rising body count in New Orleans's Garden District...

Even for an experienced NCIS agent like Alia Kingsley, the murder scene is particularly gruesome. A man killed in a fit of rage. Being the long-estranged son of the deceased, Landry Jackson quickly becomes a person of interest. But does Landry loathe his father as much as the feds suspect?

It's clear to Alia that Landry Jackson has secrets, but his hatred for his father isn't one of them. Alia feels sure Landry isn't the killer, but once more family members start dying, she's forced to question herself. What if the fierce attraction she has developed toward Landry has compromised Alia's instincts?

Don't miss other exciting titles from
USA TODAY bestselling author Marilyn Pappano:

UNDERCOVER IN COPPER LAKE
COPPER LAKE ENCOUNTER
COPPER LAKE CONFIDENTIAL

Available wherever Harlequin® Romantic Suspense
books and ebooks are sold.

www.Harlequin.com
HRS27902